Dead Center

Other Folly Beach Mysteries by Bill Noel

Folly

The Pier

Washout

The Edge

The Marsh

Ghosts

Missing

Final Cut

First Light

Boneyard Beach

Silent Night

Dead Center

A Folly Beach Mystery

Bill Noel

Hydra
Publications

Printed in the United States of America

ISBN: 978-1-942212-53-9

Cover Photo by Bill Noel
Author Photo by Susan Noel

 Hydra
Publications

Hydra Publications
Goshen, KY 470026

www.hydrapublications.com

Chapter One

Breakfast is the most important meal of the day, or so they say. Whoever *they* are would probably say French toast slathered with maple syrup was not their idea of what the most important meal of the day should be. *They* were not with me as I took a shortcut from the house to the Lost Dog Cafe, a path through the alley behind a couple of bars, the foul-weather sanctuary of First Light Church, and the site of my former photo gallery.

The February sun had slept in on Folly Beach, a small barrier island a handful of miles from beautiful and historic Charleston, South Carolina. Fog enveloped the island like a fluffy, gray, cotton comforter, and was so thick I imagined having to part it with my hands. It was still dark and I took advantage of the feeble illumination from three security lights on nearby poles as I made my way to the restaurant. I coveted the smell of fresh coffee greeting me as I thought about a peaceful morning enjoying breakfast while celebrating another day in my retirement paradise.

I felt a twinge of regret as I passed the back door of what used to be Landrum Gallery, my lifelong dream. As with many dreams, reality had slapped it down. I had kept the never-successful business open for eight years, but expenses exceeded income tenfold, and locking the doors had become the sane choice. Six months ago, I hauled the last framed photo to my car and felt both sadness, and also relief knowing it was something I didn't have to continue to struggle with. I had experienced my share of battles during my sixty-six years, and most I had no control over. This one I did.

I was distracted from reliving the demise of the gallery when I caught a glimmer of what at first glance looked like a large laundry bag veiled in the deep shadows of a trash dumpster between First Light and the former gallery's back doors. I hesitated and waited for my eyes to adjust to the dark and inched closer to the mass. Thoughts of a peaceful breakfast evaporated. The object on the ground was folded in a fetal position and, from appearances, dead.

I blinked to be sure I wasn't imagining the body, held my breath, and turned to see if anyone was nearby. I heard a car traveling up Center Street, Folly's main drag in front of the buildings, and a dog barking for its most important meal of the day. I didn't see anyone.

I inched closer. The body was a man in his late fifties, wearing a dark-green polo shirt, tan slacks, boat shoes, and an Atlanta Braves ball cap cocked sideways on his head, most likely knocked that way from the fall to the gravel alley. He was well-dressed for the laid-back, casual beach community and didn't look like he'd been homeless. There appeared to be a puddle of blood that had oozed from under the ball cap. I stooped and touched the left arm which was twisted at a right angle to his torso. It was cold. The man had eaten his last meal, regardless how important it may have been. His right hand had a death grip on a gun.

I stepped back and tapped 911 in my phone, something I had done more times than a former small business owner should have ever done, and told the emergency operator who I was, where I was, and why I had called. I assured her I would stay where I was, and she, in a well-modulated, professional voice, said the police had been dispatched. Folly Beach was a half-mile wide and six-miles long, and its downtown was condensed into a six block area. The combination city hall, fire, and police station was fewer than three blocks from where I was standing, so I wasn't surprised to hear the high-pitched wail of a patrol car as it left the station seconds after I'd ended the call.

The siren was followed by the distinct sound of the city's fire and rescue truck and a second patrol car coming from the other direction. I took a deep breath and lowered myself to the concrete step leading to my former business.

Officer Bishop hopped out of her patrol car and scanned the area before moving in my direction. Her hand hovered over her holstered firearm. She gave a slight nod, said, "Mr. Landrum," and continued to peruse the area before focusing on the body.

I had met the officer two years ago when she was new to the

department and I was stuck in the middle of a murder investigation. She was pleasant and competent, one of the few female members of the Folly Beach police department, and half of the city's African-American cops.

"Officer Bishop," I said, and realized that although I'd known her for a while, I didn't know her first name. I also thought it was strange that that had popped in my mind as I sat, hands trembling, and traumatized by what should have been a pleasant early-morning, fog-shrouded walk.

She pointed a black Maglite at the corpse, and leaned down to touch his arm. She discovered there was nothing medics could do for him.

A second patrol car pulled in the alley behind Bishop's vehicle, an officer whose first name I could remember, rushed to the body. I had known Allen Spencer since I had arrived on Folly a decade ago. Bishop asked him to make sure there wasn't anyone in the vicinity and to secure the scene. He nodded and pointed his light at me. I shielded my eyes.

"Sorry, Mr. Landrum. Didn't recognize you. What happened?"

"I don't know, Allen. I was—"

"Officer Spencer," Bishop interrupted, "*please* make sure the area's secure."

Please was said with more force and irritation than politeness. Bishop was worried the killer might be nearby. It was possible, although with two cops here and more first responders on the way, I doubted whoever was responsible was hanging around. Officer Spencer didn't wait for the rest of my answer and began circling the area near the alley.

The city's fire and rescue vehicle was next to arrive, followed by a fire engine. Two EMTs moved to the body and Officer Bishop and lowered herself on the step beside me.

"Are you okay?"

I sighed. "Think so."

"What happened?"

I shared my morning from when I left home to finding the corpse. I left out my breakfast choice.

She pointed her flashlight at the group surrounding the body.

"Know who he is?"

"I didn't get a good look, since the only light was the one on the pole. I didn't recognize him."

Chief Cindy LaMond arrived and moved beside Officer Bishop and put her hand on the office's shoulder. The chief was in her fifties, five-foot three inches in stature, with curly hair and a quick smile.

Bishop looked at her boss. "Morning, Chief. Mr. Landrum was telling me what he found."

Chief LaMond and I had been friends since she'd moved to the island from East Tennessee eight years ago. She'd been promoted to chief a couple of years back after the previous long-time chief, Brian Newman, had been elected mayor.

Cindy nodded at Bishop and turned to me. "Chris, don't tell me you've stumbled on another murder."

Officer Bishop stood. "If it's okay, Chief, I'll help the guys secure the scene."

LaMond nodded and Bishop left to join her colleagues.

"Cindy, I was walking to breakfast, minding my own business."

She shook her head. "How do you do it, Chris?"

I knew what she meant, but still asked, "Do what?"

"Manage to stumble on every dead body within twenty miles; stumble on it before anyone else; manage to get in the middle of police investigations; manage to stay alive while surrounded by dead people and murderers." She rubbed her chin. "Oh yeah, and manage to piss off every law enforcement official from here to Timbuktu."

I smiled. "It's a gift."

Cindy, God love her, had a way of dredging up smart-aleck remarks in me while at the same time calming me even in the most serious situation. Besides, much of what she'd said was true.

She shook her head. "I suppose it's just coincidence your latest find happened to be behind the building that was your gallery for what, eight years?"

I nodded and said I was sure it had been a coincidence, and that I hadn't stepped foot in the building since shutting down the business.

Spencer moved to Cindy's side and waited for a break in our conversation. She turned to him. "What?"

Spencer glanced at me and looked at the chief. "Umm, I have something." He again looked at me.

"Want me to leave?" I asked Cindy.

"No," she said, and turned to her officer. "Go ahead Officer Spencer. Hell, Chris'll find out soon enough. Might as well get it over with."

Spencer gave me a nod and turned to Cindy. "No ID on the body."

I wondered what was so confidential about that.

He continued, "I did find this."

He moved his hand from behind his back and showed the chief the small, matte-blue, semi-automatic pistol I'd seen in the man's hand. Spencer held it with his ballpoint pen through the trigger guard.

Cindy said, "I saw it."

"Doesn't smell like it's been fired," Spencer said.

Cindy looked at the gun, and then toward the body. "Don't suppose he shot himself in the head and cleaned the gun."

Spencer said, "Unlikely."

A colossal understatement, I thought.

"Crap," the chief said. "Don't go anywhere, Chris. Suppose I'd better call the sheriff."

Folly Beach had its own police force, although major crimes were handed to the Charleston County Sheriff's Office. Cindy had never been happy with the arrangement, but knew her department didn't have the resources to investigate serious crimes. The relationship between the two departments was cooperative, yet often strained.

Cindy walked to her unmarked SUV, leaned against the hood, and made the call. Spencer stayed with me and looked around like he was at a party, but didn't have anyone to talk to. The temperature was in the mid-forties, above average for early-February, but I was shivering and Spencer offered to let me wait in his patrol car. He didn't have to ask twice and we got into his car.

The chief returned and I rolled down my window and she said a detective would be here in a half hour. She turned her gaze to Spencer. "Bullet wound?"

Spencer nodded and amped up the patrol car's heat.

The chief rolled her eyes. "Where?"

Spencer pointed his finger at his forehead. "Dead center."

***

Sheriff's Office Detective Kenneth Adair stepped out of his unmarked car. He was six-foot-one, in his mid-thirties, and sported a military-style buzz cut. I had met him a year ago when he had investigated a murder and one of my friends had happened to be the prime suspect.

Adair nodded to the chief, Spencer, and me as we got out of the vehicle. He passed by us and moved to the group huddled around the corpse, so we returned to the comfort of the car. The detective looked like a high-end clothing store model in his navy blazer, light gray slacks with a sharp crease, a starched white shirt, and polished shoes. After sharing a few words with one of the EMTs and bending down to get a closer look at the deceased, Adair came over to Spencer's vehicle.

"Chief, officer, Mr. Landrum." He slipped into the back seat beside me. "Who wants to begin?"

It's satisfying to be recognized, although much of the luster is dulled when the recognition comes from a frowning police detective.

Chief LaMond twisted around from the front seat and looked at me and told Adair I had been walking to breakfast and found the body. She said there was no ID, and they found a handgun with him. She tilted her head toward Spencer who handed Adair a clear evidence bag that now held the weapon.

Adair asked Spencer to turn on the interior lights and held the bag up and inspected it like it contained a piece of fine sculpture. "Browning 1911-22," he said, more to himself than to us. "Interesting."

Cindy looked at the bag. "Why?"

"Oh," Adair said, like he hadn't meant to say *interesting* out loud. "Nothing. It's a common firearm, sold everywhere."

Nothing in that made it sound interesting. It wasn't my place to pry further.

"Anyone recognize him?" Adair asked, back on track.

"No," Cindy said.

Adair turned to me and pointed to the door where Cindy and I had been sitting. "Isn't that the back of your shop?"

I hadn't seen the detective since closing the gallery. "Used to be. I closed in September."

"Oh, sorry. What's there now?"

"Used bookstore," Cindy said. "Barb's Books opened four months ago."

Adair pointed to the door on the other side of the body. "And there?"

Spencer said, "First Light Church. They hold services there when the weather's too bad on the beach."

Adair nodded. "I remember. It's been around a couple of years."

"A little more than that," Spencer said.

Adair jotted something in a small notebook. "Give me a few minutes. Don't leave."

I assumed he meant me, since I doubted either the chief or Spencer would be going anywhere.

The detective walked fifty yards down the alley and then retraced his steps and strolled behind the police and fire vehicles. He was on the phone when he returned to the car.

He ended the call and said, "Crime scene techs are on the way. Now, Mr. Landrum, let's hear your version."

It was identical to what the chief had told him. Adair jotted some notes as I recounted what I'd found.

"Why did you take the alley instead of Center Street?"

"Short cut."

"Wouldn't it have been safer along the well-lit main street?"

"I didn't think about it since I'd gone this way hundreds of times. Could do it blindfolded. In fact, with the dense fog, I felt like I was blindfolded."

"Can anyone vouch your whereabouts before finding the body?"

I felt a knot in my stomach. "I was home."

"Alone?"

"Yes."

"You're certain you don't recognize him?"

"It was dark when I got here, but I don't think I do."

"That's it for now, Mr. Landrum. Let me have your number in case I have more questions." He jotted down my number in his book, handed me a card, and told me to call if I thought of anything else.

I was no longer hungry, but knew I needed to eat and continued my tragically-delayed walk to breakfast. This time, I took Center Street.

Chapter Two

The Lost Dog Cafe was a block off the main drag, within easy walking distance to anywhere near the center of town, and was my favorite breakfast spot. Fortunately for the restaurant, although not always convenient for me, I was not alone in singing the praises of the Dog. Most of the year, its dining room, with walls covered with photos of dogs of all shapes, sizes, breeds, and poses, was packed and groups gathered outside waiting for a table. The restaurant's two patios were canine hospitable, and there were often as many dogs waiting as there were children. February was not the busiest time and despite the traumatic delay, I was able to get a table.

The warm, inviting décor was complimented by a helpful, cheery wait staff. After what I had been through, a kind voice was as important as food, and I was pleased to see Amber Lewis headed my way with a mug of coffee. She was my favorite waitress, and we had been an item when I first arrived on Folly. It had been years since we had dated, yet she remained one of my best friends.

"Granola and yogurt?" she asked as she set a mug in front of me.

She knew I was as likely to order granola and yogurt as I was to ask for a chocolate-covered paper clip.

"French toast," I replied, sharper than I had intended.

Amber cocked her head, her long amber hair tied in a ponytail flipped to the side, and her eye narrowed. "Got up on the wrong side of the bed, did we?"

"Sorry. Bad morning."

That was all it took. She looked around, didn't see anyone

demanding her attention, and slid in the other side of the booth. Amber was in her late-forties, had been on Folly for eighteen years, and had worked at the Dog since it opened fourteen years ago. The restaurant and its staff epitomized the character of the island. The Dog was also Folly's epicenter of rumors, gossip, and occasional facts, so, for obvious reasons, it was a hangout for locals as well as a destination spot for vacationers.

She gave me a few seconds to sip the coffee before saying, "Spill it?"

She hadn't meant the coffee, and I gave her the rundown on my morning walk.

She reached across the table and put her hand on mine. "You okay?"

I assured her I was getting there.

She put her finger in the air. "Hold that thought." She headed to the kitchen with my order.

I was thinking that thought wasn't something I wanted to hold when she returned and slipped her trim, well-proportioned, five-foot-five-inch frame into the booth.

"Who was it?"

She must have figured I was okay and wanted to start collecting information, although I didn't give her much to talk about when I said the man didn't look familiar.

A couple seated at a table by the window was looking around. Amber saw them, said she needed to get to work, said my "healthy" breakfast would be up soon, and went to see what the pair needed.

I was watching Amber laughing with the diners when a woman yanked the door open and looked around. She was tall, thin, had short black hair, and was attractive in an angular sort of way. Even if the restaurant had been full, it would have been hard not to notice her attention-grabbing red leather jacket and bright-red blouse. I had seen her around town, but we had never met, so I was surprised when she headed my way.

She stopped beside the booth and looked at the seat Amber had vacated. "You're Chris Landrum?"

"I am."

"May I join you?"

Politeness and curiosity kept me from saying no, and I pointed at the open space. "You may."

She threw her jacket on the other side of the bench seat, slid into the booth, and looked around for a waitress. My first thought was she was accustomed to getting her way.

She smiled, yet her tired-looking, hazel eyes portrayed sadness. On closer inspection, I realized she was in her sixties but looked younger.

"I'm Barbara Deanelli. I own Barb's Books in a space I believe you're familiar with."

"Yes. I spent many hours there trying to make a go of it as a photo gallery. I hope you're having better luck."

She looked at me. No emotion showed. "That's what the Realtor said when he showed me the space. I think you know him. Bob Howard. He's the one who tried to tell me who you were and what you looked like."

I chuckled. "That's a scary thought."

I had known Bob since my first week on Folly. He'd helped me find a house after the one I was renting was torched with me in it. Bob had also rented me the space for the gallery. He was the antithesis of what most would expect in a realtor. His dress was slovenly at best, he was conversant in George Carlin's seven dirty words plus a few more, and he had never fallen for Shakespeare's idiom, "Discretion is the better part of valor." Despite his shortcomings, he was a good friend.

Barbara nodded. "I was beginning to wonder when he showed me the space and said, 'Yes ma'am, I'll be glad to rent this dump to you. The last person who had it went bust.'"

"Welcome to the charming side of Bob Howard. I'd hate to hear how he described me."

She stared at me. If I didn't know better, I would think she could see directly into my brain. "Howard said you were handsome back in the day when you had hair and were a few pounds lighter. Said you'd be easy to find. All I had to do was go to the Dog and look for a guy long in the tooth wearing boring clothes and drinking coffee." She grinned.

I laughed. "I'd be insulted if it hadn't come from someone who was a decade older than I am, who could seesaw with a hippo, and thinks dressing up means tying his shoestrings."

"Yes, we're talking about the same Bob Howard."

Amber made it back to our table and asked my guest what she wanted. Barbara said she wasn't hungry and coffee would do. I nodded at my mug and Amber gave me a thumbs-up.

Barbara turned to me and still showed no emotion. "I was told you found the body."

I said yes and she continued, "I'm an early riser and walked to the store from my condo to work on inventory. I didn't know what was happening in the alley until I opened the back door to get some air. The back room was way too hot." She looked at me like the temperature was my fault. "A policeman stopped me from exiting and said it was a crime scene."

"I imagine that was a shock."

"A surprise. I went out the front door and walked around to the alley to see what was going on. A young officer was standing guard at the yellow tape; his name was Spence or Spencer. He said there was a body. I asked what happened and he said he couldn't say more than that."

I was beginning to wonder where she was going with this. I waited for it to unravel at her pace.

"One of the other cops said your name, so I asked Spence, or whatever his name is, if he knew you since you'd owned the gallery. He said not only did he know you, you found the unfortunate soul. I looked around and didn't see anyone who fit your description, and asked the officer if you were still there. He said no and thought you had headed here." She tapped the table. "So there you are, and here I am."

That explained how she arrived at the Dog, but not why. "Officer Spencer was correct. I found the body. How long were you in the gall—the bookstore before you opened the back door?"

"A little while."

Vague, I thought. Before I could get a better timeline, Amber returned with Barbara's coffee and my refill. The comforting aroma of bacon coming from the table beside us filled the air. It was the only comforting thing this morning.

"Sure I can't get you something to eat?" she asked.

Barbara said no without looking at the waitress.

The lady at a nearby table leaned toward us. "Bacon's mighty good. You ought to try some."

"Thank you," my tablemate said, again avoiding eye contact.

Amber smiled at the bacon connoisseur, looked at Barb, and then at me. "Let me know if you need anything."

Barbara gave a sideways glance at the next table, watched Amber move to the other side of the room, and leaned toward me. "People here are friendly."

Her tone made it sound like she said they had malaria.

"Yes, they, we, are. A great place to be. Where are you from?"

She sipped her coffee and then set the mug down. "Out of state."

I waited for her to elaborate. Nothing.

"You came looking for me," I said, hoping I wouldn't have to ask why.

She spoke in a low voice. "Did you know the deceased?"

It reminded me of a question someone would ask at a funeral visitation. I repeated what I had told the police about it being dark and that I didn't recognize him.

"Could you describe him?"

I tried. She nodded and continued not to show any reaction. The conversation, if you could call it that, was getting stranger by the sip.

"From where the body was positioned, would you speculate he was trying to enter my space?"

"I have no idea." I felt like I was testifying in court.

"Anything strike you as unusual about the circumstances of his death?"

I didn't think I needed to say everything was unusual about finding a man with a bullet hole in his head and a gun in his hand. I tried to picture the scene and the body. I also began to think if I had noticed something I shouldn't tell the person sitting across from me.

"No. Why?"

She stared in her half-empty mug and I wondered if she had heard the question.

She grinned. "Nothing. Once a lawyer, always a lawyer."

She had grinned so I hoped I could keep the mood going, and smiled. "From law to owning a bookstore."

She gave an abbreviated nod. "Yes."

Progress, I thought. "How did—"

"Have to go," she interrupted and grabbed her jacket. "Thank you for talking with me, Mr. Landrum."

She hopped up and headed to the door. I watched her leave and realized it was one of the strangest conversations I'd had in the Dog—and that was saying something.

Barbara had barely exited when Amber was back at the table. Instead of saying something like, *Would you like more coffee young, handsome gentleman?* she opened with, "Was that the woman with the bookstore in your old space?"

"Yep."

"What did she want? Something about the body you found?"

"She wanted to know if I knew who it was."

"Why?"

I shook my head. "Don't know. A little strange. What do you know about her?"

"Not much. I think this is the first time I've seen her in here. Jason's been in her store a few times and described the owner as tall, skinny, and old, so that's why I figured it might be her."

Jason was Amber's seventeen-year-old son. I'd known him since he was eight and he was the reason she and I had stopped dating. A few years ago, he had been exposed to a murder victim I was standing over. I had nothing to do with the death, nevertheless Amber thought it was too dangerous for him to be close to me. She'd called me a "murder magnet." I'd regretted her decision, and occasionally wondered how things would have turned out between us if she hadn't made it.

"Old?" I said.

Amber smiled. "Figured you caught that. He's a teenager, Chris. We're all old to him."

"Know anything about her, other than being *old*?"

"Heard she's all business, not easy to make friends with. She's also a bit snobby." Amber paused. "That's from women. A couple of the guys, older than you, if you can believe that, said she was intriguing. That's their word, and they say if they weren't married, they'd be buying lots of books."

"Where did she come from?"

Amber shrugged. "First I heard about her was when someone said a truck was unloading a bunch of shelves over there. Said some woman seemed to be in charge of the unloading. Haven't you been in her store?"

It would have been impossible for me not to know a bookstore had occupied my former space, but closing the gallery had been traumatic, and I hadn't visited the new tenant. It even hurt to see *Landrum Gallery* painted-out over the door and replaced by *Barb's Books*. I knew I was being petty, but having put my time, energy, and much of my life savings into the gallery, I felt the loss much as I would have a death in the family. Barbara Deanelli hadn't moved to Folly at the time I'd shut the door, yet I still resented her for being in the space. Yes, I was being irrational, and did I already say petty?

I said. "Not yet."

"Think she'll make it?"

"I hope so. From what I've heard, bookstores, especially small, independent ones, are almost becoming extinct. Suppose more people read books than buy photos, so she might have a chance."

"Jason said she's selling used books. Takes them in trade for other books and if you're not trading for them, she sells them for a lot less than they would cost new."

"That's what I heard, and if it's the case, she has a chance."

Amber said she'd better get back to work, patted me on the arm, and said she was sorry I'd found the body. I couldn't have agreed more.

Chapter Three

After talking with Amber, I realized I was more curious about the bookstore than I cared to admit. It struck me as odd how the owner had sought me out for information about the body. And, after my attempt to turn my lifelong hobby into a successful business had failed, I was curious about how successful Ms. Deanelli would be. Truth be told, not often as easy as it sounded, I was ready to move past my wounded feelings and despondency over surrendering my dream.

It was time to turn to Charles Fowler, the one person on Folly Beach who knew more about books and rumors about newcomers than all other residents combined, and that was only a slight exaggeration. I had met him during my first few days on the island, and for reasons years of psychoanalysis might take to unravel, we had become friends, best friends, if two mid-sixty-year-old guys could use such a youth-centric term. We were as opposite as two people could be. I had spent my entire professional life working in the human resources department of a large health insurance company. Charles had spent his entire professional life—never mind, he had never entered the professional work force unless you count working on the line in a Ford plant in Detroit, and that was during Richard Nixon's illustrious presidency. He—Charles, not Nixon—had *retired* to Folly thirty years ago at the ripe-young age of thirty-four.

My friend had a serious aversion to W-2 forms and paychecks, yet was addicted to books. His apartment looked like a public library, minus a librarian saying "shhh" to all who entered. He had floor-to-ceiling bookshelves made of stacked concrete blocks and irregular pine boards along three walls in the living room, four walls in the bedroom, two walls in the kitchen, and not to be neglected, one wall in the bathroom. My unlikely friend swore he had read each tome with the exception of the cookbooks. My book collection could be counted on one hand, so needless to say, I wasn't a fan of reading.

His mini-library was in a small apartment building attached to the former home of the Sandbar Seafood and Steak Restaurant, and three blocks from the Dog, so I decided to walk. I could have called first, but after everything that had happened, the walk would do me good.

Charles answered the door wearing a long-sleeve, cardinal-red T-shirt with the image of a head of an eagle dominating the front. Running second to his book collection, he had a hundred or more T-shirts, most from colleges and universities, all long-sleeve. Years ago I had made a concerted effort to stop asking about them. That didn't deter him from continuing to share comments that would be fodder for *Jeopardy!*

Charles pointed to the logo on his chest. "It's Big Stuff, Winthrop University's mascot."

I pointed to my chest, "It's Chris Landrum. You receiving company?"

"You're no fun," He waved me in and pointed to a wicker rocking chair in the corner.

I knew it had a wicker seat because I had seen it on previous visits. Today it was covered with two stacks of books, paperbacks with a few hardcovers mixed in. I moved them to the floor so they could keep three larger stacks of reading material company, and sat.

Charles pointed to the books I had moved. "Barb's Books, an answer to my prayers."

When Landrum Gallery was open, Charles had been there almost as often as I had been. He appointed himself executive sales manager and, without receiving a penny of pay, had served with pride in that position. He said it had given him purpose, something to do, and a positive identity, three things that he had been lacking. He was devastated when the gallery closed, and had taken months to get over the anger and frustration. Perhaps his comment about Barb's Books signaled the end of his funk.

"You're in good spirits," I said.

"Lincoln said, 'People are only as happy as they make up their minds to be.'"

Spouting presidential quotes came in a close third to Charles's penchant for accumulating books and T-shirts.

"Jennifer Lopez said, 'I'm Glad.'"

He cocked his head. "You made that up."

I leaned back in the chair. "Look it up. Aren't you going to ask why I'm here?"

"Why are you here?"

"To tell you about my walk to breakfast."

"Hope it was more exciting than it sounds."

"It was." I shared what had happened in the alley.

He huffed. "And when were you going to tell me?"

Charles prided himself on knowing everything that happened on his island. One of the quickest ways to exasperate him was to fail to tell him something in a timely manner. To Charles, that meant within the hour, or sooner.

I thought the answer was self-explanatory. "Now."

"And you don't know who he was?"

"No." I described how he was dressed.

"Doesn't sound like he was from these parts. Think he was walking down the alley and got in a fight?"

"No idea."

Charles looked at the ceiling and back at me. "Could he have been coming out the door from First Light or the bookstore?

"No idea," I repeated. "Add this to strange." I told him about my visit from Barbara Deanelli.

Charles looked at the stack of books on the floor and back at me. "You know she's Dude's sister—half-sister."

And I didn't think I could be more shaken than I already had been this morning.

"You're kidding."

"Who'd kid about that?"

Jim "Dude" Sloan had owned the "surf shop"—yes, without any upper-case letters in the name—for thirty years, had worn hippie garb for fifty years, and had been a surfer for all but the first three of his sixty-four years. I'd known him since I arrived on Folly, although knew little about his life before that. He had seldom talked about his past; seldom talked about anything.

"Did he tell you?"

"Nope. Got it from Rocky."

"Dude's obnoxious employee?"

"Yep. Ran into him a couple of nights ago at the Surf Bar. He'd been there a couple of hours enjoying their libations. He was so lit he almost sounded human."

Rocky and Stephon were Dude's tat-covered employees who appeared to think customers were works of the devil and should be mistreated at every opportunity. Dude had told me he kept them because he didn't have to pay them much, and they had a visceral way of communicating with fellow surfers. His actual words were: "They be hangin' on the same wave." They had treated me, and most other baby-boom-generation citizens, like we weren't from the same ocean.

"Why was he talking to you?"

He held out his hands and shrugged. "What can I say. My engaging, charming personality can win over the most obnoxious surf shop employee."

There had to be more. "And?"

"Ever since Aunt M. befriended Dude's employees, Rocky's been borderline civil."

Charles's Aunt Melinda had moved to Folly three years ago. She hadn't seen him for decades and wanted to reconnect with her last living relative. She arrived full of humor, sassiness, a love for almost everyone, and terminal cancer. She had overcome many obstacles in her life, but couldn't beat the disease and passed away two years ago. During her brief time on Folly, she had achieved the impossible when she had been befriended by Dude's employees.

"What did he say about Dude and Barbara?"

"Same pop, different mom; had seen each other only a few times in the last dozen years. Barb got divorced and Dude suggested she come to Folly."

"Did you know Dude had a sister, half or otherwise?"

Charles nodded. "Sure. Known it since way back two nights ago."

That's what I thought. "Where's she from?"

"Don't know. Rocky ran out of beer and pleasantness. Gave me a farewell growl, and left."

"Don't you think it strange she came to the Dog to ask about the body?"

"Maybe, maybe not," my definitive friend said. "Not everyone is used to hearing about a dead body out their back door. You're the only person I know who has a propensity for that. It riled up her curiosity, she heard about you finding him, and voila."

"That could be all, but it didn't strike me as normal. Something seemed off."

"How do you know what Barbara's normal is?"

"Good point," I said. "Regardless, I can't put my finger on it. Just didn't sit right."

"So, how are we going to find out who the guy was?"

His question wasn't out of mere curiosity. In addition to volunteering when I had the gallery, he had taken odd jobs for off-the-books cash from local businesses, and on a more frightening note, he prided himself on being a detective. He was unlicensed and untrained, but said he'd read enough PI mysteries that he ought to be able to figure out most crimes. The scary thing was he and I had been mired in more murders than anyone who doesn't carry a badge should be. Through luck, amateur detecting, the help of a cadre of friends, more luck, being at the wrong place at the wrong time, and a touch more luck, we had solved several of them. That reinforced Charles's self-anointed private detective status.

"I'll call the chief later and see if they've identified him," I said.

"How much later?"

"Tonight."

"And then you'll call me?"

"Yes."

"Promise?"

"Yes."

Chapter Four

Good to my word, I called Charles, not to tell him who the victim was, but to let him know the police hadn't learned the identity. The man's fingerprints weren't in IAFIS, the FBI's national fingerprint database, and Chief LaMond said none of her officers had recognized him. The handgun found on the body was with Detective Adair who was trying it trace it through the serial number. Charles was disappointed and said I should have done more to learn who he was. I asked how, and he suggested I figure it out. He often offers similarly helpful suggestions.

A cold wave swept through the Lowcountry overnight and I couldn't think of a good reason to leave the house. February on Folly beat being anywhere in the North, although the cold, damp air could still be uncomfortable. Besides, I had to start pulling together everything needed to prepare my taxes, which next to a trip to the dentist, was my least favorite event of the year. Chief LaMond would call if she learned more. If I called Charles, he wouldn't let me off the phone until I agreed to harass the chief; something neither I nor the chief needed.

I was halfway through going over my bank statements when the phone rang. I figured it was impatient Charles. I was wrong.

"Brother Chris, this is Preacher Burl. Is this a convenient time?"

I told him it was.

"Brother Chris, might I impose upon you to meet me at First Light? I have a delicate situation to discuss and would rather not do it over the phone or at a public dining emporium. I have to wait here for a plumber, or I'd come to your house."

I was intrigued enough to agree; intrigued and would rather do anything other than taxes.

I avoided the alley and rapped on First Light's front door. Preacher Burl opened it halfway, looked to see if anyone was with me, and waved me in. Burl Ives Costello was five-foot-five, shaped like a football, and fifty years old. He and I had become acquainted the first year his nondenominational church had been open when three of his members, or members of his flock as he referred to them, had been murdered. I had originally suspected the preacher of the deaths, but ended up helping save Burl after the killer had tried to electrocute him.

The preacher locked the door and pointed to one of the pews. "Thanks for coming, Brother Chris. I'm sure it was an inconvenience."

I sat and said it wasn't.

"I hope you don't find what I'm about to say as silly." He paused and smiled. His blue eyes sparkled.

I returned the smile. "Preacher Burl, you'd have a hard time competing with some of my friends when it comes to silly."

Burl knew I was referring to Charles and Dude, both semi-regulars at First Light. After I closed my gallery, which had been open on Sundays, I lost my best reason—excuse—for not attending, yet I still could count on one hand the number of times I'd been to a service.

Burl nodded. "I will grant you that."

I leaned forward in the pew. "So, what it is?"

He groaned. "If I were in your shoes, I'm afraid I would think the preacher man's paranoid. You, of all people, know how much the devil has bequeathed upon my ministry."

"You've had your share of bad luck."

"Then I hope you can understand my trepidation when I learned a gentleman's life was taken from this earth mere inches from our walled sanctuary." Burl nodded toward the back door.

Inches was a stretch. "Did you know him?"

"I don't think so. Of course, I didn't see the body. The police came by my apartment this morning and showed me a photograph. The dead don't have the spirit within them and their appearance is never as remembered as when they walked this flawed earth."

No would have sufficed.

"Do you think he had something to do with First Light or one of your flock?"

Burl stood, walked to the back of the sanctuary, opened the rear door, looked out, and returned to the pew.

"Brother Chris, I am unable to detect a connection, but as you may recall, not that long ago I was oblivious to some of the events surrounding the unspeakable murders that I hold myself responsible for causing." He pointed to the corner of the room where one his flock had been killed after being pushed from a ladder. "That's not to mention how you and your friend Brother Bob saved me—praise the Lord—from electrocution in this very room. To reiterate, I do not see any direct connection between our church and the unfortunate soul who met an untimely death in yon alley." He leaned toward the back door.

I understood his anxiety, although if he didn't see any connection and didn't know the deceased, why he had called and requested this secretive meeting?

I wanted to scream, *why am I here?* Instead, I said, "Preacher Burl, you and your flock went through a terrible time, and I admire you for continuing your ministry here. You've meant so much to many people."

I hesitated and waited for him to get to the reason. Charles would have chided me for hesitating and would have demanded an explanation from Burl.

"Brother Chris, that brings me to the reason I requested your presence."

Halleluiah, I thought, followed by a pensive nod.

"You have connections with local officials. You also have a reputation for aiding the civil authorities in identifying and catching those who have given their life over to the devil. Unlike many others, you are known for keeping confidences and not spreading rumors."

"Preacher Burl, I don't—"

He held his hand up. "Please allow me to finish."

I didn't see an upside to irritating a minister, and stopped.

"Thank you. To be candid, the events of the past two years have me, as they say, shell-shocked. I have had difficulty sleeping; I have had trouble eating, although you can't tell it from my girth. I'm startled by the most innocuous sounds. My mother, God rest her soul, would say I was a mess." He looked toward the front window, and back at me. "Please don't share this with anyone. I've put my fate in the hands of the Lord. He hasn't seen fit to help me successfully sail these choppy seas."

I felt his discomfort and pain, but didn't know how I could help. "What would you like me to do?"

"Brother Chris, I don't feel I am doing justice to my ministry and to my flock as long as I remain in this unsettled condition. The latest death at the church's doorstep has accentuated everything negative within me. With that in mind, I am asking that you grant me one wish—and a huge one it is."

I motioned for him to continue.

"It may be paranoia, but I feel the death is related to First Light. Would you use your connections, intellect, and unique power to unravel the most amorphous clues to see if the death does, in fact, have anything to do with my ministry?"

I exhaled, looked at the floor, then at the large neon cross on the wall that was the focal point at the front of the room, and turned my attention to the suffering preacher. "Yes."

Burl closed his eyes like he was in silent prayer. After a moment, he said, "I will be forever grateful."

"I appreciate it, although I don't know what I can do. The police have resources. Detective Adair, the detective in charge, is good, and you know Chief LaMond. She'll make sure her entire department assists the detective in finding who did it."

Burl shook his head. "I don't doubt they'll perform. Additionally, I would feel better if someone without the restraints imposed upon the authorities was looking at the situation. A different perspective is welcomed."

I didn't see hope, yet also didn't want to say no. "Preacher, I'll do my best. I can't do it alone. With your permission, I'd like to discuss it with Charles and one or two others. I can assure you confidentiality will be foremost in their minds as well as mine."

"I would prefer you didn't," Burl said, "Nevertheless, I trust your judgment. Do what you must."

He started to walk me to the door, hesitated, and said, "Please allow me to offer a brief prayer for your success."

I did, he did, and we shook hands. He invited me to church Sunday, and escorted me to the door. I thanked him for the invitation, but didn't commit to attending.

I stopped on the sidewalk outside the church, and thought I would have been better off working on taxes.

Chapter Five

Tuesday was open-mic night at Cal's Country Bar and Burgers; known as Cal's to the locals—first, because no one wanted to say the long name, and second, because no one wanted to associate burgers, good burgers, with the bar. The country music focal point on Folly was owned by Cal Ballew, a septuagenarian Texan who had spread country charm and music to most zip codes in the southern half of the country for forty-five years. His fame had come when he hit the country charts in 1962 with "End of the Story." It was followed by a string of records with song titles that had never become worthy enough even for the most arcane trivia question. Cal took over the bar five years ago after the previous owner slithered over to the wrong side of the law and was now residing at taxpayers' expense far from the beach.

Open-mic night often attracted a handful of local wannabes, a guitar-toting vacationer or two, and each week, as regular as clockwork, Heather Lee. She was in her late forties, attractive, plied her trade as a massage therapist during the day, had the singing voice of a rooster, and was Charles's girlfriend. Most Tuesdays, Cal reserved a table for Charles, Heather, and me. Extra chairs were nearby in case some of our friends happened to drop by in need of an adult beverage, moderately-entertaining entertainment, and to, as Cal would say, *sit a spell.*

Tonight we were joined by the bar's owner. The crowd was typical for a cold, damp Tuesday evening in February: sparse, a kind way of saying the place was almost empty. Three of the twelve tables were occupied, and each had a guitar case setting close to one of the occupants.

Cal leaned his lanky, six-foot-three-inch body back in his chair, pushed his sweat-stained Stetson back on his head, and turned to Heather. "Hon, guess you're gonna get to honor us with three songs. Carla Sims, one of the other gal singers, don't look like she'll make it. Said she'd be here by now. Bad for her, good for you."

Heather beamed, Charles smiled, and I suppressed a groan. Cal, who had listened to hundreds of singers during his years on the road - and, as he seldom hesitated to point out, during his appearances on the Grand Ole Opry - tried to limit Heather to two songs and late on the program so his patrons would have had time for their ears to be desensitized by alcohol. Tonight there was more time to kill than entertainers to fill. Wisdom prevailed when he said he'd save her for last. To her, it meant she was the headliner, and none of us had the guts to tell her Cal's thinking.

"So, Kentucky," Cal said. "Hear you stumbled on another dead body."

Cal had a tendency to call people by their state of origin. Charles and I had tried to break him of the habit and had made progress. Like many reformed addicts, he backslid.

"Afraid so."

"Hear you chased the killer down the alley. That must've been scary."

I smiled. The Folly rumor machine had been at work. "It would have been if it was true. I found the body. He was dead, and no killer was nearby."

"You did see him, didn't you?"

"Not a glance. Who said I did?"

"Three or four people. They said they heard it from a guy who was hanging around after the murder. Said he heard it from the cops."

"Sorry, Cal. No truth to it."

He looked disappointed. "Then I don't suppose you found a stack of hundred dollar bills beside the body?"

"Did you hear that I did?"

"Yep. The guy who said it was about four beers south of soused so I took it with a grain of mustard seed."

Charles glanced at me then turned to Cal. "Know who he was?"

Charles was still displeased I hadn't found out the identity.

"Old drunk Jim."

Charles rolled his eyes. "The dead guy."

"Not a clue, Michigan."

Okay, maybe we weren't making as much progress as I thought.

Heather asked, "What'd he look like?"

I gave her the best description I had, considering I had only seen him for a few seconds, in the dark, and in a condition that didn't show his best side.

Heather pointed at a bar stool. "Sounds like that fellow in here Friday. Hung out over there. Cal, remember?"

Cal looked at the stool Heather had pointed to. "Was I tendin'?"

Bar owner talk for tending bar, I assumed, which was scary coming from Cal. After six years, he had mastered the hang of ordering beer and wine from the distributor, as long as the wine wasn't more complicated than red, white, or pink. Cal's never had any intention of owning anything other than his classic 1971 Cadillac Eldorado that had been his home and transportation. When the bar's former owner went to grayer pastures, Cal, who had been a regular entertainer in the bar, stepped in and took over. A few friends pitched in and helped him learn the basics. No one was able to teach him the fine art of grilling burgers, fries, and onion rings, although that hadn't stopped him from trying. And to our delight, he had hired a part-time "chef," as Cal called his help. Calling his part-time help *chef* was like calling Waffle House a five-star restaurant. Regardless, the food was tolerable, and after a few drinks, tasty.

"Nope," Heather said. "You were in the middle of a set covering Ernest Tubb classics."

"How long was he here?" Charles asked.

"Don't know," Heather said. "I wasn't here long. Stopped by for a beer after giving a massage to a flabby conventioneer from Alabama. The guy was here when I left. Didn't—"

Cal snapped his fingers. "Got it. Know who you mean. Unfriendly-like character. He was here for a beer on Friday, but the night before he parked himself on that stool and took up space for an hour."

"Are you sure it was the dead guy?" Charles asked.

Cal smiled. "He wasn't when he was in here."

Charles sighed. "You know what I mean."

"Hang on," Cal said. "Gotta play MC." He scooted his chair back and tore another runner in the ancient, dark brown, indoor-outdoor carpet he inherited with the bar. Years ago, I had suggested he rip it out, but he said it was disintegrating fast all by itself and it'd be gone soon enough. He had added, "It gives off that good ole, stale beer, mushed in grease aroma of a fine country bar." He'd played most of them, so I figured he knew.

Cal mumbled something under his breath about the carpet, and waved for one of the aspiring musicians to meet him on the tiny elevated stage in front of the rectangular, tile dance floor. The future star unpacked his guitar and Cal switched off the old Wurlitzer juke box, cutting short John Anderson bemoaning coming home to count his memories. Cal tapped a microphone that was old enough to have been crooned into by Hank Williams Sr. He asked the musician's name, and in his best master of ceremonies voice, announced to the uninterested assembly who the opening act was, and that open-mic night was brought to you by "Folly's foremost country music venue."

Folly's only country music venue would have also been accurate.

Those who knew more about music than I did said many country tunes were made up of three chords and the truth. The young man on stage appeared to run out of guitar-strumming ability somewhere shy of three chords. His lyrics may have been the truth, but were hard to focus on. Heather may be the headliner after all.

Cal returned to his chair and shook his head. "That ought to drive customers to drink. Where was I?"

"The dead guy," Charles said.

Cal stared at the musician strumming two chords. "Oh yeah. Remember him now because he wasn't dressed like most folks here. He didn't come to town riding two to a mule."

"Huh?" Charles asked before I could.

"The boy had dough. His clothes were casual and expensive. Can you believe his shirt was pressed?"

"Wonder you let him in," Charles said.

Cal winked at him and looked toward the stage when the singer, whose name I forgot after Cal introduced him, began Kris Kristofferson's "Help Me Make It Through the Night."

Cal shook his head, again. "And I thought Kris couldn't sing."

Charles was undeterred. "The dead guy?"

"Hold your stallion," Cal said. "Where was I?"

"His clothes," I said.

"Out of place," Cal said.

"That boy could use some strummin' lessons," Heather said to no one in particular.

I wasn't as good a detective as Charles, but knew she wasn't referring to the well-dressed stranger with the, heaven forbid, pressed shirt.

Charles ignored Heather and looked at Cal. "Anything else?"

Cal looked at the singer and back to Charles. "I was playing in honky-tonk bars before that guy's daddy was hatched." He pointed his thumb toward the stage. "Been bartending here for a few years so I can tell what a customer's thinking before the thoughts reach his mouth." Cal chuckled. "Can tell you a couple of things about the stranger. First, he got his hackles up when anyone tried to talk to him. Two tried; two failed. The second thing is, he wasn't here to pick-up some lovin'. No he wasn't."

Charles said, "How do you know?"

"You miss the first part of what I said? Trust me on that one. I know."

I knew that wasn't good enough for Charles. In a rare fit of wisdom, he didn't pursue it.

I asked, "What's your gut tell you about him?"

He started to say something, hesitated, and instead put up his hand. "I'll be back."

He headed to the stage, encouraged everyone to give a nice round of applause for *what's his name*, and asked the second vocalist to make her way to the stage. The smell of grilling burgers came from the small kitchen by the bar and reminded me I hadn't had supper. I'd only had one glass of wine, but figured I could stomach one of Cal's burgers. The next singer was in her twenties and I'd seen her perform a couple of other times before. Her voice was pleasant, and her guitar playing about fifty times better than her predecessor, although her song selection leaned more toward 1970s soft-rock than the traditional country Cal and most of his patrons preferred.

Anita, I remembered her name from her previous performances, began her set with Carly Simon's "Haven't Got Time for the Pain," and Cal headed toward the small kitchen to "rustle up a burger." Charles added, "Make it three, and a heaping serving of fries."

Charles watched Cal say a few words to the group at the next table and head to the kitchen, then turned to Heather. "Remember anything else about the dead guy?"

"He paid more attention to his beer than Cal's singing. Something heavy was on his mind."

Anita continued on her Carly Simon track with "Anticipation," and Cal returned with our burgers and fries.

"While you're up," Charles said, "how about another round?"

Cal tipped his Stetson. "Your wish is my command."

Heather put her arm around Charles and said, "Chucky, ain't this terrific? I'm the headliner."

Charles bristled when anyone called him anything other than Charles. To him, Chuck or Charlie were overgrown four letter words. No one other than Heather could get away with an occasional Chucky; other offenders would incur the wrath of Charles, and that wasn't pretty.

Charles—Chucky—kissed her on the cheek. "Terrific, sweetie, terrific."

Cal arrived with our drinks and leaned back in his chair while Anita transitioned into Jim Croce's "Time in a Bottle."

The bar's owner shook his head. "Ain't bad; ain't country."

His review appeared to be over, so I asked, "Remember anything else about the guy?"

"Had a fondness for Bud Light. That's it."

"How'd he pay?" I asked.

"Andy Jacksons."

Charles waved his hand in Cal's face. "Don't suppose you made him show a driver's license."

Cal stared at Charles. "In case his bucks bounced?"

Charles said, "Trying to figure out who he was."

"He was a loner who liked Bud Light, had a pocket full of Jacksons, and was as cold as a cast-iron commode in Alaska."

I figured we were at the bottom of the well of information about the stranger and it was time to mosey another direction. Cal was rubbing off on me.

"Cal, what do you know about the new bookstore?"

"Been there once. Checking to see if it had songbooks—nary a one." He paused and looked at the stage. Anita was sliding her guitar back in its case.

He stood to return to the stage. "Don't drift off."

Since Heather was one singer closer to being in the spotlight, he couldn't get her to drift off if the building was in flames.

Cal thanked Anita for sharing her version of country, and then said, "Our next crooner's been with us a few times and is always a favorite with the gals. Make welcome Ed Robinson."

Ed smiled at the rousing round of applause he received from the middle-aged couple and another woman at his table. Someone slamming the men's restroom door at the side of the stage was the only other noise in the room.

Cal returned to the table and Ed began Conway Twitty's "Hello Darlin'."

"Bookstore," I said, trying to rechannel Cal's thinking.

"Bunch of books, no songbooks. Gal that owns it'd be a looker if she put some meat on her bones and cracked a smile. I tried to welcome her to Folly, and all she did was nod. It was cool outside that morning, but her look was as cold as a frosted frog." He shook his head. "If she wasn't Dude's sis, I'd never go back. She—"

Charles leaned toward Cal. "How'd you know she was Dude's half-sister?"

Cal leaned away from Charles. "Don't know much about fractions, but Dude told me."

"When?" I asked.

"Been a while now. Don't recall for certain, a few weeks maybe."

Charles leaned closer once again. "How come you didn't tell

us?"

He was peeved because he thought he was the only one who knew about Dude's *half*-sister.

"Figured you'd already knew, being you're such a good detective and a friend of Dude." He smiled when he said detective.

"Well, umm… sure, I knew," Charles stammered. "Wondered when you found out."

I suspected Charles's feelings were more hurt because he hadn't heard it from Dude than he was Cal knew.

Heather had pushed away from the table and stared at her guitar case. She was focused on her pending performance and had no interest in our conversation.

"Did Dude say why she was here?" I asked.

"He surfed-talked about seven words that meant she'd split from a bad marriage and needed somewhere to lick her wounds. He told her Folly was a 'boss hangout' and she had moved lock, stock, and barrel of books to our fine seaside community."

Dude had never met a sentence he couldn't butcher. He didn't believe in using ten words, when one would almost do.

Charles asked, "Moved from where?"

"Dude didn't say, or if he did, I didn't understand."

Two other couples drifted in and grabbed tables. A man I hadn't seen before came in and sat at the bar. Ed had finished the late Merle Haggard's classic "Okie from Muskogee" and was introducing his wife, Gretchen, and two of his friends "out in the audience" who'd travelled "all the way" from Summerville to hear him. It was a whopping thirty-five-mile trip. Heather applauded loud enough for the rest of the table; most likely so Ed and his wife and friends would reciprocate at the end of her set. Cal headed to the new arrivals to welcome them and take their orders.

I now knew a bit more about the body and an equal amount new about Barbara. I didn't need to know more, but I was still curious.

Chapter Six

Heather tapped her fingers on the table, looked at her watch, and then glared at Cal who was delivering drinks to a table of recent arrivals. Ed finished his introductions and broke into "I'd Be Better Off (In a Pine Box)." Heather frowned and agreed it was where Ed should be. He was bullying into her stage time. The first two performers had exited, taking their fan base with them, leaving the crowd sparser than when we had arrived.

Cal returned from playing bartender. Heather put her hand on his arm, gave him her best stage smile, and tilted her head toward Ed. Cal nodded.

Charles said, "Who's the newcomer?" He pointed his beer bottle in the direction of the man at the bar.

"First time I've—"

Ed strummed the last notes of the Doug Stone cover, and Heather yanked Charles away from Cal. "Let Cal go to work."

It was her turn and she wasn't about to let a stage-hogging musician play another chord. Cal pushed away from the table and headed to the stage. Heather grabbed her guitar and followed.

Cal said, "Let's have a big hand for Ed."

Three people at Ed's table and the newcomer at the bar applauded.

"Now ladies and gentlemen," Cal's spine curved toward the mike, his long, gray hair poked out of the sides of his Stetson. "Let's make welcome one of our regular girl singers, the pretty and talented Miss Heather Lee."

Charles stood and applauded, while the two tables of

newcomers gave a polite acknowledgment. The man at the bar looked around the room and smiled.

Heather moved to the antique mike, tipped her wide-brimmed straw hat she wore to each appearance, gave the audience an aw-shucks smile, and broke into the country classic "Crazy." In addition to making a living as a massage therapist and singing for tips, Heather claimed to talk to ghosts, was handy with a divining rod, and, as she said, could spot a demonic apparition a mile away. Her weakness as a psychic was her voice which fell far short of channeling Patsy Cline. Regardless, nothing could stop her from trying. Her endearing smile, unending enthusiasm, and overblown desire combined to make up for her lack of vocal skills.

Charles knew better than to let Heather see him doing anything other than paying rapt attention when she was performing. Cal hadn't answered his question about the man at the bar, so Charles faced the bandstand and leaned closer to Cal.

"Who is he?" Charles said out of the corner of his mouth.

I looked at the man sipping a Budweiser. I didn't see why Charles was interested other than it was someone he didn't know. The stranger looked to be in his forties, had short-cropped hair, and one of those three-day-old beards that was too short to be intentional, yet too long to have been shaved. He wore jeans and a North Face jacket over a plaid shirt. Nothing unusual for February on Folly.

Cal said, "Don't know."

And Charles had waited all this time for that.

Charles gave him a look that screamed, "Why not?"

Cal shrugged and said he had to tend to his paying customers. He headed to the bar to see if the person Charles had been so interested in needed another beer, and Charles turned his attention back to his main-squeeze who had transitioned to "I Fall to Pieces."

Cal's closing time in winter was as predictable as a puppy. Most nights, he closed as soon as the last customer left; often before eight o'clock. On open-mic nights he stayed later. Participants brought their own fans, and the quality of the performances brought out the beer in higher quantities. It was approaching ten and Cal was moving slower by the minute. He looked at his watch and wiggled his index finger at Heather. It didn't take a degree in music management to know what it meant.

Our table, one other couple, and the man at the bar remained. Heather finished "I Fall to Pieces," put her hand over her heart, and said she was going to close with "Sweet Dreams," Patsy's most popular song and the one that was released after her death.

Heather said *Patsy* like they'd been best buds. A psychic thing, I suppose.

The couple waved at Cal for their check, the man at the bar wrote on a business card, and Heather performed a passable version of the country standard.

It had been a long day and I was anxious to get home, but knew Heather, like most performers, needed all the positive reinforcement she could get once she left the stage. She finished her set, and Cal returned to the mike. "Fine job, Heather. Fine job," and then he thanked everyone for coming. He also reminded them he was open every night and he'd be performing "a set or two," Friday and Saturday.

Heather started to the table when the man at the bar waved her over. She set her guitar case beside Charles and moved to the bar. The stranger shook her hand and pointed to the adjacent stool.

Heather and the man were in deep conversation. Charles glared, Cal cleaned tables, and I yawned.

Charles continued to glare. "He better not be flirtin'."

"She can take care of herself. Perhaps he's a new fan."

"Smarmy sleazebag'd be more like it."

Charles pushed his chair back and I was afraid he was going to save his damsel in distress—whether she was in distress or not. The man patted Heather on the shoulder and headed to the exit.

Heather returned to the table with a bigger smile than she had shared with her adoring audience from the stage and waved the business card in the air in front of her. "Guess what? Guess what?"

Something told me whatever it was wasn't as good as Heather thought.

Charles, through gritted teeth, said, "What?"

"That's Kevin. He's a music agent. Holy moly, he's from Nashville."

Heather handed the card to Charles, and I looked over his

shoulder as he read: *Kevin Starr, Starr Management*. That's all that was on the front of the card—no address, no phone number. Charles turned it over and stared at a handwritten phone number beginning with 615.

Heather squealed, "That's Music City."

"What'd he want?" Charles asked, not sharing a glimmer of her excitement.

She ignored his lack of enthusiasm. "Said he liked my singing. Said if I ever get to Nashville to give him a call. Hinted he'd like to represent me. Oh, Chucky, isn't it fantastic?"

"He came to hear you?" Charles said.

"No, silly goose. He's been at the Tides since Friday meeting with record execs from New York, something about them being on a retreat, recharging their batteries, or something. He said he was sick of listening to them brag on themselves and found Cal's. He's heading out in the morning. Lucky he was here and heard me. Ain't it great?"

Charles nodded. He didn't say how great he thought it was. "Have you heard of his agency?"

"No. That don't mean a bunch. I haven't heard of most of them since I've never been to Nashville. He represents some of the biggest stars out there."

"He name any?" I asked.

"Don't think so. If he did, I was too excited to remember."

"That's great, Heather," I said. Not because I thought it was, but Charles wasn't sharing in her joy. "He say anything else?"

She rubbed her chin and looked at the bar where they had been sitting. "No, I gave him my number and got his card. He said he had to leave early in the morning and needed to get back to the hotel."

Charles sat ramrod-straight. "You gave him your number?"

"Why sure, Chucky. He said he might call if he had any news I'd need to know about." She paused and put her hand over her heart. "He said there might be some paying—yep, paying—gigs he could get for me."

I wondered what news or gigs that could be. I kept my mouth closed.

Charles looked around the room and caught Cal's eye. "Mosey over a sec."

Cal flipped the bar towel over his shoulder. It knocked his Stetson sideways. "Dang. That always works when bartenders do in the movies." He straightened his hat and walked over to us. "What'cha need?"

Charles handed the card to Cal. "Ever hear of this guy or his agency?"

Cal squinted at the information. "Can't say I have. There are more agents in Nashville than turds in a zoo." He shook his head. "Smell as good too."

During Cal's years on the road, he had been exposed to numerous corrupt and sleazy promoters, managers, and agents, and had been taken advantage of by several of them. He was not a fan of anyone who made a living off performers' talents, yet had become a good judge of people and I would trust his take on Starr.

"What do you think of him?" I nodded toward where the agent had been seated.

"Nice enough. He was polite, didn't say much, no red flags. He was a lot more pleasant than that dead guy."

I didn't take it as a ringing endorsement. At least Cal didn't label him as being anything but what he claimed to be. I hoped Heather didn't get her hopes too high. I was no judge of talent, yet suspected Heather didn't have the skills to hold a paying singing job on Folly, much less in the country music capitol of the galaxy.

Charles waved the card over his head. "What's with no address? Doesn't he have an office? How's that possible for a big-time agency?"

"Got an answer for that one," Cal said. "Many Nashville agencies don't list addresses, or they only list a PO Box. If their location got out, they'd have a stream of unwanted hopefuls flitting through their doors. Everyone's a star, or thinks so."

"See Chucky, Kevin's smart. And he's gonna call."

So much for hoping she didn't get her hopes too high. Cal headed to the back room to start turning lights off, I headed home, and Charles and Heather left for their apartments walking hand in hand.

I'm usually quick to fall asleep. Not tonight. The conversation about Heather and Nashville weighed on my mind. I had known Heather for years and thought the world of her. She may have been flighty and off-kilter in most of the country, although on Folly she fit in like the candy coating on a Skittle, and often dressed as colorfully. She was the first person Charles had dated in three decades. Their needs were minimal, they would do anything for anyone, they both loved animals, and could find good in almost anyone, a trait the rest of us could learn from.

Heather lived in a small dilapidated former bed-and-breakfast and had been across the hall from Charles's Aunt Melinda during the short time she had been with us. They had become co-conspirators in trying to get Charles to propose to the singing, psyching, massage therapist. Before Melinda left to entertain God with her charm, wit, and enthusiasm, she'd convinced Charles to pop the question. He did, and at the time, had meant it. Then reality set in. He had been a lifelong bachelor, and had one serious romantic relationship in all that time. He had told me two mice had moved out of his apartment because it was too small, so there was no way within the laws of physics for Heather to share it with him, and he was as addicted to his residence with wall-to-wall books as he was to oxygen.

After weeks of painful soul searching, and an even more lengthy discussion with Heather, the engagement was called off. Their apartments were less than a block from each other and in Charles's world they "sort of" lived together. The important thing was it worked for him, and Heather had confided she enjoyed having her own "psychic and physical space," whatever that meant. The main thing it meant was their relationship thrived, which was more than could be said for many couples.

What worried me and kept me awake was how her eyes lit up and her voice quivered when she spoke of her brief encounter with Kevin Starr, the alleged agent. She had never made any secret about her ambition to become a star. I had hoped her dreams had been couched with knowledge she might not have the talent. Charles and the rest of us had politely shared her enthusiasm and attended most every performance. The reality was, besides her regular appearance at Cal's open-mic night, and an occasional appearance with the Folly Beach Bluegrass Society that brings together bluegrass performers from the area for its regular Thursday jam session, no one else had heard her. None of us dared share our thoughts about her shortcomings. Could the agent, alleged agent, from Heather's dream destination have heard something we'd missed?

Chapter Seven

Mr. Coffee had gurgled the last drop of its namesake into the carafe when a knock on the door jarred me out of my half-awake state. I wet my hands in the sink, pushed my mostly-gray, receding hair back in the same direction, and went to see who had the nerve to pester me this time of day.

Dude and Pluto stood grinning on the screened-in porch. The last time they had showed up at my door was in the middle of a thunderstorm and they'd looked like they'd stepped out of the wash cycle at the Laundromat. Today the sky was clear, the temperature cool, and they looked human—human and canine. Dude's 1970 Chevrolet El Camino was parked crooked in the drive.

"You be here?" Dude asked with a straight face. Pluto continued to grin.

Dude was in his typical winter garb of a tie-dyed shirt, a multi-colored jacket that looked like it had spent decades living in a cardboard box under a bridge, faded orange slacks, and bright-white Nike tennis shoes. Pluto, a fifteen-pound Australian terrier, was dressed in a rhinestone-covered, fire-engine red collar. Dude and Pluto looked a lot alike, although there was a five-foot height discrepancy.

I didn't think I needed to answer and waved them in.

Dude nodded at Pluto. "Water?"

I pointed at Dude. "Coffee?"

"Tea?"

"No."

"Coffee okeydokey."

Dude and Pluto followed me to the kitchen and two minutes

later Pluto was lapping his drink of choice, and Dude was sipping his second choice.

"What brings you out this chilly morning?" I looked at Dude, since I didn't expect Pluto to answer.

"To say howdy."

There's a first for everything, although Dude showing up didn't strike me as a *howdy* visit. "I'm glad you did," I waited for him to boogie nearer to the real reason.

"Howdy done," he said and looked at his look-alike canine. "Pluto be worried. Me, too."

"About?"

"One half sis."

"Barbara?"

"Affirmente."

I didn't know if it was Dude-speak or a foreign language, and without Charles, my Dude-speak translator, I was on my own. I took it as yes.

"Why worried?"

Dude looked at the Mr. Coffee. "History lesson be comin'."

I took the hint and refilled his mug while he lifted Pluto and set him on his lap. Pluto rested his chin on the table, and I nodded for Dude to continue.

"Dudester entered world in Altoona, P A. Chug-chug town named after Allatoona, an injun. Most peeps think named for Latin word altus, meaning high. Most be wrong."

All many of us had known about Dude's past was he arrived at Folly about a hundred years ago. I will now be able to tell Charles that, despite rumors, Dude hadn't immigrated from another planet.

"Interesting."

What else could I have said?

"Pop worked for Pennsy—that be Pennsylvania Railroad to those not from P A. Dudester hatched for twenty-four full-moons when mom died birthing a bro. Boss snowstorm, hospital slick road far away." He hesitated and looked in his mug.

"I'm sorry. Was the baby okay?"

He shook his head. "Never saw sunrise."

I didn't repeat sorry. I shook my head.

Pluto licked Dude's hand.

"Pop rehitched. New momster birthed Barbara when I aged thirty-six full-moons."

After what I knew about Dude, and what little I had observed about Barbara, I suspected I knew the answer. yet asked anyway. "Were you close?"

"Close as Saturn to Jupiter."

Next to surfing and butchering sentences, astronomy was Dude's favorite hobby. My knowledge of the science was that there were a bunch of planets, stars, and other stuff up there, but took a leap and guessed Saturn and Jupiter weren't in the same hood. I motioned for him to continue. Pluto continued to lick his hand.

"Childhood, she go right, I go left. She be tall, I be Dude. She be pretty, I be Dude."

I was beginning to be glad Charles wasn't here. Otherwise he would have had to know how many pets they had, their names, breeds, and eating habits, who Dude's friends were, who Barbara dated, what posters were on their bedroom walls, what books they read. That would have been for starters.

"After childhood?"

"Me moved to Pittsburgh and hired by dumb dumbs at US Steel. Me took gig and sweated in steel mill too many full moons." He waved his hand over his head. "Got fed up to here and skedaddled to Laguna Beach, Cee A. Surfin' be more fun than steel-millin'."

This was the longest I'd heard Dude talk and didn't want to interrupt, but wished he would get to why he was worried about his fractional sister.

I said, "California to South Carolina?"

Dude pointed to my back door and then toward the front door. "Got tired of seeing sunset over ocean. Thought sunrise over boss waves be cool. Packed two bourbon boxes of stuff in Chevy Nova—that be before bought luxury wheels drivin' now—then stomped on gas, and skidded to a halt here day Sonny Bono elected mayor of Palm Springs, C A." He nodded. "You be knowin' rest."

I didn't know when Sonny had been elected mayor, but did remember hearing that Dude had bought the surf shop in 1988. That I knew, and still had no idea why he was worried about Barbara.

"What about Barbara?" I hoped to move the story along before another full moon passed.

Dude took a sip and set Pluto on the floor. "Half-sis be smarter than half-bro. Barb colleged at Penn State and became lawyer from Penn State Law. Got sheepskin and hubby named Karl, with a K. Both got low-pay, long-hours job at big law house in Harrisburg." He stopped and looked around. "Any eatins?"

Silly me, how could I have forgotten to offer my uninvited guests a full breakfast.

"Cereal, no milk. Cheetos. Maybe a stale bagel."

Dude smiled. "Cheetos boss."

As unlikely as it sounded, he seemed serious so I grabbed a cereal bowl and filled it with the non-Breakfast of Champions and placed it between us on the table.

Dude grabbed two Cheetos, or as Frito-Lay described them, "playfully mischievous cheesy crunch that add a little lighten-up moment to any day." Yes, I looked it up; remember, I'm on Folly. He offered Pluto one, but the offer was rebuffed. Pluto didn't need his day lightened.

Dude shrugged and stuffed two morsels in his mouth. I ate one and waited for the history lesson to continue.

Dude asked, "Where be in story?"

"Barb and Karl with a K working for a large law firm."

"They dumped *grande* law store, opened legal lobby shop. Two biggest hirers in H-burg be state of P A, and feds. B and K made tons of lucre sellin' large corporation BS to law writers. Me visited couple of times. Karl be slimy, said if he ever wanted to escape world, would move to Folly. Said he told all his *amigos* about here. Me be thinkin' yuck. No way Jose-Karl."

Was it possible the story was getting closer to current history? If not, Dude would next be asking what's for lunch and I'd have to say he's looking at it. He then moved the story along.

"Karl then thrown into same wave with Dick Nixon, Spiro Agnew, and innocent O. J.'s lawyer, Beetle Bailey."

"F. Lee Bailey."

"That's what me say. Pay attention."

I rolled my eyes and motioned for him to continue.

He shook his head. "Karl be disbarred."

"What happened?"

"State of P A. frowns on lobby guys giving fishing boats to state employees. Go figure."

"Was Barbara involved?"

"No proof. Guilt by wedding ring."

"What happened?"

"D-I-V-O-R-C-E. Crookster hubby wrangled a no-pokey-time sentence and moved to New Jersey. He now be scribing legal briefs and counting sixty full moons till can beg to get back in the P A. bar." He stuffed another Cheeto in his mouth.

"And Barbara?"

"He, she had major blowout. Accused her of taking his money. Decided law not her cup of oolong tea, and called Dudester. Can you believe, Barbster asking Dudester for advice? Hit me like salami."

"Tsunami?"

"What me said."

I nodded and didn't tell him it stretched the limits of my imagination as well. Instead, I asked what he told her.

"Said Folly favorite hangout of Sun God; said judging others frowned on by Folly-folks; said snow be as rare as clocks in Vegas; said good place to hide, especially from history."

"And?"

"She said last reason be boss and blah, blah, blah. Here she be: Barb and Barb's Books."

I knew we must be closer, but I still didn't know what Dude was fearful of. "Now what are you and Pluto afraid about?"

"Karl with a K."

"Why?"

Dude lifted Pluto up again, and said, "Barb's no big jabberer. She, me never dialogued much sproutin' up." He stopped and waved his hand around the room. "She got to Dude-land and say not much. Dude know she be fearing something."

"Why?"

"Half-bro intuition. She not say afraid, but that Karl being wantin' moola back, said get it one way or another. Me be fearing another." He kissed Pluto on the head and looked at the empty Cheeto bowl. "Me know she fearin' him. Don't know her good, but know she no fear fast. Chrisster, me be afraid for half-sis."

The thought flashed through my head that the man murdered outside her door could have something to do with her situation. I still wondered why Dude was here.

"Why tell me?"

"Pluto and me trust you." He pointed his forefinger at Pluto, and then at his chest. "You helped before. You be one friend I can tell puerile things to and not be cackled at. Maybe half-sis will talk to you."

He lost me at puerile.

"What do you want me to do?"

"Bod found behind half-sis's door." He held out his left hand, palm up. "Omen." He then held out his other hand. "Or related? She be in danger." He wiggled his left hand. "Or Dude's imagination gone willy-nilly?" He wiggled his right hand. "You figure it out."

"Dude, I don't—"

He waved both hands in the air, almost knocking Pluto off his lap in the process. "Whoa. Trula say copsters know nothing. Need help."

"Trula?"

"Coptress Bishop. Like faux-sugar except she be like brown sugar and older than faux-sweet."

It was interesting that Dude knew Officer Bishops first name, even though Truvia was the sugar substitute and not Trula. Regardless, he knew more than I did about the mysterious officer.

I frowned. "Did Officer Bishop—Trula—say they needed help?"

"Not same words. Hinted be clueless." He nodded. "You figure it out."

I was trying to figure out how and why I should figure it out when Dude said, "Gotta skedaddle to shop. One of clerksters won lotto and got handful of Benjys. Bought big-buck board, took day off, and surfin'. Clerkster Two need Dudester."

I hadn't heard anything about it. "Won the lottery?"

Dude shook his head. "Not zillion dollar lotto. Few hundred buckeroos."

"Oh," I said, as Dude and Pluto headed out.

First Burl and now Dude. Both friends, both asking the impossible, both asking me to do something I was unprepared to do. What now?

Chapter Eight

After my American Heart Association disapproved breakfast, and a headache caused by hunger and Dude's visit, I headed to the Lost Dog Cafe for a substantial lunch. It was a little after the traditional lunch rush and two tables were vacant and another had a single occupant, Charles. He wasn't hard to spot. He wore a long-sleeve T-shirt with a large *C* on the front with an orange camel stepping through it.

I shook my head and slid in the other side of the booth. He had a good start on a quesadilla, and his ever-present cane was on the seat beside him, along with a stack of paperback books. A discussion about his shirt would do nothing to sooth my headache. I was saved when Amber appeared carrying a Ball jar of water, and asked if I was ready to order. I resisted asking for a dozen ibuprofen and ordered a chicken salad croissant.

Amber patted me on the shoulder. "Almost healthy."

"I'll get over it."

She chuckled and headed to the kitchen.

Charles looked up from his food. "You look like someone stepped on your pet pelican."

I translated it to mean he didn't think I looked good. "Got a headache and, I've been talking to Dude."

"Redundant."

I smiled. "True."

"What were you doing at the surf shop?"

"Wasn't. He came to the house."

Charles set his fork down, wiped a crumb off his straggly face, and stared at me. He knew a home visit by Dude was as common as a submarine surfacing at the Folly pier.

"Let's hear it."

I shared Dude's concerns and that he wanted me to look into it. Charles, the wannabe detective, perked up.

"Hard to believe, but Dude could be right."

"Why?"

"I've been in Barb's several times. Don't suppose that's a surprise."

"Hardly, besides I already knew it." Book collectors of a feather flock together.

"She doesn't know much about books. I thought it was weird for someone with a bookstore. Anyway, I traded her some of mine for some I didn't have. Two for one. It beat having to pay real money."

I was shocked that she had books Charles didn't have, and that he would trade away any of his collection. I still didn't hear anything to reinforce Dude's concern.

"Why do you think Dude's right?"

"Barb's not a big talker, not a big smiler either. Took a whole passel of Charles's charm to get much out of her. Of course, I did."

"What'd you learn?"

"Did you know she's a lawyer?"

"She'd mentioned it."

He huffed. "You didn't think it was important enough to tell me?"

"Nope."

He huffed again. "Anyway, she's articulate once she starts talking. No doubt she and Dude got their talking skills from different mothers." He glanced at his lunch. "She came here to get away from her ex and for a new start on life. She said she'd talked to Dude four or five times in the past twelve years before he'd encouraged her to come here. I asked her if she was going to open a law business on Folly and she said no. She was kaput with the law. She said it better than that. It's what she meant. I innocently asked if she ever heard from her ex."

It was unlikely his question was innocent.

"The second I said it, she tensed up like a fiddle string. Our pleasant conversation, that was just getting started, skidded into a brick wall." He clapped his hands. "Smack!"

Amber arrived with my almost healthy lunch and asked if we needed anything else. We said no and she moved to the next table. I took a bite and nodded for Charles to continue.

"Was Pluto with him?" asked Charles, the master of awkward transitions.

"Yes."

"Good."

"Back to Barbara?"

"Right. She didn't say anything about the ex. She got all nervous. Her eyes shifted around the room, she stood up straighter, either it was a shadow or the veins in her neck looked like they were going to pop. She was afraid. I didn't think anything of it when—"

"Hey, Charles," interrupted a man standing in the spot Amber had vacated moments earlier.

"Hey, Russ," Charles said. The newcomer was in his mid-50s, six-foot tall, stocky, with a full head of dyed brown hair graying in the temples, and a well-groomed, full beard.

"Didn't meant to interrupt, wanted to say hi."

I'd often wondered what the phrase *didn't mean to interrupt* meant. Of course he meant to. He wasn't walking by and for some unconscious reason, his mouth started talking—interrupting.

"No problem," Charles said. "Have you met my best friend Chris?"

"Don't believe I've had the pleasure," said the interrupter. He cocked his head and snapped his fingers. "You're the one who found the body. Heard about you; seems stumbling on the dead and who made them that way is something you do."

"No. It was bad luck finding him and worse luck for him."

"The murder was all people were talking about when I got back in town."

"Where'd you go?" nosy Charles asked.

"Las Vegas."

"What's in Vegas?" continued Charles's inquisition.

"Trade show. T-shirts, other logo wear. Boring." Russ hesitated and looked at me. "Who killed him?"

"Don't know."

"I don't know either," Charles said. "I've known Chris since

Justin Bieber was a babe in swaddling clothes. Chris used to have a photo gallery down the street. Now he's a bum like me."

Russ leaned down and shook my hand. He had on a *Folly Beach Forever* T-shirt, tan Dockers, and scuffed deck shoes. "Nice to meet you."

Russ pointed to Charles's T-shirt. "Story?"

"Glad you asked," Charles turned and winked at me, and looked at Russ. "Gaylord the Camel. Campbell University, up the road, Buies Creek, North Carolina."

"Cool," Russ said.

"Thanks," Charles said, and then turned to me. "Russ owns the new T-shirt stores on Center Street. Wised up and moved here from Delaware to live happily ever after."

I hadn't known who owned SML Shirts and Folly Tease, although I wondered when they opened how the small island saturated with gift shops could support another one, much less two. Charles had said there could never be enough T-shirt stores. Since he had the largest collection outside their manufacturing plants in China, I wrote off his biased proclamation. SML Shirts selection was similar to the other island gift shops. Folly Tease's slogan was "Folly's finest shirts of all colors with off-color messages." A niche, albeit a popular niche, market.

"Oh," I said.

"Again, good to meet you." He then turned to Charles. "Gaylord, that's good. Be sure and let me know." He saluted at Charles, or at Gaylord, and headed to the exit.

Charles watched Russ leave. "Nice fellow. Good to have someone to talk Ts with. Maybe he'll take me with him to the T-shirt hootenanny next year."

That would be as close to heaven on earth as Charles could get. "Let him know what?"

"Nothing," Charles said.

I didn't believe him, but knew him well enough that if he didn't want to tell me, he wouldn't. "How's his business? Seems like there were already enough shops."

Charles nodded. "I think SML Shirts is sucking wind. It has too many shirts that are like all the other stores shirts. Folly Tease's another story. Never a shortage of vacationers wanting shirts that say things like *Tell your boobs to stop staring at my eyes*."

Maybe Gaylord the Camel wasn't so bad after all. After the unintentional interruption, I wanted to get Charles back on track. "You think Barb's afraid of something?"

"Yeah. Except, I don't know what, other than she seemed nervous after talking about her ex."

"Have you seen her since the body was found?"

"You mean since you found the body?"

I sighed. "Yes."

"No." He had finished his lunch and watched me pick at mine. "Tell you what. I'm going over there now to trade more books." He pointed at the stack beside him. "Want to go?"

I still had bad feelings about having to give up the gallery, and wasn't ready to make an appearance in its former home. I couldn't shake the feeling of loss.

"Not today," I said and took another bite.

"How was Pluto?"

I smiled and said fine. Of course, that wasn't enough information for my canine-loving friend. I had to tell him about giving the dog water, about how he hadn't shared in our breakfast Cheetos, and that he had on his red collar.

Charles must have figured he'd milked me for all the Dude and Pluto details and headed to Barb's Books.

My head had stopped hurting, my stomach was full, and I still had no idea what I was supposed to do to allay Burl and Dude's fears. So I did what I have been doing more of, I went home and took a nap. Inspiration didn't often come while sleeping, but I was determined to keep trying.

Chapter Nine

I wasn't overwhelmed with inspiration about how to learn if the death in the alley was related to Burl or Dude. What I was inspired to do was overcome my irrational anxiety and visit Barb's Books. That inspiration came after I had reduced the contents of a box of Oreos and stared at a reality show where ten contestants were dumped in Paris and had to survive French food, hostile locals, and an irritating host who kept throwing embarrassing challenges at them. I made a mental note not to apply for future seasons. I decided visiting Barb's Books couldn't be as bad as what the dimwitted contestants had to endure when subjected to televised humiliation for a chance to win fifteen dollars after taxes, agent fees, and years of therapy.

After a decent night's sleep, I wasn't as inspired to visit my former hangout, yet willed myself to do it anyway. I grabbed a lightweight jacket, my canvas Tilley, and headed out. It was before ten o'clock, but the temperature was in the upper forties, and it should be a nice day. Bert's Market was next to the house so I stopped in for coffee and some local conversation. Bert's was as well-known on the island as the Folly Pier and the view of the Morris Island Lighthouse. It billed itself as the grocery that never closes, although I'll admit I don't frequent groceries in the middle of the night, and couldn't verify that claim. The smell of fresh coffee drew me to the back of the store where a coffee urn met the needs of even the most addicted coffee drinker. I got my morning's first caffeine fix, talked to Ted, one of the store's employees, about his latest boating misadventure, and headed to Barb's.

I took a deep breath, a sip of coffee, and entered the bookstore.

I was jolted by how different the space looked than how it did the day I carried the last box out. During its tenure as Landrum Gallery, framed photos lining three walls, a couple of aluminum and canvas photo racks stood along the back wall, and little else. The center of the gallery was open and potential customers could see the framed images from anywhere in the room.

Now, I faced a five-foot-high, four-foot-wide, pine-colored wood bookcase with six rows of shelves filled with books with their covers staring at me. It looked like a mix of new and used books. *T*ing into it was another bookcase, nine feet long; a walkthrough, and another nine-foot section. There were two bookcases, each fifteen feet long and six feet high lining the wall to the right. They were crammed with used paperbacks, standing at attention, spines facing out. To my left, there was a waist-high counter. On top of the counter were two shell-shaped bookends sandwiching four books, and Barbara Deanelli perched on a bar-height chair behind it. Everything in the store, other than the used books and Barbara, looked new. The fixtures alone cost more than I took in the entire time I occupied the space.

The proprietor stood and came around the front of the counter and held out her hand. I gave her soft hand a brief shake. "Welcome, Mr. Landrum. I've been wondering when you would make an appearance." She wore another bright red blouse and black slacks, her face unsmiling as she waved her hand around the room. "What do you think?"

From my new vantage point, I saw twenty more feet of shelving along the left wall and two additional sections of bookshelves that matched the ones behind the front end cap.

I hated to admit it, but I was impressed and told her so.

She smiled. "Thank you. I suppose it looks a bit different than it did when you had it."

About as different as a kayak to an aircraft carrier. I smiled. "I'd hardly recognize it."

"I never saw the gallery. How did you have it laid out?"

I walked her through an abbreviated description. If she cared, it didn't show, but she'd been kind to ask.

The door was closed to the back room and I didn't feel comfortable asking to tour the small space that had been the unofficial meeting room for my friends. Back in the good-ole-days, it featured a Mr. Coffee, a refrigerator whose contents contained a high percentage of alcohol, and an old, beat-up table and chairs that held many memories—mostly good, but with a couple of horror stories mixed in.

The front-section of the store was only nine hundred square feet so the entire tour and description of how it looked took two minutes.

"Are there any books I could interest you in?" she asked, businesslike. Her smile had disappeared.

"Afraid I'm not a big reader."

"That's too bad. To my good fortune, there are several locals who are, and from what I understand, there should be many more when vacation season arrives."

"True. There are three or four places on the island where you can buy books, but they only carry a couple of local authors."

Since Charles didn't generally sell his books, I didn't mention his collection would exceed the number of books available in many small bookstores.

She grinned. "That's my hope."

"I hear you're Dude, umm, Jim Sloan's sister."

Her grin disappeared. "Yes."

I waited for more, but after an uncomfortable silence, I decided it'd be best if I left. Where, I had no idea. I didn't see an upside to staying.

"Before you go, could you tell me how you regulated the heat? When it's comfortable out here, it's hot enough to melt plastic in back."

"Poorly." I explained that the furnace and ductwork were as old as the building and all I had figured to do was to block the vent in the back room to keep the temperature tolerable. She thanked me and I offered to answer other questions that might come up. She nodded and looked at me like it was a trick offer, yet still thanked me.

I reached for the doorknob and she said, "One more thing, Mr. Landrum."

"Call me Chris."

She nodded and pointed toward the alley. "Have you learned anything else about the body?"

"Nothing new. The detective on the case is good, so it's in capable hands."

She started to say something, but didn't; her fist was clenched, and she gave a curt nod. "Good seeing you again."

Her message couldn't have been clearer than if she'd shouted, "Go away."

I told her I hoped her business was a success and repeated my offer to share whatever I knew about the building.

She shrugged.

I closed the door behind me and shook my head. Strange, I thought. Ms. Deanelli was courteous, but not friendly, something that did not bode well for her success. Her total response to being Dude's sister was, "Yes." And, it was clear she wanted to learn more about the body. It was more than mere curiosity. Strange—strange and interesting.

Chapter Ten

Cindy LaMond called as I walked away from the bookstore and wanted to know if I could meet her on the Folly Pier. There are a few requests I wouldn't turn down. A free meal, an invitation to attend a state dinner at the White House, and a request to meet the police chief were near the top of the list.

It was an hour before we were to meet, and I had nothing to do so I headed to the thousand-foot iconic structure to take a stroll. There were several fishermen on the wood deck and an elderly couple walked hand in hand along the rail and was gazing toward the horizon. I was approaching their age and wondered what they were thinking. Were they seeing their past in the waves rolling in as regular as the beats on a metronome? Or, could they be pondering their future, regardless how few years may be remaining? I shook my head and refused to go down that same road.

What I couldn't shake was Barb's terse acknowledgement of her brother, even if only half-brother, and her interest in the body. Did she know more than she was telling? Did she know the victim? I even wondered if she'd shot him; although, if she had, why come to the Dog to get his description?

I had often ventured to the Atlantic end of the pier where I convinced myself that I'd done my best thinking. I had also spent hours there without a significant thought, and on occasion had found myself dozing after listening to the soothing waves and looking back on the island I called home. Today was to be a day without significant thoughts, so I headed to the beach. I nodded to the older couple who was still at the railing.

The woman gave me a contented smile that only one who has been around for many years can pull off. "Have a pleasant day, young man."

I smiled. "You, too."

I don't know if it was from being called a young man, a salutation I hadn't heard in years, or because I was going to meet one of my favorite people, but I felt lighter and my step quickened. Before I started down the stairs to the parking lot, I saw the chief headed my way.

"Undercover?" I said and smiled. She was dressed in a white turtleneck sweater and jeans instead of a uniform.

"Off work."

"Good," I said.

"Get a day off every seven months whether I've earned it or not."

"Poor chief."

"Hell's bells. I asked for this rodeo. Gotta take the bad with the badder."

"How come you're not spending the day with Larry?"

Cindy was married to another of my friends, the owner of Pewter Hardware store. Both Larry and his store were small in stature; Larry was 5'1" standing on a surfboard and if he weighed in triple digits it was the day after Thanksgiving. Cindy was a couple inches taller and had her twenty-five pounds on her spouse—a fact that wasn't wise to mention in her presence.

"The boy would rather work to make enough money to eat rather than hear his adorable wife gripe about work all day. Can you believe it?"

"His loss."

She laughed. "Keep that up and I'll dump the shrimp and run off with you."

Despite their differences, the LaMonds were the happiest couple I knew. I also knew Cindy didn't ask to meet me to flirt. She suggested we find a vacant bench on the pier.

"I don't get out here as much as I'd like," she said by way of explanation. She stared at the choppy waves and didn't appear to want to get to the meat of the meeting. She told me about how she and

Officer Bishop had chased a middle-aged drunk two blocks down Erie Avenue before he decided he'd rather stop and throw-up on a kid's scooter. The hardest part of the capture was holding him, since he thought summer was just around the corner and all he had on was orange racing Speedos. She took more delight in telling the story than a police chief should.

She finished laughing about Speedo man, and asked, "How's Karen? Haven't seen her in a while."

Cindy still wasn't ready to talk.

Karen Lawson and I had dated for the last four years. She was a detective in the Charleston County sheriff's office, which was how we had met several years before we'd started seeing each other socially. She had been lead detective on a murder I'd stumbled on. To compound our relationship, her father was Brian Newman, Folly's mayor. He and I had been friends before his daughter and I had started dating. Prior to a shake-up in the sheriff's office, Karen had been assigned major crimes on the island. Nearsighted governmental minds prevailed, and she was banned from investigating criminal activity on Folly.

"I haven't seen her in a while. Something about murderers not taking vacations and continuing to kill folks in Charleston."

Cindy tilted her head and glanced at me from the corner of her eye. "Speaking of murder, I learned the identity of the vic."

Now we're getting somewhere. "Who was he?"

She leaned forward and took a small, bent notebook out of her back pocket.

She waved the book in my face. "Butt-contoured. Latest in police-chief fashion." She flipped a couple of pages. "Lawrence Panella, age fifty-eight, Caucasian, five-foot-eleven, currently deceased and residing in the coroner's office in Charleston, previous residence Myrtle Beach. Retired from various sales jobs, lives with loving wife, Elaine."

"How'd you find out? You said his prints weren't on file."

"Traced the gun. Hard to believe in this day and age, he bought it legally, registered it, and had a South Carolina concealed weapons permit. All squeaky legal. Combine that with the fact his honey reported him missing the day before yesterday."

"Why not earlier?"

"She said he was away on a part-time sales job, whatever that's supposed to mean. He'd been gone a month. If that's part-time, I'd hate to hear what his full-time job would've been. Anyway, she reported him missing. Now he ain't."

"What kind of job?"

"Here's where it gets interesting." She hesitated and looked toward the beach.

I waited.

"Wifey-pooh doesn't have a clue about the part-time gig. Said when he was working full-time he sold farm equipment, like big-ass tractors, combines, other things I haven't heard of. Made a hay bale of money doing it."

"She didn't know why he was here?"

"Didn't know he was. If you think that's the interesting part, I'm gonna scramble your shriveling brain cells." She grinned.

I motioned for her to continue.

"I'll start with the pistol he was packin'. It's a Browning 1011-22, compact rimfire semi-automatic, shoots 22 long rifle. Guess who's a big fan of that handgun."

"Gandhi, or the Dalai Lama—"

"Stop," Cindy interrupted. "Don't take the fun away by guessing it."

"Who?"

"Hit men."

I remembered when Detective Adair saw the gun and started to say something and hesitated. Did he already know it?

"Detective Adair said it was a popular gun. Don't thousands of law-abiding citizens own them?"

"No doubt. There's a tad more you haven't heard."

"That is?"

"It seems five years before out latest murder victim moved up the road to the hoppin' community of Myrtle Beach, he lived in Newark, New Jersey, where frustrated state cops spent years trying to pin a couple of hits on him. He was never arrested; seems the boy was as slick as WD-40 on ice."

"So he moved, unscathed, to Myrtle Beach, semi-retired from

'selling tractors,' and took a *part-time* job doing something his wife knew nothing about, and turns up here."

Cindy nodded, "Add dead to that and you've got it."

"Here's my question, Chief LaMond, what was Lawrence Panella doing on Folly?"

She shook her head. "Citizen Landrum, I have not a freakin' idea. I do know when he got here, at least in the area."

"Am I going to have to drag it out of you?"

"Might be fun trying." She chuckled. "Mr. Panella checked into the Holiday Inn a week before he took his perma-nap in the alley."

"Holiday Inn-Riverview?"

"That's what I said—sort of. He checked in under his name, paid with a credit card, didn't make any calls from the hotel phone, but nobody does anymore since every Tom, Dick, and Alexander Graham Bell has a cell phone. Nothing suspicious."

"What next?"

Cindy shook her head. "State and sheriff folks are wading through his things, physical and digital: bank records, electronic correspondence, phone records, other high-tech stuff. To be honest, if he managed to thwart law enforcement much smarter than our state and local guys for all those years, I can't imagine being able to pin anything on him."

"So, I repeat, Chief LaMond, what next?"

Cindy bit her lower lip, glanced at a fisherman pulling his rolling cart toward us, and nodded. "Let's see. I'm going to, umm, take an hour of my day off and go to the office, answer a couple of irate e-mails, one from one of our fine, upstanding citizens who thinks my department is playing Gestapo, and the other one from a fine, upstanding citizen who thinks we're too easy on the bad guys, and then—"

I chuckled. "Okay, okay, what will you do about the murder?"

One of Cindy's most endearing qualities, and I suspect one that helped her diffuse difficult police interventions, was her sense of humor and irreverence. It was also her way of pleading helplessness without having to say she didn't know something.

"I could go to the post office and see if the John Deere salesman slash hit man sent me a letter mentioning who hired him and who he was hired to bump off, maybe even including a signed confession by the hirer. My keen woman's intuition tells me those documents ain't there."

"So there's nothing you can do?"

"Chris, the state cops have the resources to do all the digital forensics, the fuzz in Myrtle Beach are capable of tearing the man's home and records apart, the gun's already been analyzed, and the bullet from his head is setting somewhere waiting for the tool that put it there to show up."

"But—"

She put her hand in my face. "From what I can tell, no one on our beloved island knew anything about the *hombre*. What do you suggest I do?"

I couldn't think of anything and told her so.

She started to stand. "Now I have to go start communicating with my constituency."

"Cindy, will you—"

She huffed. "Yes, Chris, I will let you know if I learn anything. You know I live and breathe so I can tell you everything that's going on, especially when it involves dead folk.

I smiled as she walked away. The smile was for my relationship with Cindy, and not for what was going on—whatever it was.

Bill Noel

Chapter Eleven

My earliest memories of Charles were of us walking down the side streets and taking photos. I focused on Lowcountry landscapes, and rustic houses and cabins encapsulated in character and inhabited by some of the finest people on earth. Charles, to put it artistically appropriate, leaned toward the avant-garde and captured images of discarded candy wrappers, flattened soft drink and beer cans, and interesting shaped, and often tire-flattened pooch poop.

Our conversations, which I enjoyed more than the photography, were as varied as the photos. My friend was one of the island's leading experts on gossip, arcane information, the lesser-known dalliances of prominent citizens, and everything related to how to get through life without a visible means of support. I brought to the table, or more correctly, the street, my experiences from many years in a bureaucratic megacorporation, and insights into human nature gleaned from human relations training and a degree in psychology. Charles also credited me with saving his life on a couple of occasions, and I gave him kudos for doing the same related to a few hair-raising situations I'd found myself in.

Charles greeted me at the door of his apartment with a broom in his hand, and on his torso a long-sleeve, gray Bowling Green State University T-shirt with a falcon's head on the front.

I pointed at the broom. "Flying somewhere?"

"Funny. It's called house cleaning. Did it last March, but figured since there wasn't a gallery that needed me, I'd do it again."

He still hadn't forgiven me for closing the gallery, but was coming closer to accepting it was gone and never to return.

"Grab your camera. Let's walk."

He grinned, and told me to give him a minute.

Twenty seconds later, he was back. He had slipped a Lost Dog Cafe sweatshirt over his college T-shirt, drooped his Nikon camera strap over his shoulder, plopped his Tilley hat on, shrugged into a bright-yellow jacket that had somehow hid in his closet void of any college logo, and he wore a genuine smile on his face.

"Where to?" he asked.

"Your call." I was interested in talking about the recent events more than our destination.

"How about Vermont?" he said with a sly grin.

"How about somewhere closer?" I was pleased with his mood.

"Party pooper. Okay, follow me."

We left the gravel and shell parking lot he shared with a few other apartments, walked past Heather's building, and away from town on West Indian Avenue. We had gone about two hundred yards when Charles came across a treasure-trove of photo ops. An opossum or a raccoon had foraged through someone's trash, and left three, empty green beans cans, a Ritz cracker box, and five Payday wrappers along the side of the street. You would have thought Charles was a paparazzi and had stumbled on a secret meeting of Jennifer Lawrence, Brad Pitt, and the Pope. He snapped photos from all angles and treated each discarded wrapper photo like it would become a Pulitzer Prize finalist.

I stood at the side of the road and watched my friend at play. I wanted to tell him about what I'd learned from Cindy, but wasn't ready to interrupt his mission to document the trash of the world, or at least our small corner of the globe. He had exhausted the angles from which to photograph the detritus and looked around for somewhere to discard the mess. While he may wait eleven months in between house cleanings, he couldn't stand litter on *his* island. He pointed to an aluminum garbage can on the other side of the street and I dragged it over while he used his foot to scoot the trash in a pile and onto a piece of cardboard to scoop it in the can.

He finished cleaning the roadway and I lugged the can back to its rightful yard.

He tapped the camera. "Too bad *we* don't have a gallery to display these photos."

I started to respond, when he said, "Kidding."

Right, I thought as we continued away from town.

We had reached the corner where Shadow Race Lane intersects West Indian when he asked, "Any news on the killing?"

"Glad you asked." I continued walking. "I talked to Cindy."

"When?"

There was a reason Charles was one of the island's top contenders in the race to accumulate the most trivia.

"Are you ready to hear what she said?"

I told him about Lawrence Panella and his alleged career.

Charles stopped, and pushed his hat back on his head. "A hit man. A hit man like in the movies who gets paid to go around killing people?" He waved his arm around his head. "A hit man like in the movies was right here on Folly Beach?"

I wondered what other kind of hit man there was. I nodded.

"Wow! And you didn't call me from the pier so I could hear what she was saying."

I looked at the pavement and shook my head. "You want to mope or hear the rest?"

"The rest."

I repeated Panella's bio and about the gun found on the body and that his wife didn't know why he was here.

"Doesn't sound like he was on vacation since he lived by the ocean at Myrtle. Don't suppose he was hired to kill himself."

"It wasn't his gun that killed him."

"Who was he here for?"

"Don't know and neither does the police. Besides, I'm not sure he was here to kill anyone."

We had reached the turnaround at the end of Shadow Race Lane and Charles had stopped to look at a small boat parked in the drive of one of the large, elevated luxury homes that dominated Folly's newer developments. He mumbled, "Who killed the killer?"

It was rhetorical and I shook my head. We walked in silence as we headed back toward Charles's apartment. I was shocked he didn't ask more questions. Something was on his mind, but something else you didn't do with Charles was to ask what was bothering him. He was obsessive about being early to everything—to Charles, on-time meant thirty minutes early—yet when it came to talking about his feelings, later, if ever, was his timeline. I was the same way so I didn't push.

He was the one who couldn't stand silence, and had a comment to make regardless of its relevance. This time I was feeling uncomfortable and shared I also had visited Barb's Books.

"Oh."

"She has a nice store," I said.

"Yeah."

I had expected an avalanche of questions since it was my first visit. I decided to drop the subject and enjoy the pleasant weather and scenery.

Instead of turning on his street, Charles continued on West Indian Avenue and headed to the pocket park behind Folly's combination community center and library. The Lost Dog Cafe shared a property line with the park and in-season there were often groups of vacationers waiting in the shade for a table. Today, the park was empty and Charles sat on a bench overlooking a wooden bridge that crossed a tiny, dry stream. He removed his hat, rubbed his hand through his hair, and moved his head around like he was working a crick out of his neck. I sat beside him and waited.

Charles turned and looked at the crepe myrtle behind the bench. "He called."

"Who?"

Charles was slumped over; he reminded me of a deflating balloon.

He glanced at me. "The Nashville sleaze ball."

"The agent called Heather?"

Charles nodded.

"Why?"

Charles looked at the ground. "Told me last night. She called and was so giddy I had a hard time understanding what she was talking about." He sighed and looked up at me. "Kevin Starr wanted to know if she's a songwriter. She told him she'd written a couple, but mainly covered hits by Patsy Cline, Loretta Lynn, and other classic country greats, or something like that."

He closed his eyes and shook his head.

"And?"

"He said a couple of Nashville's well-known bars had open-mic nights and with his connections, he'd get her appearances. Said bunches of singers and writers were 'discovered' there."

I wondered if Kevin Starr had been listening to the same Heather I knew.

"Why'd he want to know if she's a songwriter?"

"The open-mic nights he was talking about were for writers, not singers, but they'd still get to sing the songs they wrote."

"And he thinks someone would hear her and want to sign her to a record deal?"

"That's what Heather thinks. She told me she'd heard of a couple of people who had *made it big* after being discovered at these bars."

I'd been a longtime country music fan and when I was living in Kentucky had visited Nashville a few times and knew a little about its popular music venues.

"Remember the name of the bars?"

He looked up at a nearby palmetto tree, or was looking heavenward for divine inspiration. "One was Bluejay something."

"The Bluebird Cafe?"

"That's it. Heather said Garth Brooks played there before he became famous. The other one was Douglas Corner Cafe. Ever heard of it?"

"No, but that doesn't mean anything. I haven't been there in years." I hesitated and dreaded the next question. "What does Starr want Heather to do?"

"Duh. Go to Nashville. He wants to sign on as her agent and make her famous."

That was as likely as me flapping my arms and flying to Kuwait. I bit my tongue. I didn't know what Starr's game was, and suspected it couldn't turn out good for Heather. "You said open-mic nights. Can't anyone sing? Why would she need an agent to get in?"

Charles shrugged. "The open-mic nights I know about are at Cal's and showing up is his only requirement. Don't know about famous Nashville hot spots. Know Heather was babbling like a four-year old on Christmas morning."

I didn't tell him, but I would check the websites on my own to see if the venues he mentioned had other requirements for appearing.

"Is she going?"

"I love Heather. She's a kind, funny person."

I nodded at his non-answer.

He looked at the bridge and said, "She's a good masseuse; maybe good at being a psychic."

I didn't think he wanted a response.

He looked around and leaned closer. "Between you and me, her singing might not be the best in the world."

It was like saying a chipmunk *might not* win the Westminster Dog Show. I said, "You could be right."

"Heather knows her voice isn't as great as some. She also says the voice isn't all there is to be famous."

Ernest Tubb and Kris Kristofferson came to mind, and don't get me started on Bob Dylan. Compared to Heather, they would have been candidates for the Metropolitan Opera.

"Is she going?"

"Remember the other morning when you met Russ and he asked me to let him know?"

I wondered what that had to do with Heather and Nashville, but following Charles's logic was occasionally a circuitous trip, so I chose to take it with him. "And I asked you what he was talking about and you said nothing."

"Russ wants me to run one of his stores,"

I was stunned. "Like a real job?"

He nodded. "He knows I'm a big fan of T-shirts and I was your sales manager at the gallery. He thinks I would be good at the SML store since its sales ain't up to snuff."

"Are you considering it?"

"The best time I've had in years was when I felt you needed me in the gallery. It gave me a reason to get up in the morning. I miss that, and doing the same for Russ might be what's best for me."

"I'm surprised, but understand. And then the Nashville thing comes up with Heather."

"So yeah to your earlier question, about her going, I don't think I can stop her. What can I do?"

"What do you think?" I asked, channeling my counseling

training from the dark ages.

He looked at the urn-shaped concrete fountain and then back at me. "What kind of stupid answer's that? I thought I asked you."

So much for my rusty education.

"Let's try it this way, what'll you do if she goes?"

He whispered, "I don't know."

Chapter Twelve

I would love to say Charles and I came up with a perfect solution to his dilemma. I would love to say Heather had miraculously acquired a world-class voice and became as famous as she had dreamed of becoming and she and Charles would still never have to leave Folly Beach. I would love to say I knew what he should tell Russ. I would love to say I'd found the Fountain of Youth. I couldn't say any of these things. What I could say was Charles agreed to suggest to Heather that perhaps her voice wasn't up to country stardom, and I would search the Internet and see what I could find on Kevin Starr. Was he on the up-and-up? Had he discovered stars? Was he a con artist trying to take advantage of Heather? Or, and my guess, was he tone-deaf and delusional? What I was certain of was if Heather moved to Nashville to chase her dreams, Charles would follow. I would be devastated.

Karen called when I was on my way home and asked if I was interested in sharing a feast of chicken fried in eleven herbs and spices. I agreed and asked if she wanted me to meet me at the KFC near her house. She said no and would bring box suppers to my place.

I had an hour to kill before the home-delivery accompanied by a detective, so I began an internet search for Kevin Starr. I had hoped the first reference would say something like: *Fake music agent arrested for bilking thousands out of aspiring singers*. Instead, there were five LinkedIn references to Kevin Starr; two of them referring to Nashville and music agent. I wasn't a member of LinkedIn, so those sites were useless. I found a photo of him on an on-line Nashville weekly paper over the cutline: *Agent Kevin Starr with newcomer*

Sandra Ball. The photo showed Kevin with a well-endowed woman in her twenties. Both were smiling at the lens. The photo was taken at a cocktail-party fundraiser for an animal shelter, although I couldn't tell how recently it had been taken. It didn't prove anything other than Kevin was in Nashville and had told the photographer he was an agent. More digging, but I couldn't find any websites listed for Sandra Ball, Kevin Starr, or Starr Management. I understood a newcomer might not have a site, but found it incredulous there wouldn't be one for Starr or his company. I Googled yellow-pages for a phone number and an address, for Starr Management, and found a listing with a phone number, the number he'd written on the card he'd given Heather. No address was listed.

Karen arrived before I could dig further. The familiar smell of fried chicken seeped from the large sack she handed me as she stepped into the living room. Karen was pushing fifty, runner-thin, with shoulder-length, chestnut brown hair, and, in my opinion, beautiful. Instead of her typical navy-blue pantsuit work attire, she wore a dark-green blouse and tan slacks.

I took the chicken and set it on the kitchen table, placed her leather jacket on a chair in the corner of the kitchen, and took a long, mushy kiss offered by the detective. I reciprocated.

She stepped back and looked at the refrigerator. "Happen to have beer in there? This has been one gruesome week."

I told her I thought I could find one. She said she thought I could too since about the only things in the refrigerator would be beer, wine, and ice cream. She wasn't far off, and I handed her a Budweiser. I poured a glass of Cabernet from a bottle on the counter and asked if she wanted to relax in the living room before digging into the "feast."

She smiled. "No way. I'm starved."

I took the hint. I smiled at the set of steak knives Bob Howard had given me as a housewarming gift before he knew I had zero culinary skills. The chicken wouldn't need such heavy tools, and I grabbed two of my finest paper plates and four McDonald's napkins from the silverware—in my kitchen, plastic ware—drawer.

Karen had already torn open the bag and removed two box meals and was ready to dump the coleslaw on the plates. She took a bite of chicken before I was back at the table. Gruesome weeks brought out her appetite. Karen had been blessed with a metabolism that allowed her to eat huge quantities of high calorie food without gaining an ounce. I envied it, and had learned over the years it wasn't contagious.

I said, "Want to talk about your week?"

She had finished the first breast and started on the second. She took a spoonful of mashed potatoes and shook her head. "No. Two bodies and the usual suspects: drug deals gone bad and cheap guns."

"Sorry."

"Don't be sorry, nothing else to say." She took a deep breath. "My job starts after bad things happen. It'll never change."

Karen has been a detective for several years and a beat cop for years before that. She was good at her job, and seldom let the dark side get her down. I was surprised it seemed to be getting to her more than usual.

"Anything I can do?"

"Being here helps. It feels good to be away from the blood and gore for a few hours." She grinned. "What's been happening over here?"

I wanted her take on the murdered hit man, but considering what she had said, I knew it wasn't a good time. Instead, I filled her in on Heather and Kevin Starr. She started to interrupt once, but let me finish.

"What?" I asked.

"Are you talking about the Heather Lee I've heard sing?"

I nodded.

"The agent, he a con or deaf?"

"Don't know. He must be one or both."

"One of our detectives came over from the Metro Nashville Police Department. Want me to have him check with his buddies in Tennessee and see what they can find on Starr?"

"If it's no trouble."

"He's new with us and should still have friends there. I'll ask tomorrow."

"Thanks. Charles will appreciate it, though he'd appreciate it more if the cops in Nashville would arrest Starr and stick him in jail for a hundred years."

Karen smiled. "I'm sure he would."

"Unless someone proves Starr is a mass murder and bumping off all the naïve, aspiring singers he cons into moving to Nashville, I don't think anything can stop Heather for heading there to find fame and fortune."

"And if she goes, so goes Charles."

"Yeah."

"If he leaves Folly you'll lose your best friend."

"That's part of it. There's more than that. I keep thinking how traumatized Charles was when I closed the gallery. He lost his identity, his purpose, as he called it, and the gallery was only open a few years. Charles has been here more than thirty. Folly and Charles are as close as skin on your hand, and I can't imagine him in Nashville. For Heather, she'll be pinning her hopes and dreams on a man she doesn't know in a city known for chewing up and spitting out singers like mulch from a wood chipper." I shook my head. "Nothing good can come from it. They know nothing about Nashville, and don't have a way to get there."

She reached across the table and took my hand. "Don't get the cart before the horse. Let me see what I can dig up. If it's nothing bad, what's the harm in them going to Nashville for a few days? Let Heather sing, or whatever it is she does, at the open-mic nights. Can you picture someone hearing her, going gaga, and signing her to a record contract?"

I smiled at that image. "True, but I know Charles and think I have a good feel for Heather. All it takes is someone to say she has potential, or that she has a unique singing style, and she'll want to stay forever."

"As a true friend, you can't stand in Charles's way."

"I know. If he wants to go for a few days or a few years, I'll support him." I smiled. "Besides, he'll want me to take them."

She squeezed my hand. "That's what friends do. Let me see what our detective finds before getting too upset." She let go of my hand and sat back in the chair. "And speaking of friends and detectives, when were you going to tell me about finding a body?"

I wasn't ready for that transition. "Tonight." It sounded weak as I said it.

"Um, hmm. I bet." She clenched her fists.

"How did you hear?"

"Give me some credit, I am a detective." She glared at me. "Although, it didn't take much detecting. Ken, Detective Adair, told me, and then your mayor—you know, the one who happens to be the father of the lady you're eating chicken with—called to tell me. It would've been nice to tell them I knew."

"Sorry. It's that—"

"That's a sorry I accept," she interrupted. "Continue."

"I knew you were snowed under at work and I didn't want you to worry. Besides, all I did was come across the body. I didn't know the guy or anything about him. It has nothing to do with me."

"Then why did Detective Adair ask me to tell you who the guy was and where he was staying?"

"Curious, that's all."

"Chris, if I find out you're butting in police business *again*, I won't have to worry about somebody killing you. I'll do it myself."

"I'm not getting involved."

"I've heard that before." She showed no signs of softening.

"Honest. It's in good hands with Detective Adair. It's none of my business. Period."

She made a slight nod. "So you don't want to know who he was or where he was staying?"

I didn't tell her Chief LaMond had already told me. "If Detective Adair wanted you to tell me, I guess you should. Wouldn't want him angry with you."

She gave me the hit man's name and local address, and reiterated she would kill me if I got involved.

I nodded, crossed my fingers in hopes she wouldn't explode. "Does Adair have any leads?"

Karen chuckled. "Glad you're staying out of it."

I held my hand up, palm facing Karen. "Curious."

"Yeah. Adair doesn't know anything more than the basic facts: Where the vic lived, what his wife said about what he was doing, where he was staying in Folly, and the rumors about his past."

"Nothing about why he was here?"

"Nothing." She rolled her eyes. "So, I come over and you're

trying to get my mind off my terrible week by talking about murder."

I smiled. "Maybe I should try a different strategy."

Fortunately, she returned the smile. "I do know something you could do to get my mind off the week."

The next morning, she said I had succeeded. I still had a feeling something was bothering her.

Chapter Thirteen

I watched Karen pull out of the drive a little after sunrise, and turned on the radio to hear a cheery meteorologist tell me today was to be the "pick of the week with enough sunshine to keep dermatologists in caviar and temperatures to tempt listeners to buy Fourth of July fireworks." Instead of going caviar and fireworks shopping, I decided time in Charleston photographing its historic churches would be a good way to spend the day. Having my photographs displayed in a gallery was a fading memory, yet I'd been a photographer for many years and still enjoyed capturing my surroundings. Besides, it would be a welcomed distraction.

I would have invited Charles, but knew he had to deliver packages for Dude. Charles didn't have a working car, so he pedaled around the island on his pride and joy, a classic 1961 Schwinn bicycle, and picked-up a few bucks in the process.

On the way to Charleston, I took a chance my friend hadn't begun his carrier route and gave him a call. He didn't have a cell phone or an answering machine, so I was pleased when he answered, and told him what my Internet search had uncovered about Kevin Starr.

"Oh great," he said, with dejection in his voice. "He's for real. Heather'll be thrilled."

He either hadn't heard, or ignored, what I'd said about seeming strange that Starr's agency didn't have a website, and there wasn't anything about the singer in the photograph. If Cal was right about agents not listing their address, I would have thought it unusual he wouldn't have at least a post office box.

"When does he want her in Nashville?" I was hoping it wasn't soon so it would give the real detective time to dig into Starr's credibility.

"A week, give or take. Heather's going to ask around the salon to see if someone knows about a cheap car she can buy. She wants to be ready when Starr calls back. She's so excited."

"I'm happy for her." I hoped he didn't hear disappointment in my voice. "Do me a favor."

"Okay, maybe."

"The next time Heather talks with Starr see if she can get names of some of the singers he represents. He should want to brag on them, being they're stars."

"I'll try. She's mighty hopped-up about going, so I think if he said she'd be his first client, she'd still be packing."

"Try anyway."

Charles hesitated and then said, "I'm off. Surf shop customers are waiting to get their goodies from CPS."

Charles and his vibrant imagination had named his pedal-powered delivery service Charles Parcel Service. He'd said he hoped the "slightly larger" UPS wouldn't feel threatened by his moniker. I'd told him they could withstand the economic impact.

I was lucky enough to find a parking spot a block off Meeting Street and within a few hundred yards of some of the most beautiful houses of worship in the southeast. I was eleven miles from my small bohemian island, yet it didn't take much imagination to feel I had stepped into history. Seconds later, I was standing in front of St. Michael's, perhaps the most photographed church in Charleston. The crisp-white Anglican church's towering steeple was visible from numerous vantage points and left no doubt about the importance and historic significance of the building that opened in 1761, the oldest church building in the city. With more than four hundred places of worship, Charleston was dubbed "The Holy City," and St. Michael's had been the most visible symbol of religion's importance to the community. The front of the church with its impressive steeple was the subject of most photographers, though I preferred to wander through the small, brick-walled cemetery behind the sanctuary. Sunlight filtered through a large magnolia tree and illuminated the ancient tombstones with soothing light and brought to life the importance of those who had departed a century ago.

The temperature was still cool, yet I was able to shed my jacket as I walked from St. Michael's to the French Protestant Church on the appropriately named Church Street. The gothic-revival structure, better known as the Huguenot Church, was different in appearance than many of the other magnificent churches. Instead of being hidden behind a brick wall, its cemetery was surrounded by a wrought-iron fence. I took a few shots of a tombstone framed by the fence and then sat on a Charleston Battery Bench and gazed at the wide variety of foliage growing in the well-maintained area. The differences between the two churches reminded me how much their location and buildings differed from the oceanfront services at First Light. While First Light's services were held on the beach in good weather, the hope it offered its followers was no different than what Charleston's magnificent churches promised.

I understood Preacher Burl being concerned about the possibility of someone in his flock meeting an untimely demise after what had happened before with his church. What I couldn't understand was his concern over the recent death. The body was in the alley behind a row of stores along Center Street. It wasn't closer to First Light's door than it was to Barb's Books. The alley was off the beaten path, but not isolated. It was often used to get to the rear entrances of a couple of the bars, and others took the shortcut between two parallel streets. There was no evidence of anyone trying to get in First Light's rear door. Why was the preacher concerned? Paranoia? Or was there something he wasn't telling me?

There's one way to find out. On my drive home, I called the preacher and after three rings, I heard, "Good day, Brother Chris, learn anything about the poor soul?"

I detested caller ID. "Not yet, Preacher Burl, but I'd like to meet and talk about it."

"I don't." He hesitated. "But will. When's good for you?"

I told him today. He said he wasn't available and we agreed on a time and place to meet tomorrow.

It was getting warmer so I decided to park at the house, change into lighter clothes, grab a sandwich, if the bread hadn't turned blue, and walk on the beach. I needed to lose a few pounds and had been trying to get more exercise—something I'm not a fan of.

I opened the door and my day took a nosedive, I took two steps into the house when I noticed the living room looked like a tornado had touched down. A small table from the corner was in the on its side in the middle of the room. Photo magazines that had been on the table were scattered everywhere and one of the ceramic vases I'd bought at a yard sale to make the room look more homey had been smashed, shards everywhere. The ottoman was on its side and my flat-screen television was face down on the floor.

I took a deep breath and started to back out of the room, when I heard a rustling behind me and turned to see the second ceramic vase hurling at my head. A sharp pain registered in my brain, I saw what looked like the finale of an Independence Day fireworks show in my eyes, followed by everything turning white, and then black. I didn't feel anything as I hit the floor.

Chapter Fourteen

I opened my eyes and saw the living room from ankle level. My head felt like it had been hit by a meteorite. I stared at my table lamp, bulb shattered, and cord snaked out behind it on the floor beside my leg. I didn't move, because my head hurt too much and if the intruder was still in the house, I didn't want him, or her, to know I was still among the living.

A minute later, the only sounds I heard were cars passing in front of the house and blood pulsing through my aching temple. I raised my head a few inches and looked around. I blinked back a tear and pushed up to a sitting position. Still no sounds from inside the house. I glanced at the floor and didn't see blood, a good sign. I touched my head and felt a knot the size of a basketball. Again, no blood.

I inched the phone out of my pocket and tapped 911 and told the dispatcher what had happened. She asked if the intruder was still in the house. I said I didn't think so, and prayed I was right. I ended the call and moved to my lounge chair which appeared to be the only thing unharmed in the room.

My legs stopped shaking enough for me to venture farther, so I walked in the kitchen. There was little in it so there was not much that could be disturbed. Drawers by the sink were open, but nothing was out of place. I moved to the second bedroom I used as an office and storage room for prints from the gallery. Whoever had invaded my privacy appeared to have spent the most time here. The four-drawer filing cabinet where I kept most every piece of paper I had, had been ransacked, and papers from it were strewn around the room. A taped banker's box that had held hundreds of slides dating to the pre-digital age had been ripped open and the contents flung in every direction, and my photo printer looked like the visitor had taken a sledgehammer to it. Its plastic shell was shattered and magenta ink from one of color cartridges seeped out of the mangled machine.

A siren from a Folly Beach patrol car's disturbed my dismay as I looked at the disheveled room. I wanted to check the bedroom before anyone arrived. Dismay turned to anger as I gripped the doorframe for balance and looked in. One of my steak knives was plunged in the pillow and the sheets were shredded and lay useless on the floor. A piece of copy paper was on the pillow beside the knife and something was printed on the paper in red ink. I stepped closer and read: *LEAVE TOWN*.

If I had had food in my stomach, it would now be on the bedroom floor.

"Mr. Landrum, sir?" came the familiar voice of Officer Bishop from the front of the house.

"In here." I turned to meet the officer.

She looked left and right as she approached. "Are you okay?" She continued to look around.

My head throbbed, my legs were still weak. I was furious, and bile was inching its way up through my throat. "Yeah, just a bump."

The officer stepped closer and examined my head like she was trying to identify the genus of a bug. "Doesn't look okay to me. There's an ambulance on the way. Why don't we go in the living room, so you can sit down and tell me what happened?"

I thought it was a terrific idea, especially the sitting down part.

Allen Spencer was next to arrive. "Are you okay, Mr. Landrum?"

I gave him the same answer I'd given Bishop. He nodded and frowned. He knew I was lying. While Spencer went from room to room surveying the damage, Bishop asked me what had happened. I told her I came home from Charleston to find this and then someone smacked me in the head with a vase. Not insightful or detailed, but it was all I could offer.

"Did you see who?" Spencer asked from the bedroom doorway.

"Afraid not."

Bishop asked Spencer to keep an eye on me while she looked around.

He said, "The ambulance should be here soon."

I closed my eyes. My head hurt, although not as much as it had minutes earlier.

Bishop returned and Spencer asked her how the intruder had gotten in. A couple of years ago, someone had broken into the house and at the time Spencer had suggested I get stronger door locks, which I had.

"Broke the window in the office, opened the latch, and climbed in."

So much for the extra-strong locks. At least Spencer wouldn't be able to chide me for not heeding his advice.

I heard the piercing wail of an ambulance in the distance.

Spencer said, "Do you know anyone who would want to do this to you?"

It seemed like a big coincidence that within the last few days, I found the body in the alley and now this, but I said, "No."

Cindy LaMond walked through the door followed by two paramedics from the Charleston County Emergency Medical Services. Cindy stood in the background talking to Officer Bishop while one paramedic examined the knot on my head and the other one checked my pupils, reflexes, blood pressure, followed by a plethora of questions about the injury and my overall health.

The paramedic voiced what I dreaded when he said they wanted to transport me to the hospital to get a more thorough check up. I hated hospitals, and that distain had increased tenfold since I had been on Folly. I had spent more time in medical facilities the last eight years than some surgeons. I had visited my closest friends as they fought battles with death, and had been a patient myself a handful of times. I would rather swim to Bermuda than enter the emergency room doors at the hospital, and I was a poor swimmer.

"I'll be fine."

The paramedic gave me a stern look. "Sir, there's a chance you have a concussion. You should let the docs check you over."

I shook my head. "I'll keep a close watch on it. I'll have

someone stay with me a day or so. If anything happens, I'll go to the hospital."

In the background, Cindy mumbled, "Hardheaded."

"Your call, sir. I would recommend against it. If you're certain, you'll need to sign papers and we'll be on our way."

The other paramedic stuck a clipboard in front of me with forms attached. I didn't read the fine print. No need, I knew it released them responsibility for from anything horrible that happens because I had refused their kind offer of a ride. I scribbled my signature on the bottom. They grabbed their medical equipment, and on the way out, said, "Take it easy, sir."

The chief told Spencer he could go back on patrol, and asked Bishop to stay. Cindy then put her hand on my arm. "You sure you're okay?"

"Will be," I smiled—a mistake. It hurt.

Cindy glanced in the kitchen, took a brief look at the mess in the office, and went in the bedroom.

She returned and said, "Chris, I'm going to call Detective Adair to see if he can come over. It seems strange that this would happen so close to you finding the body. Besides, I'd like him to get his lab rats to take a look at the love note on your pillow. I think chocolate would have been more appropriate, but that's me. Doubt they'll find anything, but you never know. It looks like whoever wrote it was a five-year-old you've pissed off, or someone trying to disguise the handwriting with piss-poor printing."

Cindy stepped outside and made the call, I remained as still as possible in the comfortable chair, and Officer Bishop walked around the room avoiding the mess on the floor.

"So you're certain you didn't see the assailant?" she said, asking the question I had already answered three times.

"Yes." I pointed to the overturned ottoman. "Have a seat, relax." Her pacing was making me nervous.

She didn't say anything, but righted the stool. "Nice house, Mr. Landrum."

"Thanks, officer, and call me Chris."

She nodded. "I'm Trula."

"Nice name." I smiled. My head didn't hurt as much this time.

She lowered her head. "Thanks."

Cindy returned. "Okay, here's the deal. Detective Adair will be here as soon as he can get away. I have to get to city hall for a blankety-blank freakin' budget meeting." She turned and pointed a finger at Bishop. "Don't repeat that." She turned back to me. "Officer Bishop will stay with you until the detective arrives." To Bishop, she said, "Since our headstrong friend here told the EMTs someone would be with him all the time, you get first shift." She huffed. "Now Mr. Landrum, you stay there with your butt stuck in that chair. Don't get up. Don't touch anything. Try not to let anyone conk you on the noggin until you tell your story to Adair. Think you can do that?"

"I'll try."

"Good. I'll have Larry stop by and fix the window."

It was close to an hour before Detective Adair arrived. Officer Bishop met him at the door and pointed to where I was seated, although since he was a detective, I suspected he could have found me. I stood and shook his hand.

"We meet again, Mr. Landrum." In addition to Adair's normal preppy look, he wore a forced smile. He glanced around the room. "It appears your housekeeper had the day off."

I assumed it was his paltry sense of humor, so I smiled. Trula, standing behind Adair, grinned. Adair walked from room to room taking in the sorry sights and I returned to my chair. He came back and sat on the ottoman Officer Bishop had vacated.

"Start from the beginning."

I repeated the story. He took notes and nodded as I finished each point.

"Mr. Landrum, I doubt they'll find anything, but I'm having the crime scene techs do their thing. Who has it in for you? Why does someone want you out of town?"

I wished I had taped my earlier answers so I could play them back, although if I had a tape recorder, which I didn't, it would have suffered the same fate as my printer. I told him I didn't know anyone. He looked skeptical.

"Mr. Landrum, I've known you for what, a year?"

"Yes."

"And in that time, you've been involved in two, no, three

murders counting the one the other day. Now that's a lot even for a cop to deal with, and you, what, a retired pencil-pusher and former shop owner, are smack-dab involved in three." He shook his head. "And you don't know anyone who could have done this. That's hard to swallow."

My head still hurt and the last thing I wanted to do was get in a protracted conversation about the past. I appreciated his point of view, but the unfortunate events a year ago had been resolved, and I couldn't see how stumbling on a body in an alley could have anything to do with me.

"Regardless, Detective, I don't know anyone."

"Then I'll leave and let you get some rest. I don't know when the techs will get here, so please don't touch anything that's been disturbed until they're finished."

I thanked him for coming and Officer Bishop walked him to his car. Before he pulled away, I wondered why I hadn't told him about Barbara Deanelli's unusual curiosity about the victim, and Preacher Burl's free-floating anxieties about the death. I suppose it was because I couldn't see how either could be relevant. Was I right?

Two hours later, the techs from the Charleston County Forensic Services Unit arrived; two hours of awkward conversation with Trula Bishop. The techs didn't comment on my housekeeping, other to say they'd seen worse. They went about their business, apologized for any mess they may have made, and told me to have a good evening. I couldn't see how it could go any way but up. Officer Bishop went above and beyond her assigned duty to babysit me. She helped straighten up as much as possible. The techs had taken the tattered sheets and stabbed pillow, so she helped me make up the bed and carry the printer's remains to the trash. The flat screen television had survived the fall. It took me another hour to convince the vigilant officer I was okay enough to stay by myself. I was surprised when she hugged me on the way out the door, told me she was sorry for the trouble I had been through, and said she would drive by every hour to make sure everything seemed okay. I was touched.

Winter temperatures didn't bother me as much as the early sunsets. It was a little after seven and dark. I started to fix a glass of wine, but figured if I had a concussion I'd better stick with something non-alcoholic. I refiled some of the more current documents, before feeling weak and moving back to the living room chair. I thought about drifting into a peaceful nap, but decided against it, again, because of the possible concussion.

My headache began to get better until I tried to think who could have done this. I tried to convince myself that I had interrupted a burglary. The knife and note blew that wish out of the water. If someone wanted me dead, he or she had the perfect opportunity. Why leave me alive? Did the intruder think I was dead? Or, did something scare the person before he or she could finish me off? The who and why remained unanswered.

The conk on the head not only hurt and slammed me with new unanswered questions, but reminded me of things I had been giving way too much thought to; things I had avoided until the death of Charles's aunt a couple of years ago; things that had been bothering me since the beginning of this year. I was approaching my late sixties. Today my life could have ended; at best, I probably have thirty years left, and that's if I was lucky. What have I contributed? I had spent most of my work life plowing the fields of bureaucracy. My employer was in good shape when I was hired; was in good shape when I retired. My professional legacy will be a page of notes in an archived file in a storage room, never to be resuscitated.

My dwindling bank account shattered my dream of owning a photo gallery, and damaged the pride and purpose of the best friend I'd ever had. It was also the same best friend who will probably be following his significant other six hundred miles away to follow her dream. My twenty-year marriage ended a quarter of a century ago. I had become reacquainted with my ex-wife four years ago, only to see her murdered while trying to restart her life on Folly; a murder I may have been able to prevent. I'm in a relationship with Karen, yet for reasons I can't articulate, am avoiding taking it to the next level.

I had spent most of my years avoiding talking about myself. I was a much better listener and more comfortable being on that end of a conversation. Would I feel better if I shared some of my doubts and fears with someone? I considered myself spiritual, while not being big on organized religion. Maybe I could talk to Preacher Burl about some of the things that had been bothering me. Why not start at lunch tomorrow? I could ask about his concern over Panella's death and seek his guidance with my fears and anxieties. I smiled for the first time in hours when I thought by talking to the preacher I could kill two doves with one stone.

Despite my efforts not to, I drifted off. The phone jarred me awake, and jarred even more when I answered and Karen screamed, "Are you okay?"

"I'm fine." I shook my head to see if I was telling the truth. A headache, but that was all. "Detective Adair tell you?"

"I sure as hell didn't hear it from you."

"Guess I got busy cleaning up and didn't have time to call."

"Yet Kenneth Adair had time to be there, go back to the office, go out on a new homicide case, and still call me."

"I'm sorry. I should have called. I'm still shook up."

She sighed. "Are you sure you're okay?"

She had calmed. I reassured her I was okay and only had a little headache. She asked if I had any idea who did it, and she got the same story I'd shared with everyone and his or her brother over the last few hours.

"Want me to come over?"

"Thanks, but I need to get to sleep. I'm fine."

"You'll call if you need anything?"

I assured her I would.

"Like you did today?"

Okay, she wasn't over it yet.

I repeated that I would call.

"You better. Oh, I almost forgot. The detective who'd worked in Nashville talked to his buddy over there. His friend called back this afternoon and our guy called me. Some people do call me."

"What'd he learn?" I hurried past her snide comment.

"Good and bad news for Heather. Starr Management, owner Kevin Starr, is real. That's the good news for Heather. I know you wanted to hear something terrible about him."

"What's the bad news?"

"The cop in Nashville had to make several calls before he found someone who'd heard of it. The Music City insider told the local cop Starr Management had been around for a couple of years and

Starr's relatively new to the business. The contact called him 'A minnow in an ocean of sharks.'"

Oh great, I thought. "Because he has an agency and a stack of business cards, doesn't mean he can help Heather?"

Karen's chuckle surprised me. "I've heard Heather sing. Nothing can help her." Then she said she was glad I was okay.

Karen's call had shaken me awake. It didn't do anything to make me less depressed.

Chapter Fifteen

I was to meet Preacher Burl at eleven o'clock at the Folly Beach Crab Shack. Burl had said he wanted to meet early to avoid the lunch crowd. Being the middle of the week in February, I knew there wouldn't be a wait regardless when we arrived. I suspected it was so we could have a more private conversation, which was fine, since I wanted to know what he had been reluctant to share.

The popular restaurant had opened moments earlier and I was given a choice of tables. I would have preferred outside on the deck, but it was in the low-fifties so I picked the spot that offered the most privacy. Burl hadn't arrived and I spent time cracking open complimentary peanuts, tossing the empty shells in a blue plastic bucket in the center of the table, and looking around the brightly-colored interior. Whoever had chosen the colors avoided the beige section of the color wheel. Festive oranges, greens, and reds dominated most surfaces and left no doubt the Crab Shack was beach-centric, fun, and a casual-dining destination.

The hostess had been pleasant, the atmosphere cheerful, and I knew the food would be excellent, yet I still couldn't shake my feelings of despair and sadness. Were they the after-effects of yesterday's assault, or something deeper?

Burl approached and said, "What's with the long face?" He smiled.

I returned his smile. I didn't tell him what I found amusing was how his full, milk-chocolate colored mustache contrasted with a few stands of combed-over hair covering his balding head as well as a diaper could cover a rhinoceros.

"Welcome, preacher." I avoided his question, and pushed the peanuts toward him.

"Ah, my weakness." He grabbed three nuts from the cardboard container and started breaking them open.

"You could have worse weaknesses."

"I'm afraid that I do. Though none so onerous to render me inadequate as a spokesperson for the Lord."

Do I ask what they were? I wondered. I didn't want to get distracted. "Don't we all."

He nodded as the waitress approached and she asked if we were ready to order. I had been in the restaurant many times and knew what I wanted without looking at a menu. Burl had as well and we each ordered fried flounder and water.

"Preacher, the other day when you asked me to look into the death of the man in the alley, you said—"

He leaned forward. "Have you learned something?"

"No."

Burl leaned back, his shoulders sagged.

His reaction reinforced my thought that he knew something he hadn't shared. "You said you didn't know the man, and didn't know how he might be connected to First Light."

"That is correct, Brother Chris."

Now the delicate part.

"Preacher, the body was in the alley. He wasn't any closer to First Light's door than to Barb's Books or from the parking lot on the other side of the alley. People walk through there all the time. There wasn't any indication he had tried to break in the buildings, and he could have been going anywhere. What makes you think he had something to do with the church?"

Burl frowned and looked at a mural featuring the Ferris wheel that had towered over the beach years ago. "Brother Chris," he mumbled as he turned back to me, "you know better than most about the various trials, tribulations, and challenges God has bestowed upon me dating back to the first church He led me to establish in Mississippi."

I nodded. Burl had an unbelievably poor record of starting

churches before he had crossed the Folly River two years ago. One burned, one was run out of business by other local churches, and one closed after Burl was accused of killing a member of his flock to inherit a substantial sum of money. After arriving here, three of his followers were murdered and suspicion fell on their preacher. Some friends and I found the real killer and First Light survived the rumors and innuendoes.

"Preacher, help me understand why you believe the death may be related?"

"As you have heard me espouse, the Lord works in mysterious ways. I have also said, albeit on not as many occasions, the Devil follows a parallel path. He weasels into our lives, plants seeds of sin, and can appear at the most inopportune time and place."

Burl paused and stared at me. Was the answer to my question in there somewhere? Did Burl believe the hit man was at his doorstep at the behest of the Devil?

"I'm dense this morning. Tell me again why you believe the death was related to First Light."

Lunch arrived before he could clarify, and Burl asked if he could offer a prayer. I said, "Of course." He thanked God for the food, our friendship, and asked him to offer solace to those who were in pain. He said "Amen," and pounced on his fish like he hadn't eaten in a week. Was he hungry, or avoiding answering?

He gulped down his drink and coughed as he swallowed. "Brother Chris, there are only so many times one can be pricked by a pin before believing he is a pincushion."

"You think since you've had horrific experiences with your churches there could be a connection with this recent death?"

"Possibly." He didn't make eye contact.

I didn't have to be an expert on body language to know he wasn't telling me everything. If he wanted my help, whatever that might be, he had to level with me.

"Preacher, please don't take this wrong. There's more than you're telling me."

He looked at me and grinned. "Heavens Brother Chris, how could I take offense from you calling me a liar?"

"That's not what—"

"Brother Chris" he interrupted, "no need to explain. I was teasing. The reason I asked you in the first place was because you have a gift of sorting through the, shall I say, excrement, most others slip and slide in and never get past. I know you have no law enforcement training, but returning to my belief about the mysterious ways God works, He has allowed you to see what others fail to get a glimmer of."

Those were some of the best suck-up lines I'd heard. "Preacher."

He waved a peanut in my face. "Brother Chris, allow me to finish."

I closed my mouth and stared at him.

"I have lied to you." He tilted his head to one side and the other. "Not a lie, but more of a failure to share additional information that may be helpful in your quest for answers." He cracked open a peanut and continued, "I'm conflicted. You see, one of my flock confided something I believe is tied to the incident in the alley."

"What?"

He sighed. "I take seriously my duties as a minister for the Lord. People of all ilk share with me their darkest secrets. To serve both the Lord and my flock, I must hold their words tight to my bosom. You understand, don't you?"

I did, and thought he could use a lesson in brevity from Dude.

"Hence my conflict," Burl said looking at his plate. "The individual who shared his secret did so while he was under the influence of the devil's juice. Now don't get me wrong, on occasion I will consume an adult beverage and once upon a time made ends meet by tending bar. Excess is a tool of the devil. Plastered, you might say, was the condition of the gentleman to whom I am referring." He looked up. "Under soberer circumstances, there is no question what my actions would be. His words would not be shared with anyone." Burl hesitated and looked around the nearly empty room and back at me. "I believe the gentleman is in danger; his life may lie in the balance. I feel I have to tell you."

"If that's true, you need to tell the police."

"That was my first reaction. I have no more than suspicions. The man didn't indicate there was an immediate threat. And, to be honest, I promised him I wouldn't tell the authorities. That word I can keep by telling you."

I wasn't up on the ethical or legal constraints between a preacher and a drunk, and still thought Burl should tell the police. I was curious enough to not let it go with what he'd said, or hasn't said.

"I understand." I waved for him to continue.

Burl closed his eyes. "Lord, please reassure me that this is the right thing to do."

I couldn't help with that and remained silent.

He sighed. "I received a call from a bartender on James Island with whom I have been counseling on issues I will not divulge. He said one of my flock was in his establishment and had consumed an inordinate quantity of alcoholic beverages. Unbeknownst to the bartender, someone had been buying the man drinks, and if the bartender had known, he would have cut him off. Regardless, I was asked if I could collect the gentleman. I, of course, said I would."

"That was kind of you."

"It is my duty as his spiritual leader. I rushed over and with aid of the bartender, was able to load him in my car. I knew where he lived and was headed there when he said." Burl stopped and put his hands on the table. "Lord, should I continue?"

I waited and Preacher Burl must have received an affirmative answer.

"The gentleman said his name wasn't Douglas Garfield, the name I know him by, and that he was Harlan Powers. Said he had been placed in the 'wit pro pro,' which I looked up and learned was the US Witness Security Program. He didn't confide what he had done to be assigned to the program or where he had come from. I didn't ask." Burl looked at me for a response.

I had known someone else on Folly who had been in the witness protection program. Someone once joked Folly wasn't dubbed the Edge of America for nothing.

"When was this, Preacher?"

"The night you found the body at our door."

"Go ahead."

"Brother Douglas, or Harlan, was both fragile and piano-wire strung at the same time. He kept looking around like someone was following us, and when I got to his apartment it took me a long time to get him inside. I tried to assist him to the bedroom. He flopped on the couch and I didn't possess the strength to move him. One second he was cursing and saying things like 'the nerve of them,' and 'I'm a dead man,' and then he passed out. I'm not naïve to the ways of the world or to those under the influence, yet to be honest, I didn't know what to do. I left him on the couch."

"Did he say anything else?"

"Nothing coherent."

"Are you thinking he thought someone from his past found out where he was and hired the man in the alley to kill him?"

"Yes."

"Have you seen him since that night?"

"Two days later. I stopped by his apartment to see if he had, umm, recuperated."

"Had he?"

"He was sober, although I wouldn't say he was okay. We were in front of his building. His head flicked back and forth like a sparrow at a large bird feeder."

"He say anything about the body?"

"No. I felt so sorry for him and told him I wasn't going to the police, but I had a friend who might be able to find out what was going on."

"What'd he say?"

"Funny thing is I thought he'd be relieved seeing he was so upset before. Instead he stared at me and shook his head, and made some excuse about needing to get back to doing something in the apartment."

Great, I thought. "Did you tell him who I was?"

"I may have mentioned your name. I didn't tell him anything else. Will you please help?"

I nodded that I would.

Burl returned the nod. "It might be helpful to know Brother Douglas might come across as a bit obnoxious."

"Might?"

Burl smiled. "In the spirit of candor, Brother Douglas is obnoxious. He's rude, only interested in himself, and is hard to converse with in a positive nature."

Who wouldn't want to meet Douglas, I thought. I also wondered if it had entered Burl's mind Douglas Garfield could be the person who killed Lawrence Panella if the man thought Panella was on Folly to kill him? I also wondered if it had entered Burl's mind that he told the potential killer I was looking into the murder. My head began to ache again. This time, it wasn't from contact with a vase, a vase Douglas may have shattered on my skull.

Burl asked the waitress for a water refill, took a sip, and tilted his head. "Brother Chris, I'm not prone to meddle. I can't help but observe that something seems to be bothering you. Care to share?"

Let's see, I find a body; and then someone ransacks my house, before the ransacker uses my head as a vase catcher; and with good intentions, a local minister fingers me to the possible murderer as the person who will try to find out who murdered the man in the alley. Add to that, my best friend may be leaving Folly; my business goes bust; and I'm on the downward side of my life. Why would it appear something's bothering me?

"I'm tired, Preacher." Why not compound everything with lying to a man of the cloth?

"You sure, Brother Chris?"

I needed to work on my lying. This wasn't the time to seek pastoral counseling. It was time to change the subject. "Yes. By the way, what do you know about Barbara Deanelli?"

Burl tilted his head down and his eyes rolled up to stare at me. "You saved my life last year and I owe you big time. I'm here if you ever need to talk." He paused and took another sip of water. "Sister Barbara, the lady with the bookstore?"

I told him yes.

"Not much, I'm afraid. She attended our seaside service three consecutive weeks, and then stopped coming."

"When was this?"

"About the time she opened the store. I may be underestimating the lady's spiritual quest, although I had the impression she was there to promote her new business. As far as I know, she may have visited each church on the island on weeks thereafter to get better known. Marketing, you know."

"Did she spend more time with anyone more than with others

before or after your services?"

"Good question. To be honest, as preachers are prone to be." He hesitated and smiled and I returned his smile, more to keep him talking rather than seeing humor or truth in his statement.

"I said I suspected she was there to promote her store, yet she didn't appear good at it. You've partaken in our pre-service sharing of fellowship, lemonade, and coffee, so you know it's an opportune time to catch up on what's happening with the others."

"That it is."

"Well, Sister Barbara was in physical attendance, and shared what I perceived to be a forced smile with those nearby. From what I could tell, she never spoke to anyone to say more than hello. Granted, I was often enveloped in conversation and didn't observe all of Sister Barbara's interactions, yet it struck me that she wanted to market her store, and perhaps herself, but because of shyness, distrust, or not enjoying communicating with others, she was not successful. Chris, I observed her three times at the most, so please don't take this as gospel. I could be off base."

Burl's observations were consistent with my impressions of the store owner and I told him so.

"One more question. The other day you told me you didn't think you knew the man who was killed."

Burl nodded. "Correct. I've given additional thought to it and I still hold to that conclusion. If he was looking to find Brother Douglas, or whatever his birth name was, he didn't seek him out at a First Light service. Of that I am certain."

My phone rang before I could respond. I would have let it go to voicemail and not interrupt our conversation, but I didn't recognize the number and thought I'd better answer.

A familiar female voice said, "Mr. Landrum, this is Barbara Deanelli. I hate to bother you. Is it possible for you to stop by the store in the next day or so? It's about this confounded thermostat."

I looked at Burl and said, "I'm nearby and could be there shortly."

"Perfect, thank you." The phone went dead.

"I appreciate you breaking bread with me," Burl said. "I'll get the check if you need to go."

I almost asked the waitress to take a photo of this historic moment: someone offering to buy my lunch. God does work in mysterious ways.

Chapter Sixteen

Barb's Books was fewer than a hundred feet from the Crab Shack so including a sidewalk conversation with Jamie about this week's performance of the Folly Beach Bluegrass Society, I was at the bookstore five minutes after leaving Preacher Burl gobbling down peanuts for dessert.

Barb was the only person in the store. She wore black slacks and the third red blouse I'd seen her in. She smiled and asked if I could follow her to the backroom where I could explain the fickle thermostat. When Landrum Gallery had occupied the space, the backroom was a hodgepodge of mismatched yard-sale and clearance items. The refrigerator had been discarded from a nearby house being remodeled; Mr. Coffee had come from the clearance shelf at Walmart; and the distressed table that had been the center of social, and occasional work, activities had been surrounded by four chairs that would have looked at home in a condemned trailer park.

Night-and-day popped in mind as I looked around. The sole similarity between then and now was the four-foot-long fluorescent light fixture in the ceiling. My refrigerator had been replaced by an apartment size, shiny black model. The space where my battered table and chairs had resided now held a glass-top rectangular desk with black, steel legs. On the desk was what I assumed to be the latest iSomething laptop, and a portable Bose sound-system was playing an orchestral arrangement being broadcast from satellite radio's Classical Snob channel. An expensive oriental rug was centered on the foot-worn wooden floor.

Despite feeling like I was in a parallel universe, I was

impressed and shared the feeling with Barb.

Her smile widened. "Thank you." She pointed at the thermostat.

Having spent countless hours in the space, I knew what the problem was and had previously told her my solution was to block the vents in the office. She didn't think that was the best plan and said she wanted to make sure the "gadget on the wall" was operating as it was designed to before she blocked the vents. I stared at it like a mystical cure would appear, and wiggled the toggle that set the temperature, before saying, "It's doing the best it can."

"That's what I feared. Can you recommend a reputable repairman?"

She said it like finding someone reputable would be a rarity. I offered her two company names I had heard good things about. She entered them in her laptop, looked at the thermostat, and then at me. "Would you like some water?"

"That would be nice."

"Tap or sparkling?"

Many things had been said by my friends and even a foe during the years I'd occupied the room, yet I was certain that was one question that had never been voiced.

"Tap, please."

She got two glasses—another first for the space—out of the cabinet, the distinct green bottle of Perrier Mineral Water from the refrigerator, filled each glass with ice and poured the Perrier in one and pedestrian tap water in the other. She set both glasses on the table and moved to the door leading to the gallery, whoops, bookstore, to see if potential customers had wandered in. Like the hundreds of times I had made a similar move, the store was quiet.

I took one of the seats and after she realized she was customer-free, lowered herself in the chair on the opposite side of the table.

"How do you like Folly?" I asked.

She sipped her Perrier and tilted her head left and then right. "Seems pleasant. I like the mild winter compared to what I'm used to."

Ah, a door into her life had opened. "Where was that?"

"Pennsylvania."

Okay, that's a slight crack in the door.

"Always live there?"

She looked at her glass. "Yes."

The history lesson was over. "Like anything else about Folly other than the mild winter?"

She looked at me like I had asked her bra size. Had I pushed my questioning to its limits?

She paused, and said, "I find Charleston fascinating. Its history, architecture, waterways, thriving art community, all outstanding."

I couldn't disagree, although she still hadn't said anything about Folly. "I've been here going on nine years. I think the people are wonderful and I love the laid-back atmosphere on the island."

Priming the pump might help get her talking about where we were.

"My brother, biological half-brother, told me the same thing before I moved."

"Dude?"

She glared at me. "How do you know that?"

"Small island, few secrets," I said and was surprised because she'd acknowledged being his relative during my first visit. "I think it's great. Dude's a friend and I think the world of him. I didn't know he had any relatives until I heard about you."

"You may have noticed we have little in common."

I'd been thinking nothing in common. "I have."

She smiled—the crack widened. "I hear you have a strange way of helping the police."

"An exaggeration, I'm sure. Rumors are never in short supply."

"Rumors and friendliness." She continued to smile. "Folly folks could friendly a body to death."

"Over the top is an alien concept to some residents. Folly is chock full of passionate people: passionate about their independence, passionate about keeping Folly Folly, and passionate about their friends." I stopped and looked at Barb, hoping she would comment. She gave a slight nod, nothing more. "Anyway," I said, "newcomers tend to either love it or hate it, not many in-between."

"You've been here a long time. I assume you're in the love it category. I know Jimmy does."

It took me a second to realize Jimmy was Dude. I nodded, and didn't want to interrupt her first extended comment.

She looked at me like it was my turn to speak.

"Dude's one of the people I think everyone would hold up as a perfect example of what Folly is."

"I hope his two employees aren't good examples. I don't know what Jimmy, Dude, sees in them."

I grinned. "You mean other than being insolent, obnoxious, and rude?"

"That describes the two. The taller one, Rocky I believe, tried to be nice, but fell short. When I met him he said something like, 'Oh, chick, you're Dude's snooty sister. He's stoked you're here.'"

I laughed. "Rocky's a charmer."

Barb chuckled. "Steven, the other one, turned his back on me."

"Stephon," I said. Charles's propensity for correcting others' mistakes was rubbing off. "His ignoring you could be a blessing. It's neck-and-neck to who's the rudest. Back to your question about what your brother sees in them, it's loyalty, and many of his customers identify with them. They're protective of Dude. They'd do anything for him, well maybe not anything, I doubt they'd be polite if he asked them to. Anything else, probably."

"Yes, I noticed how Stephon hovered on each of Dude's truncated words. I'd as soon stay far away from him." She closed her eyes. "I ran into him in Bert's Market, and he was trying to be polite by asking me how I was doing, if everything was okay." She looked at me. "It was like he'd never spoken the words before. He's weird."

I told her each had a kinder side and I shared the story of them participating in Charles's aunt's funeral. Barb said she was surprised; I told her I would have been shocked if she wasn't.

"You live in that house next to Bert's."

"Yes." I tried to hide my surprise she knew. "How'd you know?"

She hesitated and then said, "I saw you coming from there one day as I was leaving the store.

"Yeah, I've been there most of my time here."

"Cute house." She walked to the sink and refilled my water glass.

The front door squeaked open as she set the glass on the desk.

"I'll be back."

I took a sip, stared at the door leading to the store, and thought maybe Barb wasn't as bad as I had thought. We were having a pleasant conversation and she seemed more comfortable. Then another thought struck me. Was she the person who'd broken in my house and smacked me in the head with the vase? Did I think that because she knew where I lived? That didn't make sense; it was no secret and many people knew about it. And, what possible reason could she have? I barely knew her and couldn't imagine a motive. Then why had it occurred to me?

She returned before I overanalyzed it further.

She sighed and pulled another Perrier out of the refrigerator. "I hate romance novels."

"Oh," I said, not knowing a better response.

"Doesn't matter what I like. They outsell every other fiction genre two to one, especially in used books."

I wasn't much of a reader and doubted I'd ever touched a romance novel, much less read one. I moved to more familiar territory and shared how some of my least favorite photos were my best sellers and I had to keep reprinting them. She seemed interested and added that mystery novels were her second best seller.

"Speaking of mystery," she said. "Have you learned more about the man in the alley?"

Why did she keep coming back to that? I told her what the police had learned about his background, his alleged career, and that they didn't know why he was here.

"Think the killer's the person who broke in your house and conked you in the head?"

Now it was my turn to be surprised. "How'd you hear about that?"

She smiled. "As someone told me a few moments ago, it's a small town."

"Who told you?"

"Someone. Are you okay?"

"Only a headache left." I grinned. "You didn't do it, did you?"

She tilted her head, started to say something, paused, and said, "Why, Mr. Landrum, would I do that?" She gave me another smile.

"Did you have the secret to operating the thermostat hidden there?"

"Is that a no?"

"What do you think?" She continued to smile.

So far she sounded like an attorney with a sense of humor not giving a direct answer.

I returned her smile. "I think you're avoiding the question."

She looked at the door to the shop and then at me. "Sorry. I've spent too many years deflecting questions both at work and well, elsewhere. Of course I didn't break into your house. Why would I? I am sorry you were hurt."

To believe or not to believe? That was the question; one I couldn't get a handle on. I doubted she was going to help. More than anything, I wanted to see her reaction.

"I can't think why you would." I said, although there was one huge reason she may have. She killed the hit man.

"Are you working with the police on finding the killer?"

"No, all I did was stumble on his body."

"You've helped in the past." She glanced at me and then at the door, either a nervous habit, or wishful thinking someone would come in and end our conversation.

I shrugged. "Ancient history." Once again it popped in my mind about the possibility that she had been the person in my house. I wasn't about to tell her Preacher Burl had asked me to look into the murder.

"Interesting. I'd better get back to running a bookstore. Thank you for your assistance with the thermostat."

She stood and motioned to the door. I was being dismissed.

Why interesting? I wondered as I closed the door on the way out.

Chapter Seventeen

I was on my way to bed when the phone rang. It was a little after ten and I couldn't recall ever receiving a call that late bringing good news. I was pleased to see the caller ID indicated it was Karen.

"I'm a couple of miles off-island wrapping up an interview. Have a few minutes for me to swing by?"

I said of course. There had been nothing in her voice to indicate my streak of bad evening calls was about to be broken.

"I hope it's not too late to bother you," she said as she came in. Her eyes were red and her usual confident gait was absent.

I said it was fine and asked if she wanted something to drink. She said beer as we moved to the kitchen.

I handed her a Budweiser and sat beside her at the table. "Rough night?"

"Yeah," she said and took a long swallow. "Tracking down a suspect in that high-profile murder on East Bay the other night."

"The tourist from Arizona?"

She nodded. "It was a wasted trip. The guy has an alibi. I'll verify it tomorrow, and if it holds, I'm back to square one." She took a deep breath and shook her head. "That's not why I wanted to come by."

She took another drink and I waited for what was coming. I feared it nevertheless.

"I wanted to talk about it the other night, but … to be honest, I didn't have the nerve. Then you started about Charles and Heather leaving, and I chickened out." She exhaled. "I've been a cop my entire adult life, and I'm pretty good at it. I rose through the ranks quicker than most, and with an exception of one or two, I have the respect of my colleagues."

I agreed.

She stared out the window and said, "I'm thinking of quitting."

I was shocked, and as calmly as I could asked, "Why?"

She shrugged. "A mid-life crisis, or maybe I'm sick of seeing society's underbelly. Crap, I could be worn out." She looked at the ceiling and back at me. "Or, a combination."

Karen thrived on her work. According to her colleagues, she was one of the best, and from what I could tell, seldom let it get to her.

"What would you do?"

"That's a great question. If I had the answer I wouldn't be struggling with this as much."

"Options?"

She smiled; her eyes screamed anything but happiness. "I could live off my savings, tap out my 401k, pay a bunch of penalties and taxes. That'd carry me a year."

"Not the best option."

She looked down at the table and then at me, yet didn't make direct eye contact. "There are two possibilities." She paused. "I've been approached by a large company that has two corporate security openings. I met one of their big-wigs in November, after he and his wife were witnesses in a fatal hit-and-run I was investigating. One of the jobs is in Charleston. It doesn't pay near what I'm making, but it's convenient." She rubbed her hand through her shoulder-length hair and bit her upper lip.

"The other one?"

"It's at the corporate headquarters. A VP position and I'd be over security at seventeen locations, looking into corporate espionage, theft management, and other stuff I know enough about to get by." She grinned. "The pay's twice my salary."

"It sounds great." I tried to appear enthusiastic, although felt there was a but coming.

"It is." She paused. "But, it's in Charlotte."

More than two hundred miles from Charleston.

"Oh."

She glanced at me. "Yeah, oh."

"What company?"

"They asked me not to divulge their name unless I take it."

"They've made an offer?"

She nodded.

"Is it what you want?"

She looked at the floor. "I'm leaning that way."

"The job in Charlotte?"

"Yeah," She mumbled and continued looking down.

After spending umpteen years in human resources with much of that time conducting exit interviews and negotiating contracts with employees who were being hired or promoted. I'd learned to ask one telling question when someone was talking about changing jobs.

"Are you considering it because you're running to something you want, or away from something you're tired of or frustrated with?"

"When I was lying in the hospital bed, gosh, two years ago now, I gave a lot of thought to why I was a cop. I've suppressed a lot of fear since then. I can't shake the feeling I'm not ready to get killed for a paycheck."

Karen almost died from two gunshot wounds sustained while trying to stop a restaurant robbery. It was touch-and-go and the doctors had all but given up on her. She was young and in excellent shape, both things contributing to her recovery. She was off-duty at the time and stopping at the restaurant to get supper.

I thought about reminding her that since she wasn't working when she was shot, it could have happened to her regardless what her job was. I kept those thoughts to myself. "I suppose it would be safer chasing corporate crooks."

She nodded.

"When do you have to let them know?"

"They want to know now, but I bought a few days." She scooted back from the table and went for another beer.

I stared off in space. She returned and I said, "Have you talked to your dad about it?"

She smiled. "Sort of."

Before becoming mayor, Brian Newman had been Folly's chief law enforcement official, and before that had been a military cop.

"What'd he say?"

"Before or after the steam stopped rolling out his ears?"

"After."

"He said he didn't like it; said I wasn't cut out to be a paper-pushing, pseudo-cop; said I'd be bored out of my gourd. He then said he knew where I was coming from and he'd support me either way. He wasn't happy. After grousing about it, he put on a smiley-face and hugged me."

"Back to my question, running from or to something?"

"I wish you didn't have such a good memory. It's both. I'm tired and frustrated with the job, tired of the sadness, tired of the increasing politics that are seeping in, tired of being tired. Then again, the thought of new challenges is appealing and I feel young enough to take them on with enthusiasm."

That was more of a non-answer than I was hoping for, although it led to the real issue for me. It wasn't many hours ago when Karen was telling me if Charles was Heather's true friend, he wouldn't stand in her way of chasing her dream in Nashville. Was I more selfish? Could I leave Folly and move to Charlotte? Could I give up my dream home, at my dream location? Was I too old to make the drastic change?

"That brings up the big question: you and me?" I said. "Charlotte's hours away."

"I've given it a lot of thought, Chris, and I don't know if you'll like what I have to say." She looked me in the eye. "If I take the job, I don't want you to leave Folly. I know how much it means to you."

"Karen."

She held up her hand. "Wait, please. We've dated what, five years? Our relationship isn't much different than it was in the beginning. Doesn't that tell us something?"

I started to interrupt. Instead, I bit my lip and remained silent.

"Would I like us to be married?" She nodded. "I think so, yet after this long, I'm not certain. You don't have to say anything. I believe it's the same with you. Besides, if we're destined to be together, whatever that means, we'll find a way to make it work. The good thing about the position is it has regular hours, five days a week. After what I'm used to, it'll be like a part-time job."

She was right. You would think after dating that long, I would have been ready to settle down. There was no one else in my life, and as much as I hated to admit it, I wasn't getting younger. We had a relationship based on love and convenience. There was a good chance of that changing—changing dramatically.

"Separating the new job out of the equation, if that's possible, do you want to give up your job? Is it that bad?"

She sipped her beer. "If I had to make a decision tonight, I'd say yes. Have I thought about it enough to feel I'd be making the right choice? Maybe not, I don't know. That's why I asked for a few more days."

"Is there anything I can do to help?"

"Listening helps. I've still got to think about it, and," she chuckled. "I need to get some sleep and look at it with a clearer head."

I said she could stay the night. She said she'd feel better at home. I walked her to the door, gave her a lingering hug, and tried to hide the tears that were beginning to roll down my cheek. She left the porch and didn't look back.

Chapter Eighteen

I had never fallen victim to migraines, but knew they were debilitating. Perhaps it was from the blow to my head but if this wasn't a migraine it was its evil cousin. The pain, feeling like a chainsaw ripping off the top of my skull, kept me awake three hours. I stared at my bedside clock for forty-five minutes after Karen had left. That was after I'd spent the first fifteen minutes trying to wrap my mind around what she'd said. I'd spent the next fifteen minutes feeling sorry for myself, a condition I detest, but one that slips in more as I get older. In the last few days, my best friend was considering moving away, my significant other, or whatever others would refer to Karen as, may be leaving, and I, out of everyone on Folly, had to be the one who stumbled on a body.

Had it only been ten minutes since I looked at the clock? Sleep, where are you?

Is there anything I can do to stop any of these things from happening? The simple answer was no when it came to the body. It gets more complicated from there. Charles will make up his own mind. As a good friend, and if he asks, I'll do whatever I can to help him make the best decision, and if it's to follow Heather, I'll step out of his way and support his decision. That would be much easier if I felt Heather had a snowball's chance in a microwave of becoming the star she so dearly covets.

Then there's Karen. She's a good cop; she loves Charleston; she loves her work; and she may, or may not, love me. Is the job in Charlotte something she wants? Is she running to it, or is there something more? Could that something be me?

Love was a four letter word we'd seldom mentioned. On a few

occasions she had said she loved me; I'd done the same. But, we had never talked about taking our relationship to the alter. I suppose I knew before tonight it was something she would have wanted.

Five more minutes. Come on clock, either speed up or let me go to sleep. Do I have anything to take for a headache? No. I could go next door to Bert's, the headache cure headquarters on Folly. Never mind. Try to fall asleep—again.

I closed my eyes, but instead of sleep I realized I was the problem. I've been single for a quarter of a century. My marriage ended poorly and while on occasion I appeared to be a glutton for punishment, I wasn't ready to give the sacred institution another chance. Why not? I'm more mature, or think I am. I've learned many lessons about relationships over the last few decades; most were positive. What am I afraid of? I'm set in my ways and look askance at change. Does that make me selfish? Possibly—okay, probably. Could I find anyone I could like more than Karen? Therein lays the problem; why did I think *like* instead of love? Was it poor word choice or intentional? I confess, I'm not certain what love means. Am I trying to overanalyze it? And even if I said I wanted to get married and Karen took the job out of state, was I willing to leave the one place where I feel more at home than anywhere ever; the place where I had more friends than I had accumulated in my first six decades?

The answer didn't come, but sleep had.

***

The chainsaw in my head was out of gas. The excruciating pain had mellowed to a dull ache. Two things popped into my mind. I hadn't solved a thing during the three hours of pre-sleep misery, and I was starved. Did I feel good enough to walk to the Dog? Would food calm my head and help me find answers to the questions that had seemed so acute in the middle of the night?

I concluded no to both questions, so I ran water over my face, and drove to the Lost Dog Café instead of walking. The restaurant had just opened, but Dude was already at a table sipping on a mug of tea. He was dressed in his ever-present Day-Glo, tie-dyed T-shirt with a peace symbol on the front.

He pointed to the chair facing him. "Yo, Christer, two for tea."

I had hoped to have a quiet breakfast and not have to talk to anyone, and decided eating with Dude would be the next best thing to silence. Besides, I didn't want to be rude being that we were the only two customers. I smiled—yes, it hurt—and joined him. He waved a current copy of *Astronomy Magazine* in front of me.

"Wanna gander?"

The cover had something that looked like a zillion stars, or planets, or space gnats on it. I declined.

He set the magazine on the chair beside him. "Your loss."

During the winter, Dude spent most mornings in the Dog, and by most mornings, I meant five or six days a week in two or three hour blocks. Much of that time was spent with him pondering the solar system, and why the surf shop wasn't as busy as it was in the summer. Years ago I had stopped reminding him about the definition of *off-season*, and now when he asked, I limited my answer to *don't know*. He made enough money the rest of the year to support his tea-drinking habit. You couldn't tell it looking at him, but Dude was one of the most successful business owners on the island.

"Be out early." he said.

I nodded and didn't burden him with the reason.

"Business be slow last sunshine," he said and shrugged.

"Oh," I said, my common comment either when I had no idea what a person was talking about, or didn't care to get in a discussion about it.

"No board bidness today. Rocky be back after spendin' lotto fortune. He plus Stephon be handlin' no customers."

"Oh," I repeated, as Amber delivered coffee, water, and a smile. She asked if I wanted to order and I said not yet.

"Didn't think so. Could tell since you look like you've been run over by a shrimp boat." Her smile faded. "You okay?"

I thanked her for her kind comment and said I was tired.

She looked at me like I had told her the sun wasn't coming up today, but nodded and didn't push about my condition.

Amber went to greet another tired looking couple, and Dude said, "Hear you be visitin' fractional-sis."

"She tell you?"

Dude grinned. "No. Have bookshop bugged."

He had the ability to bug the bookstore as much as I could calculate the square root of seventy-three. It was safe to ask the next question.

"You seeing much of each other?"

"More than since she surfed off to grade thirteen."

"How does she like it here?" I'd heard her version and was curious about what she'd told her *fractional* brother.

"She be adjustin' slow, but not warmin' to Dudester."

"Why not?"

"She don't appreciate smarts, charm, and wit of fifty-percent bro."

I smiled. "That explains it."

"That, plus she not accustomed to small berg. She be hanging with lawyersters too long. She be pleasanter with Stephon than be with bro."

"Your employee?" I tried not to show disbelief.

"Employee be like people who want train cats—no can do, but he and Rocky be on job each day."

"Showing up's half the job nowadays. Haven't they been with you for years?"

"Who else be hirin' them? Yes, been around many moons. Some days, want to blast them with my AK-47. Other days, man hug them."

I didn't know Dude had an AK-47 and cringed at the image of him hugging anyone, man hug or not.

"Where'd they come from?"

"Earth moms," Dude said with a straight face.

"You sure?" I said with an equally straight face.

"No."

"They have a past?"

"Odds and biology say yes. Be at tat-shop being inked, but that be all. Me don't know it—don't ask; they don't tell. Both take fondness for part-sis, like they did for Aunt M. Look like puppies around Barb. Tat-covered pit bull pups, but pups."

Dude was spouting more words than usual, and I was trying to figure them out when Russ Vick arrived. I waited for him to say he hated to interrupt. He didn't have to, because Dude invited him to join us.

"You know Russter?" Dude asked as he moved his magazine for the newcomer to sit.

I said I'd met him a few days ago.

Russ shook my hand and said he hoped he wasn't interrupting anything important. With Dude I never knew what was important and told him no.

Russ turned to Dude. "Question, Dude."

"Answer, Russter."

Russ gave me a *huh?* glance and turned to Dude. "You've run a business here for a long time—"

Dude waved his finger above his head. "Many a moon."

This time Russ shared his *huh* look with Dude. "Anyway, I'm trying to do things right. I've joined the business-owners group. I've kept my prices competitive with other stores. I've participated in city events, even gave away T-shirts for that auction the women's group had in December. I've not badmouthed anyone—tempted once or twice. Never did." He paused and looked at me and back at Dude.

Dude said, "What be question?"

I was on the same wave with Dude.

"It seems like others in the business community are treating me like a piranha. They're not saying anything, and when I ask a question, I get one-word answers. I hear grumbling behind my back. I feel I'm not wanted."

I was amused he complained to Dude about one-word answers. It wasn't the time to point out the irony.

Dude rubbed his straggly beard and nodded. "Stealin' money from other businesses be frowned on."

Russ jerked his head back like he'd been punched by an invisible fist. "Stealing?"

"Old saying *competition be good* be wipeout bad. Two-bucks-in-wallet vacationster spend at place already here, store get two bucks. If two places, store get one buckaroo. Store one be pissed. You be store two, the piss-causer."

That's a lesson you won't find in marketing textbooks. The frightening thing was I understood what he meant. Dude was making my headache disappear. I glanced at Russ.

"Are you saying they're afraid of competition?" Russ asked.

The *piss-causer* was quicker than I'd given him credit for.

Dude gave a thumbs-up.

"Your sister's new to town. How's she doing? Is she being snubbed?"

"She be selling *libros*. Who else doing that?" Dude asked as he looked around the restaurant like he expected to find someone selling books, umm, *libros*, in the corner.

"Point taken," Russ said. "So there's nothing I can do?"

Marketing 101 by Professor Dude was sinking in.

"Stop hawking T-shirts. Sell penguin suits or totem poles," Dude said. "Be only one in town—be a mono polly."

Russ looked at me.

"Monopoly," I said.

To his credit, Russ laughed. "Good suggestion. I'll pass. You're nothing like your sister."

"She be log taller, times two smarter, and chick."

Russ nodded.

I started to say a store named Tuxes and Totems had a nice ring to it, but knew Russ was serious. I said, "Newcomers to Folly, especially if they're opening a business similar to one already here, go through a period feeling like they're being snubbed, or worse, ignored. It's the nature of most businesses. It sounds like you're doing what you can. After a while, you'll be accepted as another business struggling to make it. It takes time to overcome rejection."

Russ frowned. "I hope you're right." He turned to Dude. "Sorry to take up so much time. I'd better get back to not selling T-shirts." He stood, looked around the restaurant, and headed for the door.

Dude watched him go. "Okeydokey *hombre*. FB need new T-shirt bidness like need nuclear power plant."

I agreed and told Amber I was ready to order. She looked at me and said, "French toast?"

I grinned.

"Barb be okay," Dude said.

I told him I had visited her store and had a pleasant

conversation.

"Fractional sis say be afearin' ex?"

"No. Is she?"

"Yes sir."

"Why?"

"You know she be art major?"

I didn't and wondered what that had to do with her being afraid. "I didn't know that."

"Yes sir. She be makin' clay sculpture thingees before headin' to legal school. Me never grasped vector change."

"Dude, what does that have to do with her being afraid of her ex-husband?"

"*Nada.* Be trivia."

I wondered if Dude was taking Spanish lessons during the off season.

"Why is she afraid of her husband?"

"Ex. Don't know. Think has to do with him crossing legal lines and bribin' bureau-krats. Be frowned on by fuzz."

"Is that why they got a divorce?"

Dude shrugged. "Hope so."

"Does she think he would harm her?"

He nodded.

"Would it help if I shared this with Chief LaMond? She could talk to Barb and keep a closer eye on her."

"Barb would kill if you do. Not real kill, figure-like kill. Wants no one to know her bidness. What happen in Harrisburg stay in Harrisburg."

"It's your call, Dude."

"I be watchin' over her. You no worry." Dude grabbed his magazine and started to stand. "Thanks for offerin'. You be good *amigo.*"

Dude headed for the door. I hadn't thought about it for a while, but realized my head hurt again. I took a deep breath and wondered what the Spanish word was for headache.

Chapter Nineteen

French toast and a half-hour without talking or listening had worked wonders for my head. Its ache was reduced to a dull thud and stayed that way until I tried to make sense out of the death in the alley. I wanted to push it aside, yet, regardless of how hard I tried, it lingered. The more I thought about, the more questions and scenarios came to mind.

If Lawrence Panella was on Folly to ply his trade, was Barbara the subject of his attention? Did her ex hire Panella to kill her? Did she find out and kill him instead? Were Burl's fears about Douglas Garfield valid? Was Panella here for Garfield? If so, did Garfield find out and get to him first?

Did the break-in at my house have something to do with Panella's death, or was it simply a burglary I had interrupted? The note on the bed all but eliminated burglary. On the other hand, I couldn't imagine anyone would think I had something there related to the murder, nor would anyone have any reason to leave the note.

Was the alleged hit man walking through the alley and found himself in an argument with someone who settled it with a bullet; a senseless killing that had nothing to do with Barb, Garfield, Burl, or me? Was I thinking about it to avoid thinking about Karen and Charles's possible moves?

I looked around the near-full restaurant, and, as incredulous as it may seem, not a diner had ventured over and answered my questions. It was up to me, and so I did what many wise people on Folly did when they had difficult questions or wanted to hear the latest rumor. I waved for Amber.

She returned with a coffee pot and a smile. "And how may I be of assistance, Chris?"

Her smile was infectious and I've never stopped looking forward to seeing her. "Ms. Amber, I have a question?"

She continued to smile. "Make it easy."

"I'll try. Do you know Douglas Garfield?" I realized with that question I had told her everything I knew about him except what Burl had confided to me.

"Chemically-induced thin, six-foot-three, long black, greasy hair, with evil-looking, dark-brown eyes?"

"Don't know, never met him. How do you know him?"

Amber shrugged. "We're engaged."

"You're kidding."

"Yep. Seeing if you were paying attention."

I breathed a sigh of relief. "I always pay attention to you."

She batted her eyes. "That's why I've always loved you."

"Am I blushing?" I teased.

"Not enough. What else do you want to know about Douglas?"

"Everything you know."

"That's about it. He's been in a few times. His breath smelled like bad habits and beer, and it was eight in the morning. He's familiar with the brew. He's a hundred pounds shy of a beer belly, so I figure drugs are a staple in his diet. He's tried to be hospitable. My gut tells me it doesn't come easy. He could be as mean as a snake without working up a sweat."

"Does he work over here?"

"He never said and from his clothes he could work in any store, or sit at home and watch soaps all day. He's been in at different times, so I don't think he works off-island. That help?"

I smiled. "Not much. Know where he lives?"

"No, but if you wanted to find him, I'd start at the bars. A dollar to a donut, I bet you'd catch him at one of them."

"Thanks."

"Now, I've got a one for you. Why the interest?"

I skirted the question and said I was talking to Burl who said Douglas was one of his flock and he was concerned about him and thought I might talk to him.

Amber stared at me and her eyes narrowed, but didn't pursue it. Instead, she said, "I lied about asking one question. Think Charles will leave with Heather?"

"You want to know what I want to happen or what I think will happen?"

Her smile faded. "Crap."

Two men at a nearby table waved for Amber so she patted my arm and left to see how she could be of assistance.

It was almost lunchtime and since I had nothing else to do, I decided to peek in on some of Folly's bars in hopes of finding someone who fit the sketchy description of Douglas Garfield. There were at least a dozen bars and restaurants with bars so finding him was a longshot, although the odds were better than waiting at home in hopes Mr. Garfield stopped by selling Girl Scout cookies.

After twenty minutes of looking in doors and saying, "No thanks. Looking for someone," I hadn't found Douglas, but knew seven of the town's watering holes where he wasn't. Luck, and the law of averages, smiled at me when I stuck my head in Loggerhead's Beach Grill. If the weather was warmer, its elevated deck would have been packed, but it was cool and a crisp wind rolled in off the ocean a block away, so the deck was deserted. The inside bar was near the door and I spotted a man who fit Garfield's description.

A half-dozen customers were seated along the bar on the right side of the restaurant. Sitting alone, with three seats separating him from the others, sat a tall gentleman, wearing a black T-shirt, black jeans, and black work boots. To compliment his attire, he had shoulder-length black hair that looked like it'd been dipped in motor oil. He was in his late forties and was studying the bottle of Miller he held in a death grip. I had the impression it wasn't his first beer of the day.

I took a deep breath and sat in the stool beside him. He glanced over and gave a dismissive look like he would if a fly had perched on the stool. I ordered a glass of Cabernet and waited for it to arrive before speaking.

"Are you Douglas Garfield?"

He was staring at a car commercial on a flat-screen television behind the bar. "Why?" He didn't turn from the TV.

This was going to be fun, I thought. "I'm Chris Landrum, I—"

"Who gives a rip," he mumbled, still without taking his eye off what must be a mesmerizing commercial.

He hadn't denied it, so I assumed he was the right person.

"Your preacher is a friend of mine and he asked me to talk to you."

"Buttin'-in Burl, excuse me, Preacher Burl," he slurred and finished off the beer. He waved for the bartender and pointed at his empty bottle.

She said nothing and headed to the cooler. I waited to see if he had anything to say.

"The man gives me one ride home and thinks he's my guardian angel—preachers, guess we need them." He took a sip of his replacement beer and turned toward me. "I know who you are. Hear you stick your mug into as much of other people's business as the preacher does. Seen you walking from your house to Bert's. So why *pray* tell are you supposed to talk to me?" He smiled at his pathetic attempt at humor.

"Preacher Burl is worried. He shared a little about your, umm, situation and was afraid the man who was killed may have something to do with your past. Thought he may have been here to cause you harm."

He took a drag on his beer, slammed the bottle down on the bar, and twisted on the barstool to face me. His beer breath assaulted my face. "I didn't ask the preacher for help. I didn't give him permission to tell anyone what I told him. And, I freakin' don't need help from some damn do-gooder stickin' his nose where it don't belong. I can take care of myself." He pivoted back to facing his beer and stared at the bottle.

It didn't take my degree in psychology to grasp that Douglas Garfield didn't share Preacher Burl's concern he may need help. I finished my drink, slipped off the barstool, and started to leave and let Douglas to stew in his brew, when he twisted back to me.

"Who did you blab to?"

I stared at him. "No one."

"Keep it that way," he growled, and returned to his drink.

Not only was that my plan, I was trying to think of a way to erase him from my memory. I learned nothing from the brief encounter other than I wouldn't want to share a meal with Douglas and knew no matter what he had done in his pre-witness protection life, it had nothing to do with running a charm school. What I did begin wondering was whether he was the person who ended Panella's life. It was a short hop to think the answer was yes.

The headache began to return when I realized if I was right about him, he could consider me a threat and could have already left a love note on my bed. Scary, I thought and headed home.\/

Chapter Twenty

Despite seeing Douglas Garfield's frightening scowl and penetrating dark-brown eyes whenever I closed mine, I managed a good night's sleep. As has almost become a regular event, knocking on the door jolted me out of what should have been the peaceful period between sleep and my first sip of coffee.

Charles stood in the doorway in a navy blue sweatshirt, with Belmont Bruins in red on the front, jeans with a hole in the right knee, his canvas Tilley cocked at an angle on his head, and carrying his handmade cane. "Let's walk."

"Where and why?"

"Bert's for caffeine, anywhere for exercise, somewhere quiet to talk."

For years I had tried to avoid asking him about his massive collection of logo-wear, but knew Belmont University was in Nashville. I hoped his shirt wasn't an omen. The way to find out was to go with him.

Our stop at Bert's coffee urn was followed by a brief conversation with one of the employees. We left the grocery and Charles pointed toward the beach. The temperature was in the low fifties, so the coffee was a pleasant walking companion; so far, better than Charles. Something was on his mind and he wasn't ready to talk. I wasn't ready to ask.

There weren't more than ten people on the beach. Three surfers in their black wetsuits sat on surfboards waiting for the perfect wave that seldom appeared. Two couples were walking dogs, and a lady with a young child was throwing a stick in the surf and watching her enthusiastic Golden Retriever scamper into the water to fetch the priceless piece of driftwood.

Charles stopped to watch the retriever do what retrievers do, and turned and walked away from the pier. He slid the tip of his cane in the wet sand and walked for a couple of hundred yards. I kept pace beside him and realized this was the only time since I had known him that he had gone that long without talking.

Silence was broken when he said, "I spent yesterday and last night with Heather."

I remained silent, and we continued walking.

"We talked about Nashville."

Duh!

He pointed his cane toward the horizon. "She's got a stubborn streak as long as from here to Wales." He shook his head. "Come hell or high-tide she's set on following her dream to Tennessee."

"You try to talk her out of it?" I bumped into him as he stopped to watch a colony of seagulls perched on the beach resting after a morning hunting breakfast.

He stepped away from me and continued to look at the birds. "Chris, you know how, umm, how shall I say it, vocally challenged my sweetie is. What do you think her chances are of becoming a successful singer?"

I wanted to say nonexistent, but I was walking a tightrope. They were a couple—a strange couple—and I didn't want to insult his *sweetie*. "There's a lot of competition and much of it's in Nashville. I suspect her chances are slim."

Charles surprised me when he chuckled. "How about I'd have a better chance of being crowned Queen of England?" Charles starting walking again.

So much for insulting her, I thought. "That may be true. Have you said that to her?"

He glanced at me. "Every time I start thinking you have half a brain, you say something stupid like that."

Charles took an abrupt left turn and headed toward the beach access crossover at Sixth Street. We walked two blocks to East Cooper, and without saying a word, turned toward town. Christmas decorations adorned a house on our right and being February, that would normally have brought a smile to my face. Not today. The ominous feeling I was getting from Charles's discussion and more-telling, his silence, dimmed my view of anything humorous.

We had walked two more blocks. "She wants me to go."

I nodded.

"My life is here," He waved his cane around and pointed it toward town. "It's my home ... it's my ... Chris, it's my everything. I'm in my sixties, and after all those years, God, for some reason, sent Heather my way. She says that same God's calling her to Nashville."

I doubted God had anything to do with Heather being called to Nashville.

"You feel you need to go with her."

He took three more steps, stopped, and turned toward the ocean and away from me. "Yeah."

Perhaps it would be best. Heather could make the rounds of open-mic venues, realize stardom might not be in the cards, and return to the island where her quirkiness was normal.

"When are you going?"

"Starr said open-mic night at the Bluebird Cafe is on Mondays so we'll have to leave in the next couple of days. Chris, I've got a favor to ask."

I had been waiting for this. They didn't have a drivable car and whenever Charles and I had to make a road trip, I was the designated driver. A few days in Nashville could be fun.

"What?"

"Would you go with us to buy a car?"

I wasn't expecting that. "How long are you planning to stay in Nashville?" I was prepared to offer to drive them.

"Forever. We're moving."

After spending hundreds of hours with Charles, I didn't think he could say anything that would shock me. I was wrong. I was stunned.

"Moving," I said, trying to hide my reaction.

He stopped and moved to the side of the road. "Heather says nobody hits it big the first day. Says it takes years of making the rounds of free appearances, knocking on studio doors, and working with her agent before *the sky opens up and the sun shines in*, whatever the heck that means. She's talking like that since she started trying to write more songs."

"Where will you live? What will you do?"

"I've got dough left from the inheritance."

Charles and I had shared in the estate of an elderly lady we helped save from a horrific hurricane that destroyed her house a few years back. She had no family and left her estate to us. I had spent most of my share on the failed gallery, while Charles had hardly spent any of his.

I said, "True."

"We can find a cheap place to live and what do I do here? Nothing. It shouldn't be harder doing nothing there. She said she planned to take singing lessons; said they'd help tune up her voice. She has her massage skills so she could get a job anywhere."

I couldn't think of a kind comment about her taking singing lessons, and said, "What if she doesn't find what she's looking for?"

"Suppose it'll be no different than her not finding it here, except without an ocean in the backyard."

While I had to support my friend, I felt like someone had rammed a knife in my back. I put my arm around his shoulder, pulled him close, wiped a tear from my eye with my other arm, and stepped back.

"So when do you want to go car shopping?"

Charles looked at the sandy berm and mumbled, "Today."

***

A good chunk of Charleston's car dealers were west of town on or near Savannah Highway, so that's where I headed with Charles in the front seat and Heather, along with her guitar that was as ever-present as Charles's cane, in the back. When she got in the car carrying the guitar case she said she wanted it to be as happy with the car they bought as she and Charles would be. I thought she was kidding, although I wouldn't have bet on it.

Charles's previous car buying experience had taken place twenty years ago with a used Saab 900 convertible. I knew because the Swedish vehicle was still sitting in his parking lot in a spot it hasn't moved from in the last five years. As a piece of yard or parking lot art, it was attractive, but as transportation it had as good a chance of moving on its own as did the Folly water tower. I wondered who would inherit the Saab after they moved, but didn't ask; more out of fear it would be bequeathed to the person who was driving them car shopping.

After a back-and-forth discussion between Charles and Heather, they decided they wanted to find something large enough to carry Heather's worldly belongings and Charles's clothes. Charles's apartment was rented for three more months, so he would have time to come back for his books. Unless they bought an eighteen-wheeler today, he would have to rent a U-Haul to move the collection to Nashville. Heather said she wanted them to get a Toyota because she had a dream last night where she was driving one through a field of sunflowers and a quartet of rabbits were propped up on their hind legs singing "You Are My Sunshine."

I was proud of myself for not laughing. I said, "Okay." After all, she was a psychic.

Charles felt he was being ignored and added, "George W. Bush said, 'More and more of our imports come from overseas.'"

I was beginning to feel I was in that sunflower field. Instead of laughing or crying, I pulled in the parking lot of a Honda dealership. Heather asked me to drive through the used car area so she could see if the car *of her dreams* was there. It wasn't and she said to keep going. Charles gazed at four long rows of used vehicles and shook his head.

After the same results at three more dealers, Heather yelled for me to stop. We were in the second row of used cars at the Fred Anderson Toyota of Charleston. She hopped out of the car and made a beeline for a red metallic Toyota Venza crossover, and a middle-aged man wearing a Toyota logoed jacket made a beeline toward Heather.

In the next five minutes, the helpful salesman, who told us his name was Thom, with an *h*, shared that the three-year-old "almost new" vehicle had thirty-nine thousand "easy" miles, had one owner, was accident free, packed with everything Toyota put on a car, and the color was called Barcelona Red. He said since it was February, he could offer a fantastic deal on the "pristine" vehicle. I was almost convinced he was going to give the car to Charles and Heather.

Instead, he said it was a steal at a hair under twenty thousand grand. That probably was more than Charles had earned during his thirty-plus years on Folly, and he gasped when the salesman threw out the number. I didn't think it sounded bad, and when the salesman learned Charles would be paying cash, he said he would twist the manager's arm and might do better.

To Thom's delight, Heather was jumping up and down and had a huge grin on her face, so Charles agreed to a test drive. The four of us climbed in, and if the salesman was surprised when Heather insisted on taking her guitar, he didn't show it. I was pleased how well the vehicle drove and was impressed by how low-key Thom had been. He pointed out each feature, but didn't apply high-pressure sales tactics. Charles appeared to get more in the swing of things, and when we returned to the lot, told the salesman to give us a few minutes, and if we were interested we would join him in the building.

Our discussion didn't take long.

"That's it, that's it," Heather said and giggled. "That's what I was driving in the field. It's meant to be."

And it was. It took fewer than twenty minutes for us to negotiate another thousand off the price, for Charles's trembling hand to write the check, for the title and registration paperwork to be filled out, and for Thom to say they could pick the car up in the morning.

Our ride back to Folly consisted of Charles mumbling over and over again, "What have I done?" and of Heather singing "You Are My Sunshine" over and over again.

Chapter Twenty-One

I was exhausted after ferrying Charles and Heather around and watched the local news, something I did to see if there had been any murders in Charleston that Karen might be investigating. Fortunately for the citizens of Charleston and for Karen, no suspicious deaths had been reported. I wanted to call and see if she had decided about the job, but I wasn't ready to know. I had told Charles I'd meet him at his apartment in the morning, help him pack whatever he would be taking, and take him to pick up their chariot. He said with luck, and Heather's ability to get her stuff together, they would leave by mid-afternoon. Realizing Charles and Heather would be leaving tomorrow was enough for me to assimilate. I wasn't a big reader, so reading materials were in as short supply in the house as was food, and nothing of any interest was on television. It was still early, but maybe I could go to sleep and not dream about sunflowers and rabbits.

I was awakened by a strange sound and glanced at the bedside clock that glowed nine-thirty. I shook my head and had to think which nine-thirty. It was dark outside, so it was still night and I had only been asleep a couple of hours. I remained still and waited to see if I heard the noise again. Had I dreamed it?

No dream—there it was. The distinct clink of breaking glass came from somewhere in the house. I sat up and reached for my cell phone on the bedside table. The only light in the room was from the illuminated numbers on the clock and I fished around for the phone before remembering I had left it in the living room.

Nothing nearby could be used as a weapon. I didn't know if the intruder was armed or why he or she was here. I wasn't certain what to do, but figured staying in bed wasn't it.

The floor creaked as I took my first two steps. To me, it sounded as loud as a jet, but in reality, the noise wasn't enough to carry outside the bedroom. I was at the door when I heard a sharp crack of breaking glass coming from the spare room. Someone was removing glass from the window frame.

The sound gave me hope. Whoever it was may not be inside. The person didn't worry about masking noise since it was only nine-thirty and he must've thought I wasn't home. The only weapon in my arsenal was surprise. Would it be enough to scare off the intruder?

I tiptoed to the door to the spare room and reached around the corner for the light switch. I gave a second, and third thought to running for the back door, rather than doing what I was about to do. Instead, I held my breath and flicked the switch.

White light bathed the spare room and blinded me. More glass from the window shattered and I blinked a couple of times for my eyes to adjust. I saw the silhouette of someone's back falling away from the window frame. A gloved hand appeared on the ledge. One leg had been inside and caught on the sill as the body tried to pull it out. I moved toward the window. If I couldn't catch the intruder, I had to see who it was. A sliver of glass slashed into my foot and changed my priorities.

I stumbled. My foot felt like it was walking on burning coals. My knees hit the floor and I grabbed my foot. My eyes watered from pain and from the abrupt switch from pitch black to bright white light. I pulled the shard out and looked at the window. He was gone.

I hobbled to the window and stuck my head out, looked both ways, and saw the headlights of a truck was barreling down the street from the direction of the Washout. Nothing else. All I was left with was the second broken window pane in two weeks and a painful cut on the foot.

I pogo-sticked myself to the bathroom using the walls as a crutch to lean against on the way. My foot felt like it had a samurai sword stuck through it, but under the harsh bathroom light, I saw there were little bleeding and the cut was minor. I rinsed it in the tub and put some anti-bacterial cream on the wound before applying a bandage I found under the sink.

I hobbled to the living room and plopped down in my chair. I looked at the door to the spare room and despite a foot that still felt like it was on fire, realized how lucky I was, and how foolish I had been to burst in on the intruder without anything with which to defend myself. I looked at my phone on the table beside the chair. Do I dial 911 and have a fire truck, an ambulance, and several patrol cars in front of my house for a minor injury? Instead of 911, do I call Chief LaMond?

I continued to stare at the phone and wondered what calling anyone would accomplish. The intruder had worn gloves so there wouldn't be prints. He didn't get in the house so nothing had been stolen. And why would I want police, EMTs, and no telling who else, traipsing around the house and telling me there was nothing they could do. Besides, adrenaline had taken me from the bed to the spare room and now here, but I realized I was exhausted and tomorrow would be worse. I wondered what could be in my house to cause someone to break in once and now try again, and to have left the not-so-subtle hint for me to *LEAVE TOWN*. Did the intruder try a second time because I scared him off the first time before he found what he was looking for? Again, what could it be? And, could it have been a female breaking in? The question was bouncing around in my head when I fell asleep.

Another noise woke me. It was the phone that jolted me out of sleep rather than the sound of breaking glass.

"Where are you?" Charles yelled. "It's almost sunrise and you're not here."

I wanted to yell, "I'm not there because it's almost sunrise." Instead, I said, "Give me a half hour."

"Hurry. I've been helping Heather get her stuff together, and we need to get moving. The car's going to be ready in three hours."

My brain wasn't awake enough to do the higher math, but at first thought, we could get Charles's stuff together in thirty minutes and be at the Toyota dealer staring at Thom nearly two hours before he told Charles the car would be available. I didn't share any of that with my anxious friend.

I hobbled to the bedroom to get dressed and decided there was one other thing I wasn't going to share with Charles: last night's break in. He didn't need to worry about me. His mind was made up about going with Heather and as a good friend, I needed to respect his decision; respect it even though it hurt more than the gash in my foot.

Chapter Twenty-Two

Charles and I had finished packing and had his stuff by the door awaiting the arrival of his car. We had driven to Charleston, and were now sitting in front of Thom's desk an hour before the time we were to be there as he told us for the third time the features of Charles's purchase. Charles didn't appear to be paying attention and kept looking at his wrist where most people wore a watch. My friend didn't own one, but it didn't stop him from the visual reminder to Thom.

I'm sure Thom was relieved, and I know I was, when a service rep called to say the Venza was out front and ready to go. Charles beamed as Thom handed him the keys. I asked Charles if he wanted to stop at a liquor store so I could buy a bottle of champagne to break over the front fender to christen his new craft. His frown indicated he didn't see humor in my suggestion. I didn't either.

I followed him to his apartment and helped him load three copy paper boxes in the hatch. He borrowed my phone and called Heather to see if she was ready to load. After saying, "Yes, sweetie," twice and kissing the phone's screen, he asked if I could help them load the car. In a moment of weakness, he said once they got to Nashville he was going to buy a cell phone. He had never had one, nor had he ever had an answering machine or a computer, so I had to tell him how to find a store that sold phones. He promised to call with the number.

I'm not a sappy person, and was embarrassed that I had to wipe tears away on the short ride to Heather's apartment. It was finally hitting me that my best friend was leaving. I also reconsidered my decision not to tell him about last night's excitement. No, nothing good would be accomplished by raining on his parade out of town.

Heather was on the front step when we pulled up in front of her building. Her guitar case rested on her lap and a huge smile adorned her face. She jumped up and down—actually, she jumped up and gravity brought her down—when Charles opened the hatch from the driver's seat. She threw her arms around him like he'd arrived home from three years in the Sudan after serving in the Peace Corp.

I stood back and watched. I wanted to be happy for the couple and Heather's success in the music world, I truly did, but all I managed was a fake smile.

It took a half hour to haul Heather's belongings to the car. Searching for something to be thankful for, I was reminded her apartment had come furnished, so none of the furniture had to be crammed in the Venza. We did have to find room for a large, black and silver karaoke machine, a music stand, and her "favorite" chrome picture frame with crystals attached by a thin thread dangling from the top edge.

She placed her guitar case and wide-brimmed, straw hat she wore when performing on top of her possessions, and announced she was ready to *meet her destiny*.

I hated to see them go, but I was happy for Heather. On the other hand, I was sure her elation would be short lived, though it wasn't my place to tell her. I asked them if they wanted to go to the Dog for a farewell meal.

Charles glanced at Heather. "Nah," he said. "Better hit the road. Hope to get to Knoxville and spend the night before going the rest of the way in the morning."

"Mr. Starr wants me to call as soon as we get there," Heather said, and hugged me. "Thanks, Chris. You're the best thing that ever happened to Chucky—other than me. I love you."

I returned her hug and didn't say anything. I wasn't able to.

She headed to the passenger seat and Charles scuffed his foot in the shell and gravel parking lot. I noticed he wore a black, long-sleeve T-shirt unadorned with any college identification; the same shirt he had worn at his aunt's funeral, and one that was out of character from his logoed T-shirt collection. I wondered if it was intentional or the next shirt in line.

He looked at his foot that was still pushing gravel around.

"Guess this is *adios*. You know I'm bummed about leaving." He looked at me. "She's special. Don't find gals like her every day."

You can say that again, I thought.

His eyes began to water. "Now," he paused, sniffed, and said, "danged allergies. Chris, I think I've done a good job of training you to carry on my reputation. You still need to practice being nosy, and lazy, and you need to concentrate on being dumber. You've learned from the best, but you still have a way to go." He stepped back and looked at my navy blue polo shirt and lightweight tan jacket. "As Andy Jackson said, 'There goes a man made by the Lord Almighty and not by his tailor.' I never did learn you how to dress."

He was right, thank goodness. I told him I would try harder to be like him, but he could never be replaced. He said he would be back in a few weeks to get the rest of his valuables, which meant a hundred or so T-shirts and three zillion books.

"Chucky," Heather squealed. "Music City's awaitin'."

"Yes, sweetie."

He tipped his Tilley to me, winked, told me to take care of his island, and slid into the driver's seat.

Heather was ecstatic. Charles was happy. And I felt a void growing in my stomach, heart, and head.

There were a few people on the street and sidewalks, yet all I could see on my short drive home was a small town that hadn't yet realized it had lost one of its most endearing characters. The colorful exteriors of The Grill, Woody's Pizza, Planet Follywood, the Crab Shack, Taco Boy, and Snapper Jacks looked duller. Even the red signal on Folly's stoplight looked pale.

I walked in the house and tried to tell myself to cheer up. One glance at the broken window deepened my depression. Was my world falling apart, or did it just seem that way? It had been fifteen minutes since he had pulled off-island, and I was already missing Charles. I didn't know her as well as Charles did, but I also missed Heather's unique outlook, her quirky hobbies, and her ability to make him happy. I wouldn't miss her singing.

My mind switched to Karen. Would she be next to leave? I shouldn't—couldn't—stand in her way when it came to the job opportunity. She'd had a long and stressful career. She deserved to be happy, and if taking the new job met that need, I would support it. Then again, am I part of the reason for her considering it? She wanted more from our relationship; at least she did at some point. Would that have made a difference in her career decision? I moved to the kitchen, grabbed a Diet Pepsi, sat at the table, took a long sip, and flipped through a copy of a new photo magazine that arrived yesterday. Neither the Pepsi nor the magazine offered solace.

My mind switched to Preacher Burl and his concern for Douglas Garfield. After meeting with the obnoxious member of his flock, I had no interest in honoring Burl's request to help him. I wondered if Garfield was responsible for the two break-ins. He had said he could take care of himself; that's all I needed to know. So why did I feel guilty?

Now to Dude. I had known him for years and while we had little in common, I considered him a friend. If I'd learned anything since moving here, it was that friends looked out for each other, watched each other's back, and I could cite several examples of where they put their lives on the line for each other. Dude was worried about his sister and therefore, so was I. But what could I do? Was she in danger, or was she a murderer?

I moved to the spare room and stared at the broken window. Cold February air rushed through the opening, bringing a chill, but no answers. I closed my eyes and pictured Douglas Garfield smashing the glass; I could also see Barbara doing it. Or it may not have anything to do with the death in the alley and was someone high on drugs looking for the money to feed his habit.

I shut the spare room door to keep the cold from infiltrating the rest of the house, took a walk on the pier, wondered if Charles and Heather had made it to Knoxville, watched the sunset behind the Tides hotel, and tried to cheer myself up by watching a sitcom. The artificial laugh-track failed to convince me anything was worth laughing about. I prayed tomorrow would be better.

Chapter Twenty-Three

For the second time in the last few days, I called Larry to repair my window. He wasn't at the hardware store and Brandon, Larry's only full-time employee, said the owner was taking the day off and spending it with his "cutie-pie." I asked if that was any way to refer to the chief of police. He said "yep," and added if I wanted to incur the wrath of Larry, I could call his cell. Why not, I thought, and punched in the number. Larry said he was having a "delightful" day with his lovely spouse watching her select onions at Harris Teeter. I told him the problem and he said, "Thank God. A reason to get out of this frickin' grocery." For Larry, shopping ranked up there with barreling over Niagara Falls. He said he'd be here as soon as he convinced Cindy they didn't need asparagus and okra.

Fifty minutes later, Larry pulled up in his yellow Pewter Hardware pick-up truck. Instead of asparagus and okra, he carried a red toolbox and a pane of window glass wrapped in brown cardboard. He also had a police escort in the form of Chief Cindy LaMond.

Cindy said, "No way am I going to let the boy get away from me that easy on our day off."

I assumed it was her explanation of why she was with him on the emergency hardware store run. I also had a hunch she wanted to find out how the window got broken. I welcomed them and offered coffee, water, Pepsi, beer, or wine. They chose coffee. Larry said if he wasn't working with sharp glass, he would have taken beer. They grabbed their drinks and followed me to the spare room.

Cindy looked at the window and squinted. "Hmm, rock? Kid throw a baseball through it? Meteorite?" She gave me her best police stare. "Wait, I've got it. Somebody broke in. Again."

I smiled. "Don't suppose you'd buy a seagull strike?"

Larry, showing wisdom, ignored our conversation and began scraping away the caulk around the broken pane.

Cindy sat in the chair in front of my computer and leaned back. "Who and when?" She wore jeans and a denim work shirt, but had morphed to on-duty.

"Night before last," I said and took a deep breath. "Don't know who."

"Night before last," Cindy growled. "When were you planning to report it? Christmas?"

"Now."

Larry hummed "Jingle Bells," and continued his work as if we weren't there. I wished I wasn't.

"Did you think someone was taking a shortcut through your house to Bert's?" She shook her head. "Lay the details on me."

I told her what little I knew. She asked why I was asleep at nine-thirty and if I was positive I didn't see who it was. I said I didn't get a decent look and added I didn't see any reason to call the police. What I did see was an intruder wearing gloves so there wouldn't be prints, and I scared him off before he—"

"Or she," Cindy interrupted.

"Or she, got in."

Larry's cell rang and he listened for a minute and said, "Okay, I'll be there in fifteen." He put the phone back in his pocket, sighed, and said he had to go to the store and bail Brandon out. "The credit card machine—on its own, without any assistance from my computer-illiterate assistant—added three extra zeroes to a thirteen-dollar charge and the peeved customer won't leave until the problem's corrected."

Larry put the finishing touches on the new window and asked Cindy if she was ready to go. She said she had things to discuss and Larry could pick her up when he finished battling Brandon and MasterCard. He tried to plant a kiss on her mouth on his way to the door. She turned her head and he got her cheek.

"Remind me to never, never, not ever take that boy to the grocery," Cindy said, as that boy drove away.

I smiled. "Thought you two were having a fun day together."

"Yeah, right."

We moved to the kitchen and she asked if the offer of a beer was still good. I said yes and she accepted and plopped down in a kitchen chair. There was something on her mind, so I remained silent.

She took a sip and put the bottle on the table and held it with both hands like it was trying to escape. "Got a strange call last night."

I remained silent.

"Detective Adair called around ten and apologized for calling so late. That got my attention."

She took another sip and I nodded.

"He said he had been talking with a detective with the Pennsylvania State Police. They were calling about Barbara Deanelli. Seems there's an investigation going on up there and they knew she was living here and wanted to know if the sheriff's office had her on its radar. They had contacted the great detective agency in the cloud, Google, and saw where her name popped up in a Charleston TV station's report about a body found behind Barb's Books, owned by you-know-who." She paused and took a draw of beer. "Detective Adair told the Penn police person that if he knew that, he knew as much as Adair knew. He told the detective he would contact me since I was closer to what happened here and would get back with him if he learned anything. As you can imagine, he learned zero from me."

"Why's she being investigated?"

"Chris, haven't you learned by now that hoity-toity state cops look at sheriff offices like you'd look at a rabid opossum; sheriff-office fuzz look at us local yokels like you'd look at the rat bit by the rabid opossum. State cops tell county cops squat; county cops tell local yokels half squat."

"Adair doesn't know why Barbara's being investigated."

"You missed your calling. He learned a bit more than I thought he would. The Penn police said it had to do with Barbara's husband, now ex-husband."

"She's not the subject of the investigation?"

"He didn't say, but my take is no. That'd depend on what they turn up."

"Think our murder could be connected?"

"Our murder?" She frowned at me, and continued, "Doubt it,

remember, my half-squat status doesn't get me invited to many meetings about what's going on."

"Has Adair learned anything else about Lawrence Panella's death?"

"Now that you ask, Adair did share a sliver of information with Chief Half-Squat." She pointed to her face. "Seems Mr. Panella was living, as we say back home, high on the hog in Myrtle Beach; had a nice fancy house, wife belongs to an exclusive country club."

"You said he was a successful equipment salesman. Wouldn't they make good money?"

"No argument with that. Except a forensic audit of his finances showed there wasn't a legitimate source of income to keep them in the lifestyle to which they had been accustomed."

"If he was retired, there wouldn't be as large an income as when he was working."

"There you go," Cindy said. "I agree with you again, that is until he said the audit went back the last six years he had allegedly been selling those big-ass machines."

"Is this where you tell me his W-2s didn't add up to the money he was spending?"

"Lordy, Chris." She put her hand over her heart. "We've never been on the same surfboard together like we are now. You've smacked the dilemma right on its bald spot."

"If Charles were here, he'd quote a US President who said something about cash being king. People who hire hit men don't pay with a payroll check."

"Right again. The bank records show a bunch of cash deposits under the ten-thousand-buck limit that has to be reported. The cops up there would love to question him about them. Unfortunately, as you know, he's unavailable."

"Any deposits in the last few weeks?"

"You're pushing the limit on what the big-wig cops shared. If I was guessing, I'd say no."

"Why?"

"Because the Pennsylvania cops asked Adair if he found a large quantity of cash on Panella or in his hotel room."

"Cash for the hit?"

"That's my take."

"And none was found."

"Five hundred bucks rolled up in a shoe in his hotel room, and he'd paid for the room with a credit card."

"Learn anything else?"

"Cripes, Chris. Thought I did pretty good to charm that much out of Adair."

"You did."

"Speaking of Charles, do you think he and Heather are serious about heading to Nashville?"

It was a stretch to say I'd been speaking of Charles. "Not thinking about it, they left yesterday."

Cindy leaned back like I'd slapped her. "You're kidding."

"Wish I were."

"Details?"

I proceeded to tell her about their decision, Charles buying a car, their packing, and leaving.

"How long do you think they'll be there?"

I shook my head. "The way Charles talked, it could be forever."

"Damn, double damn."

***

An hour later, the phone rang and an unfamiliar out-of-state area code popped up on the screen. Great, all I need is a telemarketer trying to sell me a condo, offer a free cruise, give me an opportunity to donate to an incredibly worthy cause, or to buy a coffin at a discount. Larry had picked Cindy up after our cheerful discussion about death and Charles leaving, so I thought *what the heck*, and rehearsed all the ways I was going to say no.

"Mr. Landrum, I'm glad I caught you. This is Barbara Deanelli. Is this a bad time?"

I was surprised. "It's fine, how are you?"

It beat having to say no, but I realized how dumb it was to ask her how she was. I doubted she called to share her condition.

"I've got a favor to ask," She hesitated. "A couple more

questions. Could you stop by tomorrow?"

"Sure. Any particular time?"

"I'll be here from nine on."

I told her I'd see her in the morning. I didn't tell her it would be close to her opening because I had acquired a couple of nosy genes from Charles.

Chapter Twenty-Four

If Charles was here, he would have me standing in front of Barb's Books thirty minutes before she unlocked the door. He was hundreds of miles away, so I exerted a dollop of patience, and opened the door to the bookstore five minutes after it opened; not quite fashionably late, but the best my curiosity would allow.

"Good morning, Mr. Landrum. What took you so long to get here?"

A lighthearted comment, more progress. Barbara stepped from behind the counter and greeted me with a handshake. She wore the same red blouse she had on the first time I'd met her. She had switched from black to gray slacks.

"Please call me Chris. Would've been here sooner, but my flight was late."

Instead of looking at me like I was an idiot, she smiled.

"Call me Barb. Tap water or coffee?"

I started to ask if *Barb Tap Water or Coffee* was her Indian name, but decided not to push my luck with humor—attempt at humor.

"Coffee would be great."

She waved for me to follow her to the back room. "Good, I got a new coffeemaker and wanted to try it out on someone."

She pointed at a black and polished-chrome Keurig machine that looked like it should be in a science lab rather than a bookstore. I was informed it made one cup of coffee at a time, a feature I didn't think was efficient, as I watched her insert a cartridge in the machine, pull a lever, and push a button. My Mr. Coffee machine that had lived on the same counter for years would have been humiliated sitting next to the high-tech gadget.

We watched one cup brew and she repeated the steps and prepared one for herself. She said she should get back to the front of the store and motioned for me to follow. We sipped our high-tech coffee and talked about how nice the winter weather was as compared to the part of Pennsylvania where she'd been, and about how business had picked up. I didn't figure either topic was why she had called, and waited for her to feel comfortable enough to share.

After an awkward pause, she said, "The reason I called is I was wondering if you had a problem with rats?" She pointed to the corner of the room.

And I worried half the night about that?

"No. There are a lot of them on the island. I've had a few in my house, never in the store. Do you have some?"

She looked at the floor like one was going to step out from under one of the bookcases so she could introduce us.

"There were a few, umm, droppings in the back room," She wrinkled up her nose.

I thought it was cute, and said, "It must have scooted in when the door was open. I don't think there're any openings; none large enough for a mouse, much less a rat."

"I'll get a trap."

And that was important enough for her to call. To offer a bad, although timely, pun, I smell a rat.

"While you're here, I have another question." Barb looked around the empty store. "Let me show you."

She led me back to the office and to the back door. She unlocked the door and twisted the deadbolt.

"I'm having trouble with the lock." She gave it another twist. "It gets stuck and I wondered if there was a trick to working it."

She stepped aside and I pulled the door to and twisted the knob. It was tight, but it wasn't any different than what I had remembered.

"I'm worried about it not being locked. I'm here alone so much and worry about safety after what happened ..." She stopped, looked at the door, and at me.

The squeaky front door opened before she could continue and I followed her to the front. A man had entered and walked to the mystery section. He was my height, a few years younger, wore a black polo shirt, khaki slacks, and a red Chicago Bulls ball cap.

I leaned on the counter and Barb sat in the chair. I said, "Back to your question, the locks may be a little more difficult to turn. If you're concerned, you may want to call Pewter Hardware and ask for Larry. He'd be glad to come over and replace the mechanism. He's a good guy and will treat you right."

Barb watched the customer as he came around the shelves and down the next aisle. "Is there anything in particular you're looking for?"

"Just browsing."

Barb continued to focus on the browser, and said to me, "That's a good idea. I'll call." She jotted down Larry's name on a notecard.

The man pulled a couple of books off the shelf, flipped through them, seemed to tire of browsing and left. He was gone, and Barb continued to stare at the door.

"Do you know him?" Her fingers tapped on the counter.

"I don't recall seeing him before. Could be a vacationer killing time while his wife's in Charleston shopping. Why?"

"This is the third time he's been in since yesterday morning. He gives me the willies."

Three times in that short a time was unusual, but why the willies?

"Has he bought anything?"

Her fingers continued to tap on the counter. "No."

"What bothers you about him?"

She turned away from the door and back to me. "Want more coffee?"

I declined and wondered if she'd heard my question.

"I haven't had the store long, although long enough to learn to tell the difference between buyer and browser. I may be paranoid. It seems more like he's casing the store rather than browsing. Does that make sense?"

"Elaborate?"

She looked toward the bookcases. "I hate to admit it, and it wouldn't hold up in court, but I ran into a lot of men like him when I was practicing law. I didn't do criminal law, but some of the white collar crooks had that look in their face. There's an arrogance about them." She pointed to the door. "That guy took a few books from the shelves, like that was what he was supposed to do and each time he looked around like he was taking everything in. I can't explain it. Seemed creepy."

From other things she'd said, the man killed behind her store had bothered her, bothered her more than the tragedy of someone being killed there.

"The police chief's a friend. If you want, I'll ask her to check around and see if her people—"

"No," she interrupted. "No big deal; I'm being melodramatic. Sorry I said anything. Besides, I can handle any trouble that comes this way." She leaned down and touched something under the counter.

"You sure? I'd be glad to."

She shook her head. "I'm sure. I know the chief's your friend. Has she said anything else about the guy who was killed?"

"No." Not the whole truth, but all I was willing to share.

She sighed and asked again if I wanted more coffee.

She wanted to talk so I said yes and we headed back to the latest-greatest way to brew coffee. I still had the feeling she had called for another reason other than to ask about rats and a sticking lock.

Barb brewed two more cups, pointed to the desk, and moved her chair to where she had a view to the front door.

"Rumor is on this isle of gossip, you're someone who keeps your mouth shut when you learn something rather than spreading it around." She cocked her head to the left.

I smiled. "Where'd you hear that?"

She returned my smile. "If I told you, I'd be spreading gossip."

"If it's true, it isn't gossip."

She shrugged. "I was in Jimmy's—Dude's—surf shop yesterday; had gone over to ask him if he was having trouble with his phone system. Mine's been dropping calls and I wondered if it was a system problem or mine."

I waited.

"Anyway, he'd run out to pick up lunch and I was stuck talking to Stephon and Rocky." She giggled. "It was more like me listening to the surly employees complaining about stupid customers, wimpy waves, cold weather, and how some people like to tell tall-tales about Dude being retarded."

I smiled. "Customer service isn't their forte."

"True. I'll tell you one thing, those guys are more loyal than a hound dog would be to my brother. In another canine reference, they're like two pit bulls protecting him from what, I don't know. That makes me like them despite their attitude."

"They grow on you."

"If I'd had people around me as loyal as those two, I wouldn't be here. Anyway, my brother returned with a sack of food, and gave Stephon and Rocky lunch and took me to his cluttered office."

I may have imagined it, but I thought she cringed when she said office. I wouldn't have been surprised since hers was 180 degrees opposite of Dude's clutter-filled, disorganized work space.

I waved my hand around the room. "Looks like this one."

Barb laughed. Her hazel eyes sparkled and this was the first time I'd seen her relax. "I bet the city dump's neater." She turned serious. "After we figured out the phone problem was in the system, I was telling Dude you came in the store for the first time the other day, and he started telling me about the escapades you had been involved in and how he helped you catch a murderer a few years back. He also said if you learned anything that was none of anyone else's business, it stopped with you. That's what I meant about gossip." Her smile returned. "He also told me about giving you surfing lessons."

"One lesson, and *he be talkin'* too much," I said in my best Dude voice.

She laughed again. "Dad used to tease that I got all the words and Dude got all the trouble."

"Don't know about trouble, although he was right about words. Dude doesn't waste many."

Someone came in the door. Barb said she'd be back. I once again looked around and continued to be amazed how different the room looked. I also wondered where she was going with her stories. I didn't wait long. She returned to her seat and lukewarm coffee.

"Two books lighter."

"Two more than I ever sold this early."

She turned her coffee cup around a couple of times and stared in it like she expected to see something more interesting than coffee. "My husband, ex-husband, and I started our law firm in Harrisburg."

I already knew this from Dude who wasn't as good at keeping secrets as I was. I nodded.

"I did most of the legal work, mainly defending executives accused of white-collar crimes, and Karl, my husband, carved out a niche lobbying for corporations that dealt with state government. To be honest, we were successful beyond our wildest dreams, especially Karl's area. Don't know if you know much about it, but influencing the right legislators could mean millions, crap, hundreds of millions of dollars to companies that either deal directly with the government, or can use their government connections to get jobs or make sales outside the public realm."

"Made more than from selling two books?" I may be good at keeping secrets, but I wasn't as good at not being a smart aleck.

She giggled. "Slightly."

"So, you two were tearing up the world." I motioned for her to continue.

"Then the proverbial shit hit the fan." She frowned and gazed in her coffee cup. "A dozen law enforcement officials from every agency known to man stormed in our exquisitely-appointed offices, threw search warrants around like confetti, escorted Karl, our receptionist, our befuddled paralegal, and me into the corridor, and proceeded to turn the place upside down. It would have made my brother's office look like an ad in a design magazine. They hauled out computers, files, and my self-esteem."

Barb blinked and closed her eyes. I remained silent and hoped no customers would come in and distract her.

"Chris, I was my high school valedictorian; I was in the top five in my law school class; my IQ's in the top quartile, or so the records say. I'm not stupid. You have to believe me. I had no clue about what was going on with Karl. None."

I took her cup, poured out the cold coffee, and fixed her another one. She sat and stared at the wall.

"What was going on?"

"Long story short." She took a sip. "Karl was bribing legislators and regulatory officials, bureaucrats in charge of projects affecting his clients. He was bribing them to switch votes, bribing them to sweep reports under the rug that reflected negatively on actions his clients wanted, or to overlook roadblocks to the client getting their way. All that time, I was going about my business of defending crooks, doing the time-honored, within the law, job of helping clients." She shook her head. "No clue, Chris. I had no clue."

"I'm sorry."

"That makes two of us." She looked up from her coffee. "Before it hit the fan, our marriage was, shall I say rocky, but when everything broke, my only option was to leave." She forced a smile. "And now I'm here."

"What happened with the...the legal problems?"

"I was interviewed—interrogated—by numerous cops, my bank records received more scrutiny than the Affordable Care act, and despite their best efforts, they found nothing which would indicate I knew about his activities. Of course there are those who think I know more than I do. When it hit, some of the corporate officials who were involved scattered like cockroaches when the lights turn on. One was caught trying to sneak over the border to Canada in the trunk of his Mercedes." She smiled, more sincerely this time. "I've heard a couple are hiding in Florida under assumed names and a couple more are still on pins and needles thinking I could send them to prison if I told what I know—which is nothing."

I'd heard Dude's version and asked, "What happened to Karl?"

"It's remarkable what high-powered lawyers can do. Karl had a few 'bucks' stashed away the feds didn't get their hands on, and hired the best of the best. Instead of spending time playing Scrabble with other white-collar crooks in a country-club prison, he got off with disbarment and time served, a whopping three months. He moved to New Jersey and if you can believe tax records is making minimum-wage. He's not practicing law, but writing briefs for large law firms."

"Why tell me?" I shouldn't have said it. I had to admit some of Charles had rubbed off on me.

She smiled and nodded. "To be honest, I don't know. I had to, no, wanted to tell someone. Telling Dude would have been like telling that Keurig machine. I don't know anyone else enough to confide in. I don't want it spread around. And, Lawrence Panella." She hesitated and looked at the back door.

"What about him?"

"He was here to kill me."

Barb's declaration was followed by two families arriving in search of beach reads. There may have been a worse time to end a conversation, but I couldn't think of any. While she played the part of shop owner, I waited at her desk and ran several scenarios through my head. Was she right? If she was, how could she have known? Why was she telling me instead of going to the police? And, the most intriguing question, who hit the hit man?

Fifteen minutes later, I heard another customer enter. I was thinking there were more visitors than were ever in my gallery at any one time when Barb stuck her head in the doorway.

She was in customer mode and smiling. I was impressed how she could go from talking about a hit man out to kill her to helpful owner. She shrugged and pointed toward the group of customers. "Sorry, Chris, I'll get back to you."

Chapter Twenty-Five

I left Barb with her customers and my stomach growled a reminder I
hadn't eaten. I walked to the Dog and was almost run down by a pick-
up truck while my body was in the middle of Center Street and my
mind was in the alley behind Barb's Books rehashing my introduction
to Lawrence Panella. A horn blast stunned me back to reality. I waved
an apology and continued to the restaurant. It was chilly and no one sat
outside so I hoped I wouldn't have a long wait for a table.

The restaurant was full and after what Barb had said, I was too
nervous to stand and wait for someone to leave. I turned to go back
outside where I could walk around the nearby community park and
wait for a table.

I started to push the door open when I heard, "Brother Chris."

Preacher Burl was seated at the table behind the hostess stand
and waved me over. If I had known who was with him, I would have
pretended not to hear him. Douglas Garfield, or whatever his real
name was, glared at me. He had no interest in seeing me and didn't
hide it.

Burl said, "Join us, Brother Chris."

If he was aware of Douglas's glower, he ignored it.

"Thanks, Preacher," I said while Garfield's glare lasered
through me. "I don't want to interrupt. I'll wait for a table."

"No interruption. We'd love for you to join us."

Douglas didn't say anything. His scowl said he was not part of
we. I took the chair beside Douglas so I wouldn't have to make eye
contact with him.

Amber was at the table before I was settled. "Yogurt?" She

knew I had never ordered it, nor ever would.

I smiled. "Not today. How about French toast?"

"What a surprise," she said and started to leave, but instead stopped behind Douglas, tapped me on the shoulder, pointed at him, and mouthed, "Douglas Garfield."

She'd remembered I had asked about him and I nodded. Preacher Burl looked to see if anyone was within earshot and leaned closer to Douglas and me. "Brother Douglas and I were talking about what I shared with you the other day."

"Preacher," Douglas interrupted, "I was drunk and never should have told you. If I wanted people to know, I would have told them." He pointed his thumb at me. "I don't know this guy from Adam. It's none of his damn business. We're talking about my life."

"Brother Douglas, Brother Chris is a friend and can be trusted. God has worked through him to help solve several difficult situations. He's on our side."

I'd never considered God had a hand in me stumbling into bad situations, although have had several occasions to thank him for helping me survive them. Plus, I had no idea what their side was.

Douglas exhaled, looked at his half-eaten pancakes, then at Preacher Burl. "I don't like it. I don't like him." He pointed his thumb at me once more. "Your big mouth could get me killed."

"Douglas," I said. "I don't know what you and Preacher Burl were talking about and I don't know why you're in such a precarious situation. I assure you I understand the delicate nature of the, umm, program, and would never do anything to endanger someone in it."

"And I'm supposed to believe that crock because a complete stranger said it?"

"Yes," Burl said. "You've shared some thoughts with me and I don't have either the wherewithal or influence to provide assistance. Brother Chris does and I would recommend you give him a chance."

I regretted not leaving when Burl first called my name. Douglas Garfield was obnoxious, rude, and had said nothing to make me want to even talk to him, much less help. Instead of excusing myself and walking as far as I could away from him, I took a page out of Charles's playbook.

"Douglas, what were you and Preacher Burl talking about?"

Douglas was gripping his fork like he was afraid it would jump out of his hand and stick him in the eye. He glowered at Preacher Burl. "You tell him."

One of Burl's talents, and one I suspected had helped him through some of the bad times that had plagued his life, was his ability to look past insults and attacks on his church and find the good in everyone. If he couldn't sleep at night, it wasn't because he harbored resentment or took mean-spirited attacks personally.

Burl gave Douglas a calming smile and turned to me. "Brother Douglas believes Mr. Panella, the gentleman murdered behind First Light's foul-weather sanctuary, was sent to Folly Beach to end his life."

"The damned piece of...never mind. He was scum and here to kill me."

"How do you know?" I asked.

He stared at me like I'd asked him how he knew the ocean had water in it. "The people the damned Marshals Service are hiding me from found out where I was and want me dead."

"How would they have found you, and again, why think that's why Panella was here?"

"Can't you see?" Douglas growled.

Burl gestured toward Douglas's face. "Allow me to contribute."

Douglas looked like he was going to slap Burl's hand away. Instead, he took another deep breath, and went back to stabbing his pancakes.

"Chris," Burl said, "Brother Douglas has long had a fear the federal protection program was susceptible to leaks—"

"Like a damned sieve," Douglas interrupted.

"He believes," Burl continued as if Douglas hadn't said anything, "word has reached those for whom he was responsible for, shall we say, having their freedom removed, are now seeking retaliation by contracting with the late Panella to murder him."

I understood, but still hadn't heard anything to substantiate his claim.

"Did you see Panella?"

"No," Douglas said.

"Had you heard someone might be out to get you?"

"No."

"Has anyone from the witness protection program contacted you about a leak?"

"No," he said, continuing Dude-like responses.

I was beginning to understand why someone would want him dead, and I didn't know anything about his background.

"Help me understand. I get how the people you helped the government convict would want revenge, but I still wonder how you know he was sent for you."

He looked up from his food, his eyes squinted. "Preacher Burl said you were a bright fellow and someone who could help me out of this situation. All I see you doing is asking stupid questions and sounding like you don't think I know what I'm talking about. It was a foolish mistake telling the preacher about my past. It'll get me killed. And you're as idiotic as he is." He pushed away from the table and stood. "Forget it, and forget you ever saw me. I've taken care of myself pretty damn well."

He stormed out of the restaurant and nearly barreled over a toddler at the door.

Burl watched him go and cringed when Douglas grazed past the kid. "That went well, don't you think?"

"Couldn't have said it better," I smiled at the preacher. I appreciated his humor and composure during the difficult conversation.

Burl looked toward the door and down at his empty plate. "He's scared."

"Has a funny way of showing it."

Burl shrugged. "He's all plugged up with the past, the life he had to leave, fear that his secrets will follow him here, and a bit of paranoia thinking everyone is out to get him. He uses anger and obnoxiousness as a wall to keep people out."

"He's good at it. Did he tell you he was afraid?"

"Didn't have to. Despite his attitude, he's got a sensitive side."

"He hides it well."

Burl smiled. "That he does. He acts like he hates everyone, yet he's at our service most Sundays. He doesn't say much. He sings the hymns, and nods his head when I say something profound. Yes, Chris, on occasion I say something important. Anyway, he knows what's going on and seems to benefit from church."

"I'm glad to hear it. What do you think I can do if he doesn't want to talk?"

"I don't know. I have faith you'll figure something out."

If only I was that confident. I opened the door to something that was going through my mind the entire time Douglas was talking.

"Got a question, Preacher." I hesitated, and continued, "Do you think he could've killed Panella?"

Burl looked at me and gave an almost imperceptible nod. "Chris, I've got to tell you, my calling is to find the good in people; to help lead them down the path toward salvation; to give benefit of the doubt when no one else will. I must confess, Brother Douglas has caused me to reevaluate my position." He hesitated, took a sip of tea, and continued, "I would not be shocked to learn he's responsible."

That wasn't what I'd expected.

"Preacher, I don't know Douglas. He does seem capable of taking a life. If he found out about Panella, it wouldn't take much imagination to see him killing him before it was the other way around."

"I don't disagree, yet I still want to think he's not guilty. Please do whatever you can to determine for sure."

I said I'd try, and Burl said he had to go.

He left the Dog and I picked at my French toast and realized in a matter of a few short hours, both Barbara Deanelli and Douglas Garfield said they were convinced Lawrence Panella had been contracted to kill them. One or both were wrong. If either were correct, did he or she kill Panella? During times like this I would get with Charles, discuss it, come to some horrible conclusions, say something that made sense, and decide what, if anything, there was we could do. I missed him.

Chapter Twenty-Six

I left the restaurant and stuck my head in Barb's Books hoping to hear why she thought Panella had been on Folly to kill her. To her benefit, and with a tinge of jealousy on my part as former owner of a failed shop in the same space, she had her hands full with customers browsing, asking about books, buying books, and fighting for Barb's attention. Instead of waiting, I decided to visit her half-brother.

The surf shop wasn't as busy as Barb's, nonetheless, I still had to get past Dude's gatekeepers to get to his tiny office.

Stephon frowned at me before the front door had even closed. "What?" he asked.

"Want to see Dude."

"Don't know if he's here. Yo, Rocky, boss man here?"

Rocky was in the middle of the store fiddling with surf-board stuff, their names and purposes alien to me. "Who wants to know?"

"Old man Chris," said Stephon, taking customer un-service to new heights and throwing it off the roof.

"I'll see if he's taking *unexpected* visitors," said Rocky, who apparently had gone to the same school of customer service as Stephon.

Stephon proceeded to ignore me while I waited for the verdict from Rocky.

"Chrisster!" Dude yelled from the office.

I looked toward the back and Dude waved for me. Rocky didn't growl when I passed him, it just felt that way. Dude's surf-product, decal-covered door was another sign that the owner believed in using every square inch of wall and floor space to stick ads and logos of surf paraphernalia, or fill with items the ads promoted.

Dude slid a stack of wetsuits off the extra chair in the room and motioned for me to sit.

"I was lucky to make it past your bodyguards."

"They be protective. Charmers be not."

Be understatement, I thought. "That's a good thing. And, they're so good with customers." I smiled.

Dude waved his left hand and then his right. "Keep um, kill um, be daily dilemma. Hear Chuckster and main-squeezette boogied to surfless music town."

"Yes."

"Wipeout. Be sad for Folly and canines."

"You're right."

"Bummer." Dude looked out the door. "You be here to visit my peeps?"

"Stopped by to see you. Seeing them was an added treat."

"Lucky you." Dude smiled. "Here me be."

"I was talking to your sister a little while ago and she mentioned you so I thought I'd stop to see how you were."

"Fractional-sis."

I nodded.

Dude walked around me, stepped over the wetsuits, and closed the door. "She share worry about killer man?"

"Why do you ask?"

Dude held up his thumb. "Dead guy be carrying gun," stuck out his index finger, "reputation as never-caught hit man," and added his middle finger to the count, "fractional-sis knowing stuff shouldn't know."

Dude's lengthy—lengthy for Dude—multi-media presentation threw me. He didn't extend another finger, so I said, "She did share the thought that Panella was on Folly to kill her. What do you know about it?"

"She don't tell me more than ripple. Me be seeing fear in fractional-sis face. When we were home as tiny pup and puppette, she fearin' nothing. Scary strong."

"Do you think she has something to be afraid of?"

Dude looked at the closed door and fiddled with a ring of keys on the desk. He nodded. "Someone sent never-caught hit man, hitter be hit, bad guy be sending more." He frowned. "Fractional-sis be good gal, me do anything to keep her safe."

I changed the subject. "Why do you think the hit man was killed?"

Dude waved his arms around the room. "Folly folks fight with each other—yell, scream, give finger, bite finger. Outsider mess with us, be enemy of us all. Fractional-sis now be Folly gal."

I knew what Dude had meant. It didn't answer the most important questions.

"Dude, if Panella was supposed to kill Barb, how would someone here have known?"

Dude opened a desk drawer, pulled out a wrinkled five-dollar bill, and waved it at me. "Dude pay o-pressive taxes to fuzz to figure out killing."

I couldn't disagree. Dude is often underestimated because of his clipped and nonsensical speech pattern, but he's brighter than many give him credit for, and sees things in a much different light, a perspective that is missed by more, shall I say, traditional observers. I still wanted his take.

"True, so what's your opinion?"

"Me no detective, be store owner on way to geezerhood. Someone from her history wants her extinct; someone from her current wants her alive. Hit man stand in way of current want and got bullet. There it be."

It was a summary I couldn't find fault with, although still shy of answers. "Who?"

"How be easy, who be hard. Hit man ready to break in fractional-sis's store. Hit man hitter strolled up and put lead in head."

Two thoughts came to me. First, the most logical candidate would be Barb. Second, the other most logical suspect was talking to me.

"Who here would know her well enough to have learned about her past to know what's happening, much less find out about a contract killer and kill him?"

"Barb say she talked to you about history." He hesitated and looked at the ceiling. "Me be knowin' most of it." He slid the five-dollar bill back in the drawer and looked at me. "That be it."

A pounding on the door interrupted us. "Boss, get your ass out here," yelled the *pleasant* voice of Stephon. "Some bill collector says he needs to talk to you. Talk to you now."

Dude rolled his eyes. "Fans beck in."

I followed him to the front of the store, patted him on the back, and left him with his fan.

I thought about going home and trying to forget everything. Instead, I weathered the cold breeze, pulled my jacket tight, yanked my Tilley down as far as I could over my balding head, and walked to the end of the pier where I did my best thinking.

If Barb was Panella's intended victim, both she and Dude were the most-likely suspects. From what she had told me, Dude could be right. I doubted she had told anyone other than me enough to figure it out. She would have had the most to gain from his death. It would make sense that she would have known what had transpired to make someone want her out of the way. I watched a flock of seagulls circle a section of beach, and kept coming back to my initial reason for thinking she wasn't the killer. Why would she have approached me the morning I found the body to ask what he looked like? It didn't make sense, and then it struck me. What if she had been fishing to see if I saw anyone else on my ill-fated walk? Her, for example. It still didn't feel right, but it was a reason that made sense.

That left Dude. Their relationship didn't appear to be close, but it seemed he would have been the one other person on the island who would have known her well enough to know she was in trouble. He could have learned about Panella and killed him before he could harm her. I had never heard Dude talking about guns, but remembered he had kidded—or I thought he was kidding—about blasting his two employees with his AK-47. If he owned that powerful weapon, it would be nothing for him to have a handgun. Dude was protective of Barb, and I didn't doubt he would do whatever he could to shield her. But hadn't Dude asked me from the beginning if I could help Barb? Why would he have done that if he was guilty?

The seagulls flew to another dining spot on the beach and a young couple walked a large Greyhound under the pier. My mind wandered to my earlier conversation with Preacher Burl about Douglas

Garfield who was convinced the hit man was on Folly for him. While I suppose it was human nature, I wanted Garfield to be the intended victim. I was beginning to like Barbara and didn't want her to be involved in Panella's reason for being here, or his death. I couldn't find anything likable about Douglas and felt sorry for Preacher Burl who had become involved in the surly man's problem.

I wished Charles was still here so we could talk about the situation. The fact was, he's gone. Someone broke in my house twice and I suspected it was related to Panella's death and me finding the body. And most importantly, two people I consider to be friends had asked me to help solve the crime. At this point in my life, friends are the most important thing I have.

Chapter Twenty-Seven

I answered the phone after the third ring.

"Did I wake you?" Barb asked.

She had. It was a little after ten o'clock and I was already asleep after an exhausting day meeting with potential killers and bemoaning Charles's departure. She didn't know me well enough to know that unless it was a major emergency, along the lines of a nuclear attack, my phone and door were disturbance-free zones when the evening hours reached double digits.

Of course I lied. "No, I was awake."

"Good. I felt bad about how I left this morning's discussion. I apologize for not finishing our conversation."

"Never apologize for too many customers," I said, describing a condition I had seldom experienced.

"Thanks. Anyway, I'd like to make it up to you. Could I buy you breakfast tomorrow?"

I was often the one doing the buying when it came to my friends. I said sure and we agreed to meet at the Dog at seven-thirty to beat the church crowd and other Sunday regulars.

I turned over in bed and wondered how it would feel having breakfast with a possible killer. I smiled when I realized it wouldn't be my first time. I didn't wonder or smile long, sleep returned.

***

We had been wise to meet early. When I greeted Barb at the door, the Dog was almost full. Once again, she was wearing a red blouse, this time under a heavy, pleated, black, Patagonia jacket. I wondered if she had as many red blouses as Charles had college T-shirts. She also wore black, "skinny" stretch jeans and black-leather calf-high boots. It was in the forties, but she was dressed for Pennsylvania winters.

My favorite booth was taken and we were seated at a table against the wall. I took the chair facing the room and Barb sat facing a kennel-full of canine photos. She was quick to shed her jacket and Amber was as quick to welcome us to the Dog and ask what we wanted to drink. We said coffee and Amber started to the kitchen and stopped behind Barb and gave me the kind of look that only women could muster. It was a cross between "shame on you," and "you sly dog." Men's facial muscles weren't sophisticated enough to send mixed messages with a single glance.

Nearby tables were full and Barb leaned closer. "I left you yesterday with a strong, albeit unsubstantiated, accusation."

Strong was an understatement if she was referring to her accusation that Lawrence Panella was there to kill her.

"About Panella?"

She nodded.

"Why do you think you were the target?"

"I can't prove it, but I believe it as much as I believe anything. After my divorce and before I decided to leave Pennsylvania, I received several calls. Anonymous, disguised voice, *unknown* number. Each with the variation on the theme: *We know you know about us. Tell anyone and you're dead. Don't think about running. We'll find you and we don't have to tell you what'll happen then.*"

"Do you know what they were talking about?"

"It had to be about Karl. Like I told you, the magnitude of corruption he was involved in was never revealed. Millions were never recovered. There were enough skeletons left in closets to equip every anatomy lab in the country."

"Did you go to the police?"

"And tell them what?" She paused when Amber returned to take our order. Amber smiled. From years of observing her many customer expressions, I knew it was forced.

"Tell them about the calls," I said after Amber had moved on.

"Calls from unknown numbers. Calls cryptically implying I

knew something. And calls telling me not to run. What would the police have done with that?"

"Good point."

Barb looked at her coffee. "Besides," she was barely audible, "I didn't know anything about what was going on. I wish I did so I could have told the cops. Truly, I don't know anything."

I didn't want to argue, but pointed out, "You said the magnitude of the corruption was much greater than known and there were millions never recovered, and something about skeletons."

"I figured out most of it from Karl's court proceedings and from the little I knew about who he had dealt with before getting caught. I have no proof, and not enough information to help the police put together a case against anyone."

"Yet if you're right about Panella, someone thinks you do. Someone thinks you have enough to put him away, and enough that he wants you dead."

"I wish I did know something," she repeated. "Honest to God, I do."

Our food arrived and Barb took a bite. She closed her eyes and sighed.

"Who do you think killed him?"

"If I were the police and knew about Karl's troubles in Pennsylvania, I know I'd have a suspect."

I pointed to my tablemate.

"Yes," she said.

"Have they talked to you?"

"Not yet. It's a matter of time before they learn about Karl and come knocking."

"What'll you tell them?"

"The truth."

I assumed *the truth* wouldn't be a confession. "Could it have been one of your friends who didn't want you hurt, someone trying to protect you?"

She chuckled. "Let's see. In Pennsylvania I had two friends, both women, both attorneys, both happily married with kids, and who wouldn't be able to find Folly Beach, much less a gun and shoot someone in the head."

"And here?"

"If you don't count Jim, umm, Dude, my extended friends list would include Stephon and Rocky at the surf shop who almost speak civilly to me because I'm related to their boss, and you."

"Oh," I said, sounding more like Dude each day. "I hate to ask, but should get it on the table. Could it have been Dude?"

She sat her mug down with a clunk and scowled at me. "I thought he was your friend. How could you say that?"

I was afraid she'd react that way. I sipped my coffee, glanced around the room, and turned back to her. "Put on your attorney's hat and look at the situation like you would if someone accused of a crime came to you and asked you to defend him. Wouldn't it be prudent to look at the crime from all angles, look at all possible suspects, and look for any connection to the crime to be able to defend your client?"

She continued to stare, but nodded.

"Wouldn't Dude have motive to kill the alleged assassin?"

"I don't know the adult Dude. Why would he?"

I refrained from pointing out I had never heard adult and Dude mentioned in the same breath. "He's protective."

"He was that way as a kid. I don't know about now."

"I do, and heard someone say he would do anything to protect you."

"Really?"

"Yes, and Dude is my friend. I can't imagine him putting a gun to Panella's head and pulling the trigger unless he was provoked or Panella pulled a gun on him and Dude had to defend himself. That doesn't mean he didn't. He told me the other day his employees irritated him so much at times he'd like to shoot them with his AK-47. He was teasing, but until he said it, I didn't know he owned a gun, much less an AK. The point being, he's a man of few words, and I suspect, many secrets."

"If what you're hinting at is true, how would he have known that guy was here for me?"

"Good question. How would anyone have known? The fact is, unless the killing was a robbery gone bad or the result of a disagreement, someone found out and didn't want him to succeed."

"I still can't see Dude doing it. And before you ask by

sounding like you weren't trying to ask, I didn't do it."

"I know."

She reached across the table and patted my hand. "Thank you. How do you know? I have the strongest motive, and I knew someone was out to get me."

"True, yet remember the morning I found the body."

"Like I could forget."

I pointed to the next table. "You went right over there where I was sitting."

She glanced at the table where we had met.

"And what did you ask me?"

"Several things. I have a tendency to ask multiple questions."

"You did ask a few. The two that stuck with me were: Did I think the body was closer to your back door or to the door to First Light, and would I describe him."

"From that, I assume you think if I killed him I would have known where he was?"

"And what he looked like."

"I still have my lawyer's hat on, and to be honest, those two things wouldn't carry much weight if the prosecutor had a preponderance of evidence, albeit circumstantial, against me. They would argue that I was asking to see if you saw anything, possibly the killer—me."

"Maybe, but when you came in here that morning, you'd just learned about the death, and those were two emotionally-charged questions. They weren't you setting up a defense."

She smiled, the first time this morning. "Thanks for thinking I'm not that devious. I'm going to take it as a compliment, although they would have thrown me out of law school for that character flaw." Her smile faded and she looked around the room. "That doesn't let Dude off the hook."

"No."

I returned her smile and then turned serious. "Let me throw out another scenario. What if you weren't the intended victim?"

Russ Vick interrupted. "Hi." He was wearing one of his off-color T-shirts and a denim coat, and standing behind Barb. "Don't mean to interrupt, Chris. It is Chris, isn't it?"

I had seen the back of the burly T-shirt maven on the other side of the room with two men when we came in. I started to tell him he should put *Don't mean to interrupt* on one of his T-shirts, since he'd perfected the technique. Instead, I said, "Hi, Russ. Good to see you."

Barb's head was twisted around to see who I was talking to. "Russ,' I said, "have you met my friend Barbara Deanelli? She owns Barb's Books."

Russ looked toward the door and glanced at Barb. She craned her neck to see him and smiled.

"Don't believe I've had the pleasure."

One of the men at the door yelled, "Come on, Russ."

Russ smiled and said, "Would stay and talk, but got to catch up with my friends. Wanted to say hi. And, oh yeah, Chris, if you see Charles tell him I need an answer. He'll know what it's about."

I hadn't recalled inviting him to stay and talk, so wasn't that distraught he had to go, nor did I feel the need to tell him about Charles.

"Nice meeting you," Barb said as Russ headed to the exit.

I doubted he heard her as I watched him leave the restaurant with his friends.

I said, "Russ owns SML Shirts and Folly Tease, the two new T-shirt stores on Center Street."

"I've seen him around. I've not been in his stores, but have seen some of his T-shirts on my customers. I imagine the Folly Beach city fathers are thrilled Folly Tease is bringing near-obscenity to the wholesome families vacationing here."

I smiled. "We all contribute to society."

"Yes," Barb said. "I also suspect his stores are far more successful than the new bookstore on Folly."

"And that bookstore is far more successful than the photo gallery before it."

She grinned. "And now you can sit around and drink coffee while I'm slaving away selling books."

I shrugged. "Before we were interrupted, I started to—"

"Hey, Chris." Interruption number two. "Hi, Barbara."

Marc Salmon, one of Folly's city council members and one of the island's leading gossip spreaders, was standing where Russ had been.

"Am I interrupting?"

Of course. I didn't point out the obvious. "I see you know Barb."

"My wife is one of her best customers."

Marc and his fellow councilmember, Houston, spent an hour or more each weekday in the Dog. It was unusual to see him here on Sunday, yet not surprising. Rumors don't take the weekend off, so he had to make an appearance.

"True," Barb said. "Mr. Salmon's wife devours romance novels like a bat gobbles mosquitos."

"Please call me Marc. I'm glad your store's here. Miss B. was driving me to the poorhouse with the new books she was buying. Used's the way to go. It's also great we have a new, positive business on the island."

I wondered if it was a cut at Folly Tease.

"Gotta get to the grocery and home," Marc said. "Good to see you. Oh, Chris, before I go, rumor has it Charles Fowler and his gal friend might be moving."

You're slipping, Marc, I thought. Charles and Heather leaving wasn't a conversation I wanted to have this morning with the councilmember. "I'll check."

"You do that, Chris," he said and was gone.

Barb asked, "What's the deal with Charles and Heather? He's not saying one of my best customers is leaving Folly?"

I told her that her customer was not leaving, he was gone already. I gave her a five-minute version of a story about Charles and me that would take days to tell. She listened and interrupted with a couple of good questions. I didn't tell her about Russ's job offer for Charles, now a moot point.

"I'm sorry to hear it. I wish I could have a friend as good as Charles has been to you."

I blinked a tear out of my eye, wiped it away, and made a joke about how the sun was in my eye. Barb pretended to believe me and asked, "What's a possible scenario where I'm not the target?"

I looked around expecting another interruption. None appeared. "What if Lawrence Panella intended to kill someone from the church?

The body wasn't any closer to your door than it was to First Light. Have you met Preacher Burl Ives Costello?"

"I went to a few of his services and he's been in the store looking for used bibles. We've not talked beyond a polite greeting. Why?"

"He's a good man and is doing a great job with his non-traditional church."

"Meeting on the beach was refreshing."

"Preacher Burl has come to me to ask if I could check into a delicate situation."

"By delicate, I suppose that means you aren't going to tell me about it."

I smiled. "If I ever get in legal trouble, I want you as my lawyer."

"I hope that day never comes."

"Me too. No details, but the situation involves one of his members whose past is not available for public consumption."

"Witness protection program?"

"I didn't say that. His member has reason to think Lawrence Panella was here to revenge something he may have said or done that got the person who hired him in a heap of trouble."

Barb looked out the window, down at the rest of her food, and at me. "And my hippie brother's main selling point for Folly was it was a laid back, happy place; not his exact words, but that was the gist. He forgot to mention the murder per-square-foot ratio."

"Not be chamber of commerce friendly," I said, channeling Dude.

Barb laughed and her hazel eyes glowed in the sunlight that had allegedly caused my eyes to water.

I glanced at my watch and realized it was a half hour until First Light's morning service.

"Want to go to church?" I said, and wondered where that had come from.

"Think book buyers will wait until this afternoon for me to open the store?"

"Don't know about them. Photo buyers never kicked in the door to buy anything when I was away."

Chapter Twenty-Eight

I had attended church on a regular basis until I was in my twenties. I stopped going one Sunday and forgot to go back—for four decades. My introduction to First Light came after I nearly got killed when someone ran down one of the church's followers, killing him within inches from where he and I had been standing.

It was chilly, so I glanced in the First Light foul weather sanctuary to make sure the morning's service had not been moved indoors. It was empty and Barb and I continued down Center Street and past the Folly Pier to the opening of the beach where I saw Preacher Burl. He would've been hard to miss in his white robe made from a bed sheet. His arms were outspread and from the rear looked like a kite readying itself to be pulled skyward by the breeze. He was standing behind a repurposed school lectern and facing fifteen or so people who were moving toward the folding chairs in the sand.

Charles wasn't there to point out I was late, while Barb and I took seats in the back row. I knew, either by name or face, most of the others. When everyone was seated, Preacher Burl asked us to "silence thy portable communication devices," and to join in singing a hymn out of a photocopied songbook. The group warbled through the hymn and Preacher Burl said, "What a joyful noise to the Lord."

I grinned as I remembered when he had told me the definition of joyful didn't contain the words pretty, pleasant, or good. Burl's flock showed an overabundance of joy, and a dearth of singing ability. It was the thought that counted.

Burl was a master at preaching to the common man. He was down to earth, translated the complex parts of the Bible into language everyone from an illiterate street person to a college professor could understand and relate to. That talent, combined with the uniqueness of meeting in the midst of people walking dogs, playing Bocce ball, building sandcastles, and sunbathing, helped First Light meet the religious needs of many whose shadows would never darken the doors of traditional houses of worship. In addition to his sermons touching all comers, they tended to be long-winded and redundant, which gave me time to focus less on what he was saying, but on who was there. An advantage of being on the back row was being able to see everyone. Today, that consisted of regulars and for the first time I noticed Douglas Garfield. He wore his scowl, but was focused on each word out of the preacher's mouth. Dude was on the other end of the back row and nodded toward Barb and me, and his two employees sat in the sand behind him. I didn't know if they were his bodyguards or were church goers, which, if so, would surprise, no, would shock me.

I also did a double take when I caught the profile of the man who had been in Barb's store several times. I wouldn't have noticed him if he hadn't kept glancing our way.

The service ended with the last verse of a horrific rendition of "Onward Christian Soldiers," and Dude was quick to welcome his sister—half-sister, fractional sis, whatever—to First Light and ask her why she was here.

She explained she and I were having breakfast and I invited her.

"Woe, Chrisster be marketing for God."

Rocky and Stephon had been trailing Dude and moved beside him. Stephon looked at Barb and said, "Good to see you." He looked at me and snarled. We continued to bond. Stephon told Dude they were headed to the surf shop and the two of them left. Burl joined the group and said he remembered Barb from his earlier visits and said he was thrilled she joined the group this morning. Douglas Garfield had started our way, kicked the sand, turned, and slinked away.

Dude asked Barb if she wanted to walk with him to the surf shop. She looked over at me and gave an almost imperceptible shrug, I nodded, and she said, "That would be nice."

I was glad to see she and Dude were spending time together. From what she'd said, it was clear she needed more friends, and Dude, in addition to being her half-brother, could be a good one.

My gladness ended when Burl said, "Is it true Brother Charles and the darling Sister Heather are no longer among the residents of Folly?"

I told him it was.

"Folly will never be the same."

"You're right, Preacher." I looked around to see if the stranger who had been in Barb's was nearby. He wasn't. "Burl, do you know the man who sat in the row in front of us on the other side? He had a brown coat and a black scarf."

Burl looked toward the seat where the man had been seated. "Don't recall his name. I'm bad about those, you know. He arrived a few weeks ago. I try to meet each newcomer at the end of the service. He was here three weeks ago and told me his name, which I forgot as soon as he walked away. He said he'd come from somewhere up North and was looking forward to our warmer weather."

"Did he say where up North and what he was doing here?"

"No to both questions, and I didn't feel it was my place to ask. If, or when, the gentleman wishes to disclose details of his life, I will listen. If he seeks spiritual guidance, I will oblige."

"I understand." Understood, yet wished Burl had picked up some of the inquisitive habits of my friends.

"He seems like a pleasant sort," Burl added. "I doubt he has anything to hide and would be glad to disclose the answers to your questions upon your inquiring."

My phone rang and I pulled it out of my pocket. It was fortunate whoever was calling hadn't tried fifteen minutes earlier since I hadn't *silenced mine portable communications device.*

"Guess what I got?" came the distant, tinny voice of Charles. I could barely hear him with the ocean's roar in the background.

"Diphtheria," I said, both in the spirit of my friend, and to combat the irritating habit of most everyone who calls me skipping courteous greetings.

"Huh?"

"Never mind. Hi, Charles, what did you get?"

"I'm now in the twenty-first century. I've got a handy-dandy cell phone, with a camera, and a texting thing, and can tweet, whatever that is."

I had pestered Charles for nine years to join nine out of ten Americans who owned cell phones, and now he moves away and gets one. Progress, although irritating and belated, is still progress.

"Glad to hear it." I covered my other ear to block some of the ocean sounds that were making it hard to hear. "Did you make it to Nashville?"

"I am standing smack dab in front of the Country Music Hall of Fame and Museum right here on 5ᵗʰ Avenue in downtown Music City, USA."

"Okay. Did Heather make it?"

"She said I could stand out here and talk all day if I wanted to. She already went in, said she'd waited all her life to be this close to country music fame and couldn't wait another piddlin' second."

"Found somewhere to live?"

I waved bye to Burl and walked away from the beach. It was still hard hearing Charles and I wanted a private spot to talk.

"We're in a motel. Got two appointments to look at apartments this afternoon after Heather sniffs around every square inch of the Hall of Fame. Both apartments are in walking distance of downtown."

"That's great," I said, although my heart wasn't in it. I was happy for Heather and therefore happy for Charles.

"Guess what else? No diseases this time."

"Heather's signed with Sony Records, is appearing on the Grand Ole Opry, and you've opened a private detective agency."

"And people think I live in a fantasy world. You're not far off, though. We met with Kevin Starr last night at Starbucks. He was excited to see her and gave her the name of the man to contact at the Bluebird about singing open-mic night. She tried calling last night, but he won't be in until tomorrow."

A couple of things didn't sound right. "Why didn't you meet Starr at his office?"

"He said he meets all his artists near where they are, rather than the inconvenience of having them come to his office."

I didn't like the sound of it, but let it go. Who was I to step on Heather's boundless enthusiasm?

"If Starr is representing Heather, why didn't he contact the

Bluebird?"

"That felt funny to me. He said since he wasn't contractually tied to Heather yet, it'd be better for her to do it."

"Has he asked for money?"

"Not a dime."

He said something else, but the roar of a diesel engine from a large truck or bus on his end drowned out what he was saying.

"Can't hear you," I said.

"Tour bus. We're meeting Starr Tuesday."

"At his office?"

"Starbucks."

"Oh."

"You think that sounds fishy?"

"Do you?" I asked, the best non-answer I could come up with.

He mumbled, "Yeah."

"Be careful, I wouldn't want to see Heather hurt."

"If she fell off the cloud she's been on since we crossed the Cumberland River, it'd break every bone in her body, along with her heart."

Another country song, I predicted.

Charles continued, "Speaking of breaking things, have you broke that killer case yet?"

"Nope." I filled him in on what I'd learned since he left. I made the mistake of mentioning Dude as a suspect. If he wasn't so far away, Charles would have smacked me.

"No, no, no, to Dude killing anyone. Whoops, Heather's at the door waving for me. No to Dude. Bye."

I left the beach and headed home, missing Charles every step of the way.

Chapter Twenty-Nine

I was a block from the house when Rocky jogged up beside me. I was shocked. First, because I had never seen Dude's employee move faster than a slug, and second, because he'd stopped when we were shoulder to shoulder.

"Got a minute?" the sharp-featured, tat-covered, frowning man asked.

It was the most civil thing he'd said to me.

"Sure."

We moved off the roadway.

"You're a damned meddler." His frown deepened.

I didn't have a quick retort so I waited. Besides, I didn't think he had gone out of his way to tell me that.

"I like that about you, especially being you're an old guy." His facial expression remained unchanged. "You're not a damned poser like some old farts. Geezers trying to be hip."

I knew poser was a non-surfer who acted like one—thank you Charles for that bit of trivia. I still didn't know what to say.

"Dude's like pop to me." Rocky almost broke a smile. "Maybe like grandpa."

"He's a good guy."

Rocky looked around, kicked the weed-covered, sandy soil, and faced Burt's Market, fifty yards away. "I'd do anything for him. Subsequently, I'd do anything for his sis. Blood's thick."

Rocky's saying *subsequently* threw me momentarily. What didn't throw me was his loyalty to Dude. I still had no idea why he had stopped me; stopped me after spending years treating me like I was a splinter in his toe.

"Dude's lucky to have you and Stephon with him."

"Dude said you were going to figure out who Panella, that malevolent, was out to off."

"He asked me to—"

Rocky waved his tat-covered arm in my face. "Save you the trouble. It was Barb."

"How do you know?"

Rocky cocked his head and smiled. "Old dudes like Panella and you, underestimate guys like me. They—you—see tats, hear surfer talk, watch us ignore geezers, and jump to conclusions. Think we're stupid, the lowlifes of society."

I wasn't sure of all that, but was impressed by his vocabulary. He was a cross between Dude and William Hansel, a professor pal of mine.

"You're right. What do you know about Panella?"

"He was a strange one. He came in the shop near dark." Rocky stared off in space like he was picturing the visit. "Dude was in the office with his sis. Stephon was in back tagging boards. I ignored Panella like I do most old guys. Don't think he saw me. He started looking at our boards, so I figured he may know what he's looking at and I caved and asked if he needed help. The old guy said he was a surfer and asked what I thought was the best wax. I said Mr. Zogs Sex Wax. He asked why and I started to tell him when Barb came out of Dude's hangout." Rocky reared back his shoulders and his head jerked toward the sky. "The old guy almost, umm, defecated a brick. He turned away from Barb and slithered over behind a rack of T-shirts. He tried to be inconspicuous." Rocky paused and shook his head. "Geezers figure scum like me don't see things."

This was by far the longest, and strangest, conversation I'd had with him, but I still wasn't sure why he'd stopped me.

"You said you know he was here to kill Barb."

He looked at me. His lips turned up almost in a snarl. That was more like the Rocky I had learned to detest.

"The old guy did everything he could to keep Barb from seeing him. Was like he didn't want anyone to know he recognized her. Barb headed out the door and the old guy still pretended he hadn't seen her.

I asked him again if I could help and explain why I thought Mr. Zogs was the best. Dude calls that customer service. He says I need to get better at it." Rocky shook his head. "The geezer fiddled around some more. He was killing time. I gave it one more customer-service try. He looked at his watch and said he didn't have time to talk because he had to meet someone at their house."

"Did he say anything about Barb?"

"Don't you get it? The old man pretended he didn't know her since he was going to kill her. He didn't want someone to tell the cops they were seen together in the shop."

"Is that why you thought she was his intended victim?"

"Sure, but it didn't come to me until he turned up dead. That's when I knew he was the hit man and Barb was the target. That's why I'm telling you. You're nosy. You're known to figure out who killed people. Dude trusts you, and I figured if you knew who the old guy wanted to bump off, it'd help you figure out what's going on. The hit man was dead. It didn't mean the guy who hired him wouldn't send someone else to finish the job." He drilled a stare at me. "Barb's kin to Dude and that's good enough for me. You've got to save her."

Rocky was trying to be helpful, so I didn't want to sluff it off. "Did you tell the police? They'd be interested in hearing about Panella's activities."

"No freakin' way." Rocky was more animated than before. "The cops and I have a compound, complex relationship. We don't see eye-to-eye. Our interactions are like eye-to-ass."

The wind off the ocean had picked up and it was getting colder. I resumed my walk toward the house and to my surprise, Rocky tagged along. Something Rocky had said struck me as strange and I was trying to recall what it was when he stopped and pointed at my house.

"Is somebody staying with you?"

"What do you mean?" I looked in the direction his index finger was pointing.

"What's to mean?" He looked over at me like it was a stupid question. "Is someone at your house?"

"No," I continued to look, and didn't see anything unusual.

"Somebody looked out your front window. Whoever it was saw us and went poof."

"Crap, not again," I said to the space where Rocky had been standing.

Instead of waiting to hear my succinct analysis of what was going on, he was jogging toward the house. A Honda slammed on its brakes and skidded to a halt, and another vehicle blew its horn as Rocky darted into the stream of traffic, and charged into my front yard. I stopped at the street, waved for the Honda to continue, waited for several more vehicles to pass, and crossed to the yard. Rocky had kicked in the front door and was in the house by the time I reached the yard. The thirty-five-year difference in our ages was made clear seeing how much quicker he had made it there.

I wasn't anxious to follow him in. I grabbed a three-foot-long, broken limb from the yard and inched the door open. If the intruder was the same person who had already invaded my space twice and clobbered me during one of those times, he wouldn't hesitate to do whatever he had to do to escape. I looked from side to side as I entered.

The rear screen door slammed and I heard a string of profanities coming from the kitchen. I gripped the branch tighter and moved toward the sounds. Rocky was on the floor, leaning against the cabinet by the sink. He had a gun in one hand, and held the back of his head with the other hand. He said damn and a couple of surfer-speak profanities I didn't know. I caught the drift.

I scanned the room and rushed to my new friend. He was trying to stand, so I helped him to his feet and nudged him into a chair.

"What happened?" I continued looking around.

"Kook slammed me upside the head. I charged in here after him and he must have been behind the door." He pointed to the door leading into the kitchen. "Didn't see him. Damned sure felt whatever he hit me with."

I saw the Teflon skillet Bob Howard had given me as a gag gift for my birthday. My realtor friend knew I couldn't, and had no desire to, cook, fry, or whatever you do with a skillet. I now knew one of its uses. Bob will find it amusing.

"Let me call an ambulance?"

"Nah, I've been hit worse."

I reached for my phone. "I'll call the police."

Rocky shot up out of the chair and grabbed for the phone. "Whoa," I said. "I don't have to call them."

"Don't." He sat back down, and whispered, "Please."

I nodded, realized it was the most polite thing I'd heard him utter, and returned the phone to my pocket. I doubted the police would learn anything anyway. They might get a print off the skillet, but if the intruder had been as careful as he had been the other two times, he had worn gloves. I noticed that the back door had been pried open, wood splintered around the lock. If the police came, they would now tell me in addition to better locks, I needed a security system, twenty-four-seven armed guards, a Rottweiler, and a moat with famished alligators.

Rocky said, "Give me a minute. I'll be fine."

He focused on being fine and I went from room to room to see if anything had been disturbed. The mattress on my bed was turned sideways and the top two drawers of the dresser were pulled open. From what I could tell, nothing had been taken.

I returned to the kitchen. "You sure you're okay?"

"Will be." Rocky rubbed the back of his head. "Why would someone break in here?"

He made it sound like he was shocked anyone would think I had anything of value. More than likely it was his rude gene kicking in. I didn't tell him this was the third intrusion in ten days.

"Don't know. Could have been a drifter looking for money or something to hock."

"In here?"

He'd saved me from a concussion, or worse, so I refrained from smacking him on his sore head.

I shrugged and offered him a soft drink.

"Yeah, thanks," he said in a second burst of courtesy, probably a result of the blow to the head.

"Did you see who it was?"

He shook his aching head. "No. Couldn't tell from across the street. There was a reflection of the sun on the window and I couldn't get a good look. When I came in here he hit me from behind and boogied while I was wiped out on the floor."

He sipped his drink, stood, and looked around the room, then walked to the living room.

"Anything else I can get you?" I asked.

"Nah. Hey man, what the hell you have in here that dude was looking for?"

An excellent question, and one I had no answer for. After one dead body, two friends concerned enough to ask me to try to figure out what was going on, and three blatant invasions of my personal space and my little slice of heaven, nothing short of death was going to stop me from finding out.

Chapter Thirty

Rocky left after assuring me he was fine, and once again, I called Larry and told him I needed his hardware store expertise and carpentry skills. Once again he said he'd be right over. And, once again, he arrived with his spouse in tow.

Larry carried his tool box, gave a cursory look at the splintered wood by the front door's locking mechanism, and walked through the house and focused his energy and talents on the seriously-damaged back door. Cindy glanced at the door and pointed to the kitchen table.

She sat across from me, looked over her shoulder at the back door, put both elbows on the table, and stared at me. "Let me guess. Your door stuck when you were opening it and you kicked it with your bionic foot, and the back door was struck by one of those mini-earthquakes that erupt beneath homes of walking, talking, disaster magnets?"

"Quick, analytical mind, succinct summation, it's easy to see why you're chief," I said, to inspire a smile. I came close. I proceeded to give her a blow-by-blow description of what had happened. She patiently, patiently for Cindy, waited for me to finish.

"The same Rocky who works for Dude? The Rocky who thinks kicking canes out from under senior citizens is Nobel Peace Prize winning behavior? You sure you weren't the one hit on the head?"

I explained why Rocky had approached me, about his loyalty to Dude, and because of that, why he had been worried about Barb. She started to get huffy about why he didn't go to the cops with that information and I shared his reluctance.

She leaned back and said, "Well-founded."

"Have you learned anything new about the murder?"

She pointed to the back door. "You think that has something to do with it?"

"Yes, but before you ask what, save your breath. I don't know. Back to my question, news?"

She shook her head. "The mayor, the mayor pro-tem, the head of the merchant's association, and everyone else who has a stake in the economy of the island, has been on my case. Something about a shot-in-the-head visitor puts the kibosh on vacationers clambering to spend their hard-earned dollars on our island paradise. I don't give a cockroach about that, but I do have more than a hankering to catch the son-of-a-skunk who killed someone on my watch."

Cindy had given a broad interpretation to my question, so I tried to limit its scope. "Leads?"

"No, faux-detective Chris." She frowned. "Detective Adair told me yesterday they were at the end of the line. Ballistics gave them nothing. Their forensic auditor guru said there was nothing in his records to lead them anywhere, other than he managed to live quite well off a piddling amount of taxed income. His wife seems as clueless as their pet dachshund. And if the wonderful, loving husband was in fact a gun for hire, there appears to be no way to trace who hired him."

"So, there's nothing?"

Cindy rolled her eyes and waved both hands in the air. "Dang, can't slip anything by you."

"What's next?"

"Adair says unless we find out who Panella was after, there's not much he can do."

"So until whoever hired him hires someone else and that person kills someone here, nothing's going to happen."

"Freakin' frustrating, isn't it?"

Frustrating and unacceptable, I thought. "If I'm right and this is related to his death," I said and pointed to the door Larry was working on, "help me see the connection."

"You're the one who said it's connected."

"I found the body."

"So?"

"So, someone, I'd guess the person who killed him, thinks I

found something on the body that could lead me to him."

Cindy looked at the table and back at me. "What?"

"Money," Larry said, without turning away from his project.

"That makes sense," I said, remembering the rumor Cal had heard about me finding a pile of cash beside the body. "Everything you know about Panella indicates he paid for most things with cash, he had little legitimate income, and you said there was five hundred dollars in his hotel room and none in his car." I hesitated and said, "So, if that's the case, whoever broke in here wouldn't have been who killed him, but could have been the person who hired him."

Cindy said, "Or he would have found the money on the body after he shot him. There would have been no need to break in."

"Whoever did this is taking a big risk. It could be anyone who knew I found the body, but only the person who hired Panella would know about the money. Wouldn't he want to stay as far away as possible? Why risk getting caught breaking in?"

Larry put his tools down and moved to a vacant chair at the table and looked at Cindy. "Hon, cover your ears."

She rolled her eyes for the second time and looked at me. "He says stupid things like that when he wants to say something he thinks I shouldn't hear." She turned back to Larry. "Consider them covered."

"From my contacts years ago with folks who, umm, didn't follow the letter of the law, I heard the going rate for top-notch hit men could hit thirty-thousand bucks, and much higher for high profile or hard to get to targets. That was a quarter of a century ago. I can't imagine that high a profile target here. I wouldn't be surprised if it wasn't around forty or fifty grand."

"Breaking in here would be worth it if the person who hired Panella wasn't busting out with money," Cindy said. "Would the hirer think Panella had the money with him? He could have left it at Myrtle Beach."

"Not if he didn't get paid until he got here," I said.

"That would mean whoever hired him was here before you found the body and may still be here," Cindy said. "I'll have my guys check hotel and rental agencies to see if someone who checked in a day or two before you found the body is still around."

"The person could be anywhere in the area," I said. "You can't check them all."

"True," Cindy said. "I'll call Adair tomorrow. That'll give his folks something to do. They can't canvass each nook and cranny, but maybe they'll get lucky."

I debated telling her about Preacher Burl's concern about Douglas Garfield. Just because Rocky thought Panella was here to hit Barb, didn't make it so. Douglas was still a strong possibility, but I had told the preacher I would keep his worries away from the police. Larry helped make my decision when he said he had done all he could for the back door and had put a piece of wood over the damaged section of the front. He told me he and Cindy had better be going. Besides, I had experienced enough excitement for the day and needed to think more about Douglas before breaking my promise to Burl. I asked Cindy to suggest to Adair that he might want to talk to Barb. If Rocky was right, she could shed light on a motive. Cindy said it was on her to-do list.

I apologized for calling and thanked them for coming out on a Sunday night. Cindy said she was glad I did because it was more fun than watching Larry lay on the couch and snore while the television blared some kissy-faced movie on the Hallmark Channel.

I was exhausted after Cindy and Larry left, and slumped down in my recliner. My body may have been tired, but my mind continued to wander. Was Rocky right about Barb being the target? What other reason would someone have for breaking in the house unless it was related to Panella's murder? Was someone trying to scare me into leaving Folly with the note, or was that a smokescreen to keep me from thinking he was looking for something? And, if it was something, was Larry right about it being the money Panella had been paid for the hit?

Did Preacher Burl have a legitimate concern about Douglas? Other than Douglas being the target because of something from his earlier life, I could see how someone would want him dead because he was so obnoxious.

Where was Charles when I needed him? We had occasionally proven the whole was, in fact, greater than the sum of its parts, and found answers. Of course, more often than not, we had proven two wrongs don't make a right. I groaned at my bad clichés, and reached for the phone to make my first long-distance call to Nashville,

Tennessee.

Instead of hearing the familiar voice of my best friend, I got a mechanized voice-mail message saying the person I was calling was unavailable and to leave a message. I paraphrased another cliché, and mumbled you can lead a Charles to a cell phone, but you can't make him turn it on.

Chapter Thirty-One

In addition to being frustrated by the lack of answers, angry about my house becoming break-in-central, and my friends feeling threatened, I woke up hungry. There was little I could do about the first two problems, but a trip to the Lost Dog Cafe would solve my hunger.

Several tables were vacant, but before I could choose one, Dude waved for me from the far side of the room. His tablemate was Russ Vick and with only water in front of them, I suspected they hadn't been there long. I wasn't in the mood for conversation. Dude pointed at the chair beside him with such enthusiasm that I didn't have the heart to decline.

Dude wore his ever-present, tie-dyed, peace-symbol-adorned T-shirt and Russ had on ratty jeans and a black T-shirt with PORN STAR in fluorescent yellow on the front. They looked like two aging hippies reliving their old bad-trip days.

Dude said, "Chrisster, welcome."

"Hi, Chris," Russ said with less enthusiasm. "Good to see you."

"We be flapping lips about business," Dude said as if I had asked. "T-shirt sales sucking."

Russ looked at Dude and smiled. "Don't believe we need to share our conversation with Chris. I'm sure he's not interested."

"He be nosy, but lips be sealed." Dude mimed closing a zipper on his mouth. "Okeydokey to share."

Russ turned to me. "I suppose you know how difficult it is to break in a successful business."

I smiled, but didn't mean it. "Do I ever. Winter's a terrible time for business anyway."

Dude waved his hand around the Dog. "Be Dude's winter office."

"I see why," Russ said. "Nobody's in the stores."

Dude jerked his head away from looking at Russ and turned to me. "Speakin' about broke and brakin', hear *su casa* be boss break-in spot."

Russ, a relative newcomer to Dudespeak, said, "Huh?"

I knew what he'd meant. "Where'd you hear that?"

Dude put his hand to his ear and imitated a telephone. "Stephon thought big news since you and me be big buds. He interrupted quality time with Pluto."

"Stephon?" I said.

"He be learnin' it from Rocky Horror surf-stuff seller."

Russ repeated, "Huh?"

The waitress approached and asked if we were ready to order, before he could say more. We each ordered and Russ watched the college-age waitress walk to the kitchen.

I thought I'd better translate for Russ who already seemed confused. "Dude's two employees are Rocky and Stephon. Rocky told Stephon about the break in, and then Stephon called Dude who was playing with his dog, Pluto."

Russ looked at Dude then me. "You got all that from what he said?"

I smiled. "Clear as day."

"Ah, thanks," Russ said. He didn't look convinced.

Dude nodded. "The Rock man boogied in Chrisster's *casa* and got skilleted. Good deed, bad ending."

"Is he okay?" Russ asked, grasping the salient points of Dudespeak.

"I think so," I said. "Someone was breaking in my house and Rocky was trying to catch the guy when he got hit."

Russ looked at Dude and at me. "Why was someone breaking in your house?"

Dude said, "New popular Folly event."

"This is the third time," I said to the confused T-shirt shop owner. "I don't know why."

"Note say for Chrisster to boogie-board off island," Dude said. "The person left me a note saying I needed to leave, or else."

Russ said, "Sounds like you've got an enemy."

"Chrisster be catching dude who kilt kill-man. Somebody pissed about that. Trying to run my bud off." Dude shook his head. "No be workin'."

"It had to be terrible finding the guy," Russ said. "I can't imagine it."

"I've had better mornings."

"I'm glad I wasn't here," Russ said. "I'm often in that alley since my store is less than a block from where you found him. It could have been me who stumbled on him."

"Doubt it," Dude said. "Chrisster be early bird. He caught dead bod instead of worm. He be out before most creatures be stirrin'."

"What do the police say?" Russ asked.

Dude said, "They be befuddled."

I figured Russ caught Dude's drift and didn't say anything. I had also heard enough about yesterday. "Have you always owned T-shirt shops?"

"Nope."

"What'd you do before moving here?"

"VP of a global import business."

"Flip side of T-shirt sellin'," Dude said.

Russ smiled. "That's an understatement."

"Why'd you leave?" I asked.

Dude interrupted, "Said he be nosy."

Russ laughed. "I noticed. I got tired of the red tape and crap I had to deal with. I knew it'd do me in if I stayed. Took retirement and got the hell out of there. Selling T-shirts doesn't pay as well and I'm not wealthy, but if I stayed, I'd be dead long before my time."

"I know what you mean," I said. "My story's not much different."

"That's what I hear. At least, I think it's what Dude's been saying. I've been taking some getting-along-with-the-locals lessons. Being the newcomer is a hard nut to crack."

I chuckled. "Learn anything helpful?"

Russ looked at Dude and tilted his head. "Me be patient."

I smiled. "Good lesson."

"I was going to open one shop. The rent was so good on the second location I figured two shops would be twice as good as one."

Food arrived and feeding our curiosity took a back seat to feeding our faces. Russ asked a few questions about the other gift shops and if we knew how well they were doing. I didn't want to be too direct, but tried to hint the small island was oversaturated with similar items. Russ agreed he may have made a mistake by opening two stores and said if he kept one open, it would be Folly Tease because its shirts were different than the hundreds of others and its sales were double those at SML Shirts.

"Not be easy, being at two shops same time," Dude said.

Russ chucked. "Good point, Dude. And paying someone to work in the other store is draining. Chris, that's what I'd been talking to Charles about. With his local knowledge and appreciation for T-shirts, he would've been a natural to run SML Shirts. Now I hear he's moved. I didn't know him well, but that came as a surprise."

"A bummer," Dude said.

I agreed, more than he knew.

I wanted to move away from talking about Charles. "Have you talked to Barbara Deanelli about her experiences of opening a store? The two of you might have a lot in common, with both moving here and opening a business. I think she's having a hard time adjusting to the beach life and lifestyle."

"I haven't, but that's a good idea."

"She be my fractional-sis," added Dude. "She be lawyertress turned queen of books."

"Wise move," Russ said, and laughed. "I avoid lawyers."

"You plus everyone else," Dude said.

I nodded to that, and my phone rang.

"Chris," said the familiar voice of Preacher Burl, "did I catch you at a bad time?"

"No. I was finishing breakfast."

"Good. I don't usually call anyone this early. I knew you're an early riser and took a chance."

It sounded better than calling me a bird catching a body.

"What can I do for you, Preacher?"

"Can you meet me at the church? I promise not to put you to work."

"When?"

Dude began waving his hand in the air and pointing to the phone.

"Just a sec, Preacher. I'm with Dude and he wants to say something." I handed the phone to Dude.

"Boss sermon, yesterday. Inspired to the gills."

He handed the phone back to me before the preacher had a chance to respond.

"I'm back, Preacher."

He laughed. "Don't often inspire to the gills. Tell Dude I appreciate his endorsement."

I said I'd pass the message along and asked when he wanted to meet. He replied soon; I suggested how about now and he invited me to come on over.

***

I had left Dude and Russ continuing their bemoaning about the poor business climate on Center Street. Both had given lip-service to it being the middle of winter and off-season, yet continued to wonder why the full-time residents and handful of vacationers weren't clamoring to buy surf gear and T-shirts.

First Light's front door squeaked open and I was greeted with, "Thanks for coming, Brother Chris. All I have to offer is water."

"I'm fine."

Burl pointed to a pew near the front and followed me as I took a seat.

"I had a disturbing visit last night from Brother Douglas."

"Oh."

Burl shook his head. "I smelled Devil juice on his breath. I wouldn't call him inebriated, but wouldn't want him driving. He said his fear had exceeded his desire to remain on Folly." Burl hesitated. "Sure you don't want water?"

"No thanks."

He fiddled with the button on his shirt, wiped a cobweb off the back of the pew, and finally said, "Even though the first man sent to kill him had been taken care of, Douglas was certain there'd be others. He decided to leave the Lowcountry and despite his rude and loathsome demeanor wanted me to know he appreciated my efforts to ensure he had a better life."

I doubted those were Douglas's words.

"When's he leaving?"

"He didn't say. I had the impression it was soon. He could have been heading off-island when he left my apartment. I had asked you to assist in finding out if Brother Douglas was in danger, so I felt it incumbent to share this with you."

"Preacher, someone broke into my house yesterday. One of Dude's employees, Rocky, saw him and was rewarded with a skillet to the head for trying to catch the intruder."

"Oh, I'm so sorry. Is Brother Rocky okay? He was at yesterday's service with his associate, Brother Stephon."

"He's fine."

"Why did someone break in? It's happened before, hasn't it?"

I told him about the other two times, and he asked if I knew why. I shared what I had told everyone else who had asked, and I asked if he thought it could have been Douglas.

"I would feel better if I could say no. To be honest, it wouldn't surprise me."

"That's what I thought. Let's get back to what he said last night."

Burl nodded.

"I believe you said he told you the first man who had been sent to kill him had been 'taken care of.'"

The preacher nodded again.

"Are you certain those were his words?"

Burl looked to the door, swiped another cobweb off the pew, and turned back to me. "I can't be certain. It was late, and I was trying to figure out what he was talking about, instead of paying attention to each word. Why?"

"Is it possible he could have said he took care of it rather than it had been taken care of?"

Burl squeezed his hands together and took a deep breath. "Are you saying Brother Douglas killed the gentleman sent to kill him?"

"It's possible. I don't know what he did to get in the witness protection program. From his actions and attitude toward me, it's not a big leap to picture a violent past. He'd told me he could handle his own problems and didn't need me, or you, to butt in."

Burl looked at the floor and shook his head. "To answer your question, Brother Chris, yes, it's possible he said he had taken care of the problem. In fact, the more I think about it, the more I believe you may be right." He sighed. "As we discussed the other day, I acknowledged the possibility of his guilt, but I didn't want to believe it."

Burl would feel I was breaking a confidence, and I might lose a friend because of it, but I also knew the police were getting nowhere with the case.

I walked to the large plate glass window overlooking Center Street and glanced across the street at the combination city hall, police and fire station, and turned to Burl. "Preacher, I need to tell Chief LaMond. I know you'd prefer I didn't. The police need to find Douglas before he gets too far away."

"I suppose I knew that when I told you about Brother Douglas leaving. I prayed about it last night. God chose not to give me a clear answer. He left it up to me, and I chose to call you. Perhaps it's his will, Brother Chris." He hesitated, and said, "Do what you must."

Burl needed alone time to pray about the situation, and said he'd be there if the police wanted to talk to him. I walked home and called Chief LaMond who said she was in her office playing Angry Birds on her laptop, but figured she could break away a few minutes to catch a killer. An hour later, I met her at First Light and listened to Burl tell everything he knew about Douglas Garfield—Harlan Powers. Cindy took notes, gave Burl and me dirty looks, and told us how irresponsible we were to not tell her sooner.

She said, "Yeah, yeah, yeah," twice when Burl started talking about his role as pastor with Douglas and why he didn't feel comfortable telling the authorities. She came close to forgiving him when he told her what kind of car Douglas drove, where he lived, and where he may be going.

I felt some progress had been made on learning who had killed the hit man. And I felt better knowing Barb wasn't in danger.

Chapter Thirty-Two

The phone rang at five forty-five the next morning.

"Guess what I've got?" came the familiar question from Charles.

I knew not to guess cell phone since that train had already left the station.

"Insomnia? It's not even six o'clock."

"Not five here, but that's not it. Want to guess again?"

"No," I growled.

"You've turned crankier since I left. Okay, I doubt you'd be able to guess. Got myself a picture on this phone to send you as soon as I figure out how."

"Picture of what?"

"Not only what, but where, Mr. Crank."

I sighed. "Where?"

"The Bluebird Cafe and guess who I got to listen to?"

A six a.m. phone call, a picture, the Bluebird Cafe, and excitement in his voice; I knew the answer, although for the life of me, I couldn't imagine how it could be true.

"The Rolling Stones?"

If he woke me up, the least I could do was give him grief.

"Close, but no cappuccino. Heather got to sing at the galaxy-famous Bluebird Cafe. Can you believe it?"

No, I thought. "Wasn't she going to call them yesterday to see about scheduling a date?"

"She was, she did, and low-and-behold, they told her they didn't take open-mic singing reservations over the phone, and because of the yucky weather yesterday they told her if she was there by sign-up time at five-thirty she had a good shot at slipping in. We were there at two-fifteen, shivering, starving, and so excited about playing she made five pit stops at McDonald's down the street while I held her place in line."

"That's great," I said. "How'd she do?"

"By the time she went on at eight-thirty, a half hour before open-mic night ended, the place was two-thirds full. I was surprised how small it is; holds about ninety people. Anyway, she did the song she wrote and a few people applauded when she was finished."

A few applauding didn't sound like a rousing debut. I moved to the kitchen and fired-up Mr. Coffee while trying to comprehend Heather performing at the Bluebird. It seemed like a dream, but I knew I was awake because I stubbed my toe on the counter.

"What'd she think?"

"She was peein'-in-her-pants excited. Said it was the happiest day of her life. She left there flying higher than the space shuttle."

"Glad to hear it," I said, not as happy as I should have been. "Was Kevin Starr there?"

"Nah," Charles said. "She called him after they said she may be able to sing. He said he had to take a meeting with one of his famous recording artists last night and couldn't make it. *Take a meeting* is what big time music peeps call gabbin' with someone."

"That's too bad. What's next?"

"She has a meeting—whoops, is *takin' a meeting*—with him tomorrow."

I still didn't like the way it was going with Starr. Hadn't he told her to call the Bluebird to make an appointment? Now Charles said that wasn't the way to sign up for open-mic night. And, I didn't trust him after what Cal had said and because I knew how little singing talent was crammed into Heather's adorable body. Charles was sharp enough to know this, so there was no need to remind him.

"You're going with her, aren't you?"

"I want to. It's up to her."

"It'd be best if you went. She could use the moral support and you'd get to hear what he has to say."

"I know." He told me how excited she was in case I'd

forgotten, and said, "Caught the killer?"

I told him about Preacher Burl's suspicions about Douglas Garfield, and about Douglas leaving town and Cindy putting an APB out on him.

Charles didn't respond immediately. He finally said, "When were you going to tell me?"

He was miffed. I told him Burl had told me in confidence and I wasn't comfortable telling anyone. Charles pointed out he wasn't anyone. I agreed and halfheartedly apologized.

"I know Douglas," Charles said after letting me sulk in my apology.

"I didn't know that," I refrained from asking when he was going to tell me.

"You would if you told me earlier. The boy's bitter, he's rude, he doesn't have anything approaching a friend on Folly. Overall, he's unbearable."

That's Douglas Garfield. "True."

"Chris, there's one thing he's not."

"What?"

"The person who shot Panella."

"How do you know?"

"In addition to all those things about Douglas, you can add addicted to hops."

"He's a drunk."

"Crude translation, but true. Woodrow Wilson said, 'Never murder a man when he's busy committing suicide.' Douglas is busy drinking himself to death. I had a civil, not quite so rude, conversation with him a month ago when he was semi-soused. He told me some things about his childhood. Did you know he had a baby sister named Gail?"

"No, so?"

"Let me finish. When he was seven and Gail was five she found one of their daddy's guns. She thought it was a toy and started slinging it around like a Roy Rogers toy cap gun that Douglas had. It went off and shot Gail in the arm. The wound wouldn't have been so bad, but Douglas didn't know what to do and there wasn't anyone around. Gail bled to death."

"That's terrible."

"Yeah, for both of them. Douglas said he was sent to all sorts of doctors to help get over what had happened and the guilt he felt. Therapy helped him some, yet he never got over seeing her laughing and playing with the gun, and then dying while he held her hand and not knowing what to do to save her." Charles paused and whispered, "Chris, Douglas told me he had done many bad things in his life. The one thing he never did after that was touch another gun, and he never would."

"That doesn't mean he didn't—"

"I know. It's still possible he shot the guy, but I'd bet my car he didn't."

"So, wonderful detective from afar, who killed him? Who was Panella here to kill? Who thinks my house is a stepping stone to bigger and better burglaries? And—"

"Slow down. Too many questions. It's five o'clock."

"You called me."

"To spread Heather's glee, not to solve a murder, a puzzle, and whatever else you asked."

"Fair enough. I'm happy for Heather. Bye."

"Whoa, slam on the brakes. I'm awake now. Let's take one question at a time."

Leaving unanswered questions dangling in front of Charles was like waving a Starbucks' mocha latte in front of a yuppie.

"Question one," I said. "If Douglas didn't kill Panella, who did?"

"The person he was here—there—to kill."

"Or someone else," I said.

"Gee, that helps."

"Hear me out. At first, I thought it had to be the person he was hired to kill, but if he was good at his trade, and since he had been on the radar of cops in New Jersey for years and they couldn't get anything on him, he was good, he wouldn't have tipped his hat to whoever he was after."

"You made my argument it wasn't Douglas."

I agreed, although it didn't eliminate him from being the target.

"So, who shot him?" Charles asked.

"That's my question."

"Okay, how about this. What if it doesn't have anything to do with why he was there? He was strolling through the alley humming a tune and someone came up behind him—maybe to rob him, or to say howdy. It was dark and foggy and considering Panella's career, he would've grabbed his gun. The robber or howdy person saw Panella's gun and pulled out one of his own and shot the hit man before the hit man shot him?"

I took a sip of coffee that had brewed quicker than I had awakened. "What are the odds on that happening?"

"Better chance of me getting elected president. You have a better idea?"

"Let's skip the random act of stupidity theory. If it wasn't the person he was here to kill, that leaves someone who found out who Panella was and why he was here."

"And that person is, who, or whom, whatever?"

"You said Douglas didn't have friends, so I don't see anyone killing Panella to save him."

"True."

I said, "I suppose Panella could have been here to kill most anyone, although I don't think so."

"Was who or whom in there somewhere?"

For reasons I would have a hard time explaining, these were the kind of conversations I missed the most. I hated we were having it via phone.

"Not yet," I said. "I think the intended victim was Barbara Deanelli."

"Why?"

"The first time I met her was the morning I found the body. If I had learned moments earlier a body was found behind my store, I'd be shocked. It was in a public alley, a shortcut between two streets, near the back door to the bookstore, yet just as close to First Light. I wouldn't know what to think."

"Me either, so?"

"So, she heard I'd found the body; she asked the police about me; was told where I might be, and came to the Dog to find me. We'd never met. She comes in, shares a couple of pleasantries and insults about Bob Howard, and asked if I knew the dead guy."

"Did I miss why she was the intended hitee?"

"Not yet. Then, of all the things she could have said, she asked me to describe him. Doesn't that seem odd? It was almost like she had expected someone and wanted to know if Panella was that person."

"Following your dusty, wiggly path, why would Panella have wanted to kill Barb?"

I realized I hadn't told Charles about my recent conversations with her.

"Barb told me her husband had been part of illegal activities that involved bribes to politicians and bureaucrats in state government. It involved millions of dollars. She claims she didn't know details, but it was the main reason for her divorce and move to Folly."

"I suppose you forgot to tell me all of that."

I told him it happened when he was in the process of moving and had other things on his mind. He groused, blew out his breath, and said, "You think she either is lying to you and knows more than she's saying, or she doesn't know anything but someone thinks she does."

"Yeah, I don't think she's lying about everything. I also think she knows more than she told me. Someone's afraid of what Barb may know and sent Panella."

"I don't suppose you've told Chief LaMond, Detective Adair, or Karen your theory."

"What's to tell? I don't know anything for certain."

And, I didn't want to get into the situation with Karen. I wasn't ready to discuss it, and I didn't know how Charles would react on the heels of his leaving.

"Do you think Barb killed him?"

"No. If she had, she wouldn't have asked me to describe him."

"Do you think someone knew about the hit and came to Folly to stop it?"

"Could be. I hope that's the case, otherwise it would be someone here, and that leaves one suspect. It could—"

Charles interrupted, "I told you it wasn't Dude."

I heard Heather in the background ask who Charles was talking to. It sounded like a chair being dragged across the floor and Charles told her it was me. Heather squealed, and said, "Is he excited for me?"

Charles told her of course I was. She said something about needing to celebrate her resounding success.

Charles said, "Time to go. I'll leave you with four words: It *was not* Dude."

Chapter Thirty-Three

I stared at the phone and reheated my coffee in the microwave. Panella's death may not have anything to do with Barb. He could have been here for someone else. What I was certain of was he wasn't here selling heavy farm machinery. I had taken the first sip when the phone rang—again. I expected to hear Charles calling with more reasons Dude couldn't be the killer.

"He was in again." Barb said.

She may be new to Folly, but had caught on to the nontraditional conversation starters.

"Morning, Barb. How are you?" I was trying to bring civility to phone conversations.

"Fine."

"Good. Who was in again?"

"The man who came in when you were here."

"The one who gives you the willies?"

"The same. Listen, I feel like a fish out of water. Back home I could do this myself, but ... well, you're the one person I know, other than Dude, I trust enough to ask, and I don't think it'd be good to ask him."

"What do you need?"

"He bought three books this time; two on Early American history and a mystery by Robert B. Parker. He paid by credit card, and his name's Sylvester Lopp."

"Did he say anything?"

"He asked if I had read Parker's books. I told him I didn't read mysteries. He hemmed-and-hawed like he wanted to say something else, but gave me his credit card and left."

"What can I do?"

"I thought you could ask the chief if she could find anything about him. I had enough contacts back home to get it done, yet here, well, you know. I Googled him and didn't find anything. He could be in a police data base. I know it's not normal procedure. I'm afraid of the guy and maybe since the chief is your friend, she could check. There's been one person sent to kill me. What if that's why Lopp's here?"

I doubted a hit man he would come in the store four or five times, buy books, and give a credit card, nevertheless, she was afraid. I said I'd call Cindy.

"Thank you, and please don't tell Dude. He worries too much about me and I don't want him to do anything stupid."

I prayed he hadn't already. "I won't."

I wished it had been Charles calling.

It was before eight o'clock, but I knew Cindy was out and about, so I might as well get the lecture over about butting in police business. She answered with, "What trouble are you going to cause me now?"

"No trouble, Chief. Good morning."

"No matter how you try to sugarcoat it, you're going to ruin my morning."

Not the good mood I had hoped for. I told her I had a favor to ask and it was police business, and I didn't see how it could ruin her morning.

"You underestimate yourself. What now?"

I told her and she said I'd asked for worse. She also said she liked Barb because she brought a strong, female presence to Cindy's male-dominated world, and the island needed an estrogen fix. I remained silent and let her continue giving me grief. It was less than I'd expected, and it's the price I pay to get anything from her. She said she would see what she could find and told me to try to stay out of trouble, or invite any uninvited guests into my house until she got back to me.

I re-reheated the coffee and was determined to enjoy a full cup before another distraction. Twenty minutes later, and thinking about the events of the last few days, I realized the main reason I was having trouble getting a handle on what was going on was because there were two distinct, but related, mysteries: the murder of Panella, and the reason the hit man was on Folly Beach. If Barb was correct, it solved part of the second one, but was she right? Charles had made a reasonable case why Douglas Garfield hadn't killed Panella. He could still have been the target. If he was, who had killed Panella and why?

As much as Preacher Burl had tried to convince me Douglas Garfield was the intended victim, my gut said it was Barb. And, I could only think of three people who would have been concerned about her enough to kill Panella. It was time to talk to one of them.

The surf shop wouldn't be open for another fifteen minutes, so I walked around downtown. I passed the bookstore and wondered how things would be different if my photo gallery had succeeded. I suppose Barb's Books would have opened somewhere else. I peeked in the window of First Light and revisited my thought that Douglas Garfield wasn't in danger, at least not from a hit man. Then I remembered something Rocky said Panella had told him during his visit to the surf shop. If it was true, it gave me a different view of Panella and who may have hired him. Dude almost ran into me when I stopped in the middle of the sidewalk to think through Rocky's conversation.

"Yo, Chrisster, be imitating light pole?" said the articulate hippie.

"Sorry, Dude. I was thinking."

"Heavy thinking?"

"Believe it or not, I was thinking about asking you something and had a question for Rocky."

"Rude Rocky?"

"Yes."

"That be first."

I smiled.

Dude said, "Q and A here?" He pointed to the sidewalk, and at the surf shop. "In shop?"

"Inside."

"Boogie with me." He walked, skipped, toward the store.

My boogieing could better be called a slow walk, and Dude had unlocked the door and turned on the lights before I got there.

Stephon and Rocky followed me up the steps. If I didn't know who they were, I would have taken one look at their all-black attire, matching black watch caps, tattered leather jackets and scowls which would intimidate most anyone, and would have feared for my life. I didn't waste time talking to them and followed Dude to his office.

"Rocky?" Dude said.

"Let's talk first."

"Your party. Talk on."

I charged on. "How long have they worked for you?" I nodded in the direction of his employees.

Dude followed my head nod. "That be question not expectin'. Stephon, plus-minus sixty full moons. Rocky, ninety-seven fms. Why?"

For those who don't know Dudespeak, and it took me three years to learn to translate his full-moon calendar, that's about five years for Stephon and seven for Rocky. In either language, it was a long time for retail store employees.

I ignored his question. "Suppose you know them pretty well."

"Better than know Adele. Not as good as know Pluto—pupster Pluto, not the faux-planet. Why?"

"Know much about their background?"

"Had okay drivers' license, tax paperwork not flagged by CIA, FBI, or ASCPA. Okay by me. Why, times three?"

"One more question and I'll answer you."

"Getting old waitin'."

"Could you see either of them killing Panella?"

"Whoa! You be flingin' from left field."

The door was open and I heard surfboards being moved around in the store. I got up and pushed the door closed.

"Could you?" I repeated.

Dude looked at a colorful PREY FOR SURF poster taped on the back of the door and then at the floor, before turning to me. "Not be friendliest clerks." He squinted and nervously stroked his long, gray hair. "They suck at spelling. Pray to Sun God, pupster Pluto be as loyal as they be."

I waited, but Dude had finished talking. "Could you see them killing him?"

Dude glanced at the poster and held up three fingers. "Chrisster, chill. Be asked you one, plus one, plus one time why you askin'. Answer ain't cookin' at me yet. I be getting there."

I smiled. "Fair enough."

He blinked twice and tapped his fingers on the cluttered desk. "Here be answer. If swearin' on Bible-book and asked question." He mimed putting his hand on a Bible and raised his other hand like he was testifying in court. "I'd say yep. Sorry, yep."

I wasn't surprised, but asked why.

Dude shook his head. "Don't know why. They be loyal rude. If thought Dudester in trouble, they'd help. If thought Dudester's fractional-sis be in trouble, they do same. Blood be thicker than surf."

"Dude, this is an unfair question since they're your employees, and, I agree, they're loyal to a fault, has either one said anything that would lead you to believe he was guilty?"

He closed his eyes, his head gyrated left and right and then up and down, and he bit his lip. "No."

I was at the end of the line talking to Dude. I thanked him, told him I appreciated his candor, and asked him not to say anything to them.

He patted his lips with his forefinger. "Be Super Glued."

Chapter Thirty-Four

Instead of talking to Rocky as I'd planned, I left through the back door. I was close to figuring out part of the mystery, and had to think it through and what to do with it.

I got home and took a pad of lined paper and wrote down what I knew, and what I felt I was almost certain of. I was convinced Barb was the person Panella was hired to kill. If she'd killed him she wouldn't have sought me out to ask what he looked like. She knew more than she was saying; she knew she was in danger. She acted frightened, both to me and to Dude. I was almost certain Dude hadn't shot him. So that left the two people who would do anything for their boss, and for Barb as an extension of Dude: Rocky, Stephon, or both.

I didn't know if Stephon had talked to Panella, but I knew Rocky had. Like many others, Panella didn't take Dude's employee seriously, and figured Rocky, who looked like a burned out junkie, wouldn't remember anything he'd seen. I smiled to myself. If there was one thing I'd learned during my years here, it was not to make assumptions about anyone.

I missed being able to bounce this off Charles. And, in addition to not having Charles, I didn't have proof.

I added three question marks after Rocky's name, skipped two lines, and wrote: Who hired Panella?

If I was right about Barb being the target, more likely it was someone from Pennsylvania, but something Rocky had said nagged at me. I added two more question marks to the bottom of the page when someone rapped on the back door. Rocky was on the small porch. He was in the same black outfit he had worn in the store, and looked behind him as I opened the door.

"Got something to tell you, Mr. Landrum. Could I come in?"

To say I was torn was the understatement of the year, perhaps the decade. I could now ask him what had bothered me about his conversation with Panella, but I could also be facing the man who sent Panella to hit-man hell.

"Umm, sure."

He stepped inside and I took a couple of steps back. I wasn't ready to offer him a drink or a seat. I also didn't want him to see how nervous I was so I leaned against the counter. I turned the pad over and smiled.

His eyes darted around the room and he focused on the door to the living room. We were standing facing each other when he pushed his coat out of the way and reached behind his back. The next thing I knew, I was staring at the business end of a handgun.

"Sit." he said with nonnegotiable force.

I sat.

With his other hand, he removed two plastic self-locking cable ties from his pocket, pointed for me to put my hands behind my back, and said not to do anything foolish. I had already done one foolish thing by letting him in and wasn't about to compound that mistake. He slipped one restraint over my wrists and yanked it tight. It stung as it tore into my wrists. He looped the other tie over the one securing my wrists and weaved it though the rail in the middle of the backrest. He was silent as he went about the task, scary silent.

"What do you want?" I asked, to get him talking rather than expecting to get a reasonable answer.

"Wait." He stepped in front of me, and pulled out a third, and longer, restraint. "Cross your legs and move them against the chair leg."

He stared at me until I nodded and set the gun on the counter out of my range and wrapped the tie around my legs and the chair. It had hurt when he tightened the tie around my wrists, but it was a tingle compared to how my ankles felt when he jerked the tie tight around my legs. I grimaced.

Rocky retrieved the gun and walked from room to room; he appeared to be doing it out of nerves. He came back in the kitchen and looked out the window. He then bolted the back door and stood three feet in front of me.

"I don't want to hurt you," he said.

Too late, I thought.

"You're Dude's friend. You saved his life a while back and he thinks the world of you. Honest, I don't want to hurt you." He glared at me. "If I have to." He shrugged. "You understand?"

I nodded.

He looked at the pistol he held to his side, and said, "I killed him."

His calm voiced frightened me more than if he had screamed it. I swallowed hard. "Why?"

"He was going to hurt Dude's sis. I couldn't let that happen." Rocky had come in from the cold, and it was cool in the kitchen, but a bead of sweat formed on his forehead. "You know what I mean?"

He paced, looked around one more time, and grabbed one of the chairs and set it in front of me. He walked to the back door and opened it a crack, looked out, and returned to the chair. I squeezed my wrists apart and tried to twist them enough to restore circulation or loosen them enough to get free. All I achieved was pain.

"Tell me about it?"

It seemed an eternity before he spoke.

"Remember how strange I told you he acted when he came in the shop?"

"Yes."

"Nothing good was hiding up his sleeve, so I remembered him."

"Good."

Rocky stared at my bound feet. "I was headed to catch a wave before work that horrible morning. My apartment—not much more than a closet—is in that old building on Huron. I was taking a shortcut to the surf shop where I keep my board. It was dark—dark and foggy. Wow, was it ever foggy. I saw nothing more than a shadow of someone fiddling with the lock on the bookstore door. I was ten feet away before I got a good look at him. That stopped me in my tracks, I can tell you." He shook his head as he relived the moment. "He must have heard me because he turned. I stopped and said, 'Shit man, I'm only walking by.'"

Rocky paused.

"What happened?"

"My eyes were adjusted to the dark and I saw it was the dude who'd been hiding from Barb in the store. I took a step back and he pulled a gun out of his jacket. Aikona. She's not going to get hurt; not if I can help it."

Thanks to my Dude-speak translator, Charles, I had learned *aikona* meant *not going to happen.*

Rocky hesitated and looked at the gun. "I had this and pulled it out. The guy raised his arm like he pointed his gun at people all the time. Swear to God, he was going to shoot me. All I was doing was walking down the alley." He sighed. "I don't know how I was quicker than him. I didn't aim. I pointed my gun in his direction and yanked the trigger."

The sweat was now running down his face. His gun hand was shaking, and I thought he was going to break into tears. I held my breath.

"He flopped back like I'd smacked him with my board. I didn't know what to do. I looked around and no one came running so I went over to him. He wasn't moving. And ... and, there was a hole right in the middle of his head. He was deader than a week-old beached grouper."

"What'd you do?"

"I wanted to know his name. Don't know why, but I did. Sure as hell wasn't going to tell anybody. He was on his back, and his coat was open. I wasn't about to roll him over. Then I saw two of those money bags like Dude has when he gets cash from the bank. They were sticking out the inside pockets of his coat. Puffed him out so much it looked like he had on a bulletproof vest. Crap Landrum, they held stacks of cash, hundred-dollar bills, thirty-seven thousand bucks —more money than I'd ever seen."

"You took it?"

Rocky wiped the sweat from his forehead and nodded. "He didn't need it. Don't get me wrong, Dude treats me good, but that's more money than I take home in a year and a half. Yeah, I took it."

My hands were tingling, and my legs ached from their

awkward position.

"It was self-defense, Rocky. He was trying to kill you. Tell you what, cut these ties off and I'll forget about what's happened. We can call the police. I'm sure they'll understand."

He stood and waved his gun around the room. "Don't you think I've pondered that? It's about all I've been thinking about since that morning."

"Now'd be a good time to do it," I hoped it made more sense to him than it did to me.

"Can't."

"Why not?"

"I know how people look at me. I'm that worthless surfer at the surf shop who scares off customers. If I went to the cops, I'd be in jail before sunset, and wouldn't get out while geezers like you are still alive."

"Rocky, the police will understand, and—"

"Enough. There's more. Before I moved here, I'd spent some years locked up. I was deep in drugs—using, not selling. One night in Louisiana I was high and ran over an old dude; never saw him in the street. Convicted of vehicular homicide; spent seven years behind bars. Deserved every minute of it. I'd still be there if I didn't get clean—as if I had a choice in jail. I traversed the straight and narrow. They called me a model prisoner, can you believe that? Even got some college credits while I was 1 locked up. They let me out before my time was up."

"That's great."

"Yeah. Moved here and Dude hired me without asking anything about my past. Best thing that's ever happened to me. I owe that man my life."

"The police will—"

"The police won't ignore my past like Dude did. They'll say I killed before and now killed that dude in the alley to rob him. If I was on the jury, I'd convict my ass and ship me away forever." He pointed the gun at my feet. "That's why you're hogtied. I want you to know what happened. You're buds with the cops and'll tell them my side. They will believe what you tell them I said. You'll also tell Dude and he'll tell Stephon. They'll believe me."

I shook my head. "I'll go with you to the police. Detective Adair and Chief LaMond are good at what they do. They'll give you a fair shake. If you run, it'll look like you're guilty and they'll catch you."

"Good try. No way. Besides, I figure I can get mighty far away from here on the dead guy's cash. You're an old fart, so I figure it'll take you a while to get out of that." He pointed to my legs. "You'll call the cops and tell them what happened, and none of you'll have any idea where I went."

He started to the door and turned back to me. "Sorry for tying you up."

It struck me he wasn't going to kill me. "Can I ask you one thing?"

He grinned. "You ain't in a position to ask much. To show you I'm not as bad as you think, go for it."

"When we were talking the other day and you were telling me about your conversation with Panella, didn't you say something about him having to leave to meet someone at his house?"

He shook his head. "That's one stupid-ass question to ask while you're sitting there like that."

I shrugged, or as much of a shrug as I could muster with my hands bound behind my back. "It's important."

"Yeah, that's what he said. He'd looked at his watch like he was late."

"And you're sure he said he had to meet at someone's house, not hotel room, in a car, or anywhere else?"

"How many times do I have to say it?"

"Thanks. Good luck."

He closed the back door on his way out. I realized he wasn't the only person with perspiration running down the face.

Chapter Thirty-Five

I was alive, thank God and I suppose, thank Rocky. Now what? I was strapped to a chair in the middle of the kitchen. I couldn't use my hands or legs. The phone was in the other room and even if I could get to it, I doubted I was dexterous enough to nose dial. Frustration stuck me from all directions, yet again, I was alive, and I wouldn't have put money on my chances a few minutes ago.

I could scoot the chair a few feet. What would that accomplish? In movies, when the good guy's tied to a chair, he'd tip it over and manage to twist himself like a pretzel and miraculously escape the bonds. In the real world, I pictured myself tipping the chair over, smacking the floor, cracking my skull, and don't even think about the pretzel thing. I needed to come up with Plan B, Lord knows, I had time.

I could think of many things I couldn't do, but the one thing I could do was to scoot the chair across the floor. To what end? The steak knives Bob had given me were in the top drawer by the sink. They had remained in the drawer unused since Bob had given them to me. Unused, unless I count the one that had attached the note to my pillow. I could use my teeth to open the drawer; get my mouth around the handle of one of the knives. Then what? A knife in mouth is better than two where? *Enough foolishness, focus.* What I was certain of was there was no hope parked in the center of the room.

I inched the chair to the counter, careful not to tip over. Now what? I pulled the drawer open enough to get part of my head in and put my teeth around the plastic handle of one of the knives. My mouth slipped and I was afraid I'd slit my tongue. That would have been a poor introduction of the never-used blade to its intended use. On the second try, I got the knife out without drawing blood. I leaned up and dropped the knife on the edge of the counter. Well done, but worthless. Even if I got the chair turned around, the knife was still a foot and a half higher than I could reach. *Think, Chris, think.* I could use my Uri Geller-psychic powers and will the knife to float through the air and land in my hands so I could cut the binding. *Stop it. Get serious.*

I stared at the drawers and realized the next to bottom drawer opened at hand level. If I could get my knee close enough, I might be able to nudge it open.

I inched the chair closer to the counter, leaned as far as I could, and moved my knee to the side of the drawer. The tie around my ankles was digging into my skin and it stung more when I tried to get leverage to pull the drawer open. I failed.

I caught my breath and tried again. No better luck. I leaned back in the chair to conjure up another solution. None appeared. I had to keep trying.

The third time was more painful, but it was a charm. The drawer opened an inch. I hesitated to compose myself, and repeated the action until the drawer was open enough to have a chance to catch the knife. The knife was on the counter directly above the drawer. All I had to do was reach it with my mouth and slide it off the edge of the counter, watch it land in the open drawer, turn the chair around, grab the knife without cutting a finger off, and maneuver it around to cut the tie. Nothing to it. *Yeah, right.*

Problem. With the drawer open, I couldn't get to the knife without performing a circus act of balancing the chair on two legs while leaning over the counter to reach Bob's gift. If the chair slipped, I'd be screwed. If I slid the knife too quickly, it'd miss the drawer and land on the floor and out of reach.

Careful, Chris, I told myself as I leaned the chair to one side. It began slipping, and I quickly leaned the other direction to set it back on all four legs. I took a deep breath and inched nearer to the open drawer. Time to try again. My chin touched the knife and I nudged it closer to the edge. I said a silent prayer, and gave it another push. The knife not only landed in the drawer, its handle faced me. Proof that prayer, even a strange one about knocking a knife off a counter, worked. It also could have been pure, dumb luck. Either way, I'd take it.

After rejoicing over my knife-dropping act, I scooted the chair to the front of the drawer, turned it around, reached in the drawer, and put my tingling hand around the knife's handle. A minute later, I had cut through the tie. My hands were free. To think, Charles had said I'd never use the knives.

I rubbed my hands to restore circulation, and bent over to cut the strap that held my feet. I stood and almost fell when my legs gave way. I sat—fell—back down, caught my breath, and looked at the clock. I figured my ordeal had lasted a week or so. It had been less than an hour. I gave my legs a couple more minutes to recuperate and stumbled to the bedroom and grabbed the phone.

I tapped 9, another 9, then moved my finger off the keyboard. Rocky was rude, obnoxious, and guilty of killing Panella—in self-defense. He had stolen close to forty thousand dollars off the corpse, not to mention binding me to a chair. Still, he'd saved Barb's life, had been devoted to Dude, and had taken a risk by telling me what had happened. He'd had an hour to escape, but I figured if he had another hour, his chances of getting caught would drastically decrease. I owed it to Dude and Barb to give him the extra time. I grabbed a Diet Pepsi, moved to my recliner, and thought about how lucky I was to be alive.

***

"Lordy, lordy, what now, Mr. Landrum?" Officer Bishop said, as I greeted her at the door.

I rubbed my wrists and welcomed the way too familiar first responder.

"Good afternoon, come in please," I said, trying to allay any fear there was any immediate danger.

She stepped past me and looked around the living room. "Anyone else here?"

I shook my head. "Just us, Officer Bishop."

"Might as well go with Trula. I'm seeing you more than I'm seeing my husband. What's up?"

I began telling her about being tied up when the door flung

open and Chief LaMond stormed in.

She did the same police gaze around the living room Officer Bishop had performed. "You okay?"

"Fine, now."

The chief glanced at Bishop and down at the red welts on my wrists. "Holy recipient of bad luck, do I need to post *Warning! Hazardous to your Health* signs in your yard?"

"It might not be a bad idea."

"Okay," the chief said, "What now?"

Officer Bishop interjected, "We were getting to that."

Cindy said, "Go ahead, Chris. I'm sure this will be a doozy."

I waved for them to follow me to the kitchen and offered them a chair.

"Would you like me to start with having a gun pointed at me, being tied up, escaping using my extraordinarily creative skills, or learning who killed Lawrence Panella?"

Cindy looked at Trula. "You did hear me say it'd be a doozy, didn't you?"

Bishop nodded at her boss and turned to me. "Who killed Panella?"

I was hurt she didn't want to hear about my trials and tribulations. I "entertained" the ladies by sharing everything that had happened, up to, but not including, giving Rocky the extra hour to get the hell out of Dodge, or Folly Beach.

Bishop reached for her notebook. "What does Rocky drive?"

"No idea. Don't know if he has a car?"

"What's his last name?" she asked.

I was embarrassed to say I didn't know.

"Did he say anything to indicate where he was going?" the chief asked.

"No."

Cindy turned to her officer. "Call Jim Sloan and get Rocky's name, address, and what he drives."

Trula said, "Jim Sloan?"

"Dude at the surf shop," Cindy said.

"Sorry," Bishop said. "Didn't know that was Dude's name." She went to the living room to call.

Cindy turned to me. "And he left you tied up, and alive, so you'd tell us he killed the hit man?"

"Yes."

"Why say anything? Why risk getting caught? You know we don't have any leads and saw the case getting colder by the day. It's now a popsicle."

"I think he overheard me talking to Dude. I had begun to suspect Rocky, Stephon, or both because of their loyalty to their boss. He figured I was getting close and wanted someone to hear his side. That someone was me."

"If what he said's accurate, it's self-defense."

"I agree. He felt his past would've clouded your version of what happened."

"Didn't give us cops much credit."

Officer Bishop returned to the room. "Got an APB out on Rocky."

"Good," Cindy said. "Now call Detective Adair and tell him he may want to mosey over. Chris, the walking, talking, disaster magnet, has an enthralling tale to share."

Bishop smiled and headed back to the living room.

Cindy shook her head and looked over at the drawer that was still open. "Want to show me your knife throwing trick before the hot-shot detective from the big city comes a callin'?"

"No."

Cindy chuckled. "Didn't think so." She put her hand on my arm. "You sure you're okay?"

"Better than I was."

The next two hours were spent with me repeating my ordeal to Detective Adair. I regaled him with my circus-like escape, although he didn't appear as impressed with my creativity and dexterity as I had been. I told him for what it was worth, I believed Rocky's story that he had killed Panella to save himself, and Adair told me my opinion wasn't worth much. I lied to him when on his way out when I said I hoped they'd catch him.

My wrists were still red and stung from my escape attempt. My ankles hurt, but not as badly as my wrists, and I bounced between euphoria for being alive and learning who had killed Panella, and sadness that Rocky, trying to do a good deed, one of the few in his life, was wanted for murder, and when caught would face prison time unless he could convince the cops he was acting to save his own life.

And, there was still one huge unanswered question. Who hired Panella to kill Barb and had he or she hired someone else to finish the job? I gave it more thought before my body told me I didn't have a future as a contortionist. It was my last thought before falling asleep in the recliner.

Chapter Thirty-Six

Three hours later, the phone rang. Had the police found Rocky? The answer was not forthcoming, when I heard the excited voice of my best friend blaring out a usual, non-socially preferred, Folly greeting.

"Heather and I met Starr. She's going to cut a demo."

"Whoa. Hello Charles, how are you?"

"Huh? Oh, fine, gee. Listen, this is exciting."

I started to interrupt and share what had happened to me. I wasn't certain, but thought it would beat whatever he had to say. I knew not to waste words until he'd wound down.

"Start over. Demo?"

"It's great." Enthusiasm spewed from the speaker. "Heather and I met Kevin Starr. He's excited and said she needs to get her voice out to record execs—that's how he talks. He said she needs to cut a demo record, tape, digital thingee, whatever they do now."

"That's great," I lied—the second bigee of the day.

"Yeah, except it'll cost $2,900. She's got $735 unless she sells her guitar, which'd defeat the plan. I can make up the difference, but it'd lop a big chunk off my estate."

"Did she sign a contract with Kevin Starr?"

"Yeah. He's officially her agent."

I knew little about the music industry and wondered what Starr's responsibilities were. It seemed strange Heather would have to pay for everything.

"Why does she have to pay for the demo? If Starr's representing her, shouldn't he cover it?"

"You're asking the wrong person. I know as much about this

stuff as I know how to teach a camel to sing. What I do know is Heather's on cloud thirty-seven. She zoomed past cloud nine, as soon as she stepped in Starbucks and saw Starr sipping a latte."

That's what I was afraid of.

"When's the demo going to be cut? When does she need the money?"

"Day after tomorrow. Something about needing to reserve the studio and stuff. Starr says he can pull strings and slip her in ahead of some of the famous singers booking the studio."

Had Charles realized how ridiculous that sounded, or was he getting caught in Heather's draft?

"Does it make sense Starr could move her ahead of popular artists?"

"Chris, even if I wanted to, I couldn't stop her with a ten-foot-high concrete wall topped with barbed wire. It's her dream."

I felt uneasy, yet told him I understood. I added I had a story to share and proceeded to tell him about my day and Rocky's confession.

"When were you going to tell me? Was I going to have to read it in the *Tennessean* or hear it on CNN? Was—"

"Charles, it just happened and what part of your story were you going to let me interrupt?"

"Picky, picky, picky," he said as if it he was trying to make some illogical point. "Tell me again how you flipped the knife and didn't slit your wrists?"

"Never mind. Don't you wish you were here to share the excitement?"

He didn't say anything for a minute and then whispered, "Yes." There was another pause before he said, "Gotta go. Heather wants to go to Walmart to get a new outfit to wear for her demo session. Try not to get killed and stay away from sharp objects." The phone went dead.

Now there were two things bothering me in addition to a cut foot, sore wrists, and ankles. While I doubted Cal could do anything for my sore body parts, he was the closest person I knew to the music industry. I walked three blocks to his bar. To say Cal's mid-week crowd in February was light would be like saying a candle might not illuminate Times Square. There were two of the town's better-known drunks at a table in the corner discussing the economic advantages of Budweiser over Miller; and a young couple at another table who appeared more intent on caressing each other's arms, back, and lower extremities than listening to Waylon Jennings regretting something on the jukebox.

Cal stood behind the empty bar and was nodding his head in time with the music.

"Howdy," he said and tipped his hat in my direction. "A glass of California's finest?" he asked as he reached for a bottle of red wine.

If what Cal served was California's finest, the Golden State better gear up production of walnuts and Napa Valley better rip out its grapevines and start planting marijuana. Regardless, I nodded as he set a glass of wine in front of me.

Cal leaned on the bar and cocked his Stetson back on his head. "What brings you out? Doubt it's to peek at my packed house or listen to Hank Snow."

I shared what Charles had said and asked for his thoughts on Kevin Starr and the demo session.

"Be back," he said, grabbed a couple of Budweisers and took them to the drunks. He returned with four empty bottles. "Sorry. When they finish those, I'm shooing their soused selves out of here. They ain't driving so all they can hurt is each other on the walk home. If they weren't here, they'd be in another bar."

That was more than I wanted to know. I could tell Cal had mixed feelings about how to deal with them.

Cal gazed at the men and turned back to me. "Know how many star-struck, dreaming, country-music-star-wannabees plane, train, bus, drive, or thumb to Nashville each year?"

"How many?"

"Don't have the foggiest, but it'd fill cattle cars seven miles long. Know how many vulturin' fake agents, record producers, and talent scouts are waitin' for the wide-eyed, narrow-brained wannabees?"

I wasn't going to let him trick me again. "Seventeen thousand."

"You made that up," my astute friend said.

"Yep. How many?"

"Hell if I know, but you could be close. Without getting too numbery, it's a feed trough full of them."

"Do you think Starr is trying to rip Heather off?"

"Let me put it this way." Cal looked at the ceiling, over at the lovers, then at me. "Charles moseyed over to Music City with Heather. Heather's got herself an agent. The agent wants to make her famous."

He paused and waited for me to nod.

I accommodated him, and he continued. "It's the same Heather who's performed a bunch of times on that stage."

I nodded again.

"And you've heard her. You heard her doing what she calls singing?"

I gave one more nod.

"Did Agent Starr strike you as tone deaf?"

My head went the other way this time.

"That answer your question?"

I was afraid it did. I tried one more possibility. "Could Starr hear something in her voice that shows potential?"

Cal shook his head and put his fist to his forehead. "Yes. He hears her song of desperation, her dream, and the sweet ka-ching of his cash register."

I told him about her appearing at the Bluebird for open-mic night and asked if anything good could come from it.

"Depends."

"On what?"

"The Bluebird's open-mic nights are for songwriters. They're hawking songs, not their singing. A good singing voice ain't a gift God bestowed on many writers. If Heather was there to plug her ditties, and someone liked them, she could sell a song or two. Songwriters have used the Bluebird's tiny stage to leapfrog successful writing careers. It's possible one in a zillion kicked off a singing career there."

To my knowledge, Heather had written two songs, and they weren't anything to kick her to a higher tax bracket. Her sole reason for going was to find fame as a performer. Cal also said Starr should be fronting the demo fee, and even if he didn't, for what Heather needed, it shouldn't cost more than half of what he was charging. Cal said there were millions to be made in Music City, although newcomers were often on the spending end. Regardless how we tried to spin it, we decided Heather's chance of achieving anything beyond emptying her bank account was no better than Cal being elected into the Rock and Roll Hall of Fame. We also concluded there was little, if anything, we could do to dissuade her from moving full-speed ahead. I told him I would let Charles know what Cal said about the cost of the demo. After that, it was up to Charles and Heather.

"Another question?" We had exhausted our fame for Heather discussion.

"That'll cost you another glass of vino." Cal filled my empty glass. The couple of lovers had taken their laying on of hands to another venue and the town drunks had staggered out. From the jukebox, Tom T. Hall was telling us how much he loved beer, and Cal and I were the only occupants of the tired bar.

"Do you know a man named Sylvester Lopp?"

"Takes a mighty strung out woman named Lopp to name a kid Sylvester, don't it?"

I nodded. "You know him?"

Brenda Lee was singing "Big Four Poster Bed," Cal was pushing his Stetson farther back on his head, and taking his time answering. "Sure."

"You do?"

"Yep."

"Tell me about him."

"He's a salesman. Sells those imitation Tupperware containers you see at groceries and dollar stores. Or, that's what he says. The boy does have a strange way about him. Sometimes it looks like he should be talking and he's not. A little shy, I think."

"Known him long?"

"No. Started sipping a brew or two the last couple of months, maybe not that long. Why?"

"He'd been in Barb's Books a few times and she thought he seemed strange."

The room got silent and Cal smiled. "Makes sense." Cal went to the jukebox and punched in a few numbers.

Jim Reeves began "He'll Have to Go," and Cal moved to one of the tables and pointed for me to join him.

"These old clodhoppers don't keep the feet from painin' like they used to."

I waited to hear why Lopp's visits to Barb's Books made sense, and motioned for Cal to continue.

"Sylvester's single, divorced, been that way for three years. Born in Missouri. I'm not a good judge of age, but I'd say he's in his late fifties, early sixties. Anyway, I think he's got a crush, or whatever you call it when someone that old's likin' someone." Cal smiled. "Think the boy's besotted with Barb."

"Why do you say that?"

"Let's see." Cal said, as he took off his Stetson and looked in it like it was full of tea leaves waiting to be read. "His first time in he asked if I'd been in the bookstore. I said no, reading ain't my thing. Second time he asked me if the bookstore lady was hitched. I told him I didn't think so. Next time I saw him, he was right over there." Cal pointed to the stool at the end of the bar. "Heard him ask Chester the same things about Barb. I didn't hear all they said, but remember Chester saying, 'Go for it.'"

That would explain Lopp's visits to the bookstore. Could he have been working up the nerve to ask her out? It had never made sense if he was hired to kill her he would be that conspicuous.

"Know where he lives?"

"Must be around here. This ain't the neighborhood bar for folks in Idaho."

"Anything else about him?"

"Good tipper."

"While we're alone, let me ask another question?"

He rolled his eyes. "Charles may be in Music City, but a hefty bunch of his nosiness has rubbed off on you."

"Someone's got to do it. What do you know about Rocky, the guy who works for Dude?"

"As much as I want to know, and that ain't much. He's been in here twice I know of. Seems like a hateful little prick. Demanding and gave my regulars the dirty eye like he thought they were covered with jellyfish. If he has friends, which I doubt, they weren't with him. Why?"

"Wondering," I sipped my drink and looked down in the glass. "He pointed a gun at me today, tied me to a chair, and told me he shot the hit man who came to town."

I peeked at Cal who was staring at me like I had recited the Declaration of Independence in Hungarian.

"Holy heifer. When were you going to fess up about that?"

I smiled, and felt good I still could after my day. I gave him an abridged version of Rocky's visit and what he had told me.

"He telling the truth?"

"Think so."

"So Bookstore Barb was the hit man's target?"

"Yes."

"So who hired the hit man?"

"Don't know, but I'm going to find out."

"How?"

"No idea."

Chapter Thirty-Seven

Overnight, the bottom dropped out of the thermometer. I awoke after a fitful sleep, with the temperature hovered around freezing, several degrees below average. I was surprised when Karen called and said she had to go in to work late and wanted to come over and walk on the beach. I was more surprised when she said she'd be at the house in a couple of minutes, and less than a minute later she was at the door.

She looked more like she was heading to the North Pole than to the beach. She wore a black barn coat, a wool, red and black plaid, Tilley Aviator hat I'd given her a couple of years ago, black jeans, and old boots, the kind that'd be more at home on a ranch rather than a fashion magazine. I asked if she wanted coffee and she looked at her watch and said she didn't have time. I grabbed my heaviest coat and my hat and followed her. I tried not to venture out when it was this cold and didn't have appropriate outerwear.

We walked to the beach and limited our conversation to the weather and how deserted the streets were. My fellow residents had more sense than the two of us. The palmetto trees were shivering in the wind along with me. Other than a lone walker, we had the beach to ourselves and Karen turned left when we reached the shoreline. We nodded to the walker as we crossed paths. Karen started to say something and hesitated.

We walked a few more yards and she said, "I've decided."

I couldn't imagine her wanting to be out here in this weather if her decision was to stay. The icy breeze off the ocean felt like daggers of ice blowing right through me. A deeper freeze grabbed my heart.

"You're taking it," I said and looked toward the ocean. I didn't want to look at her when she answered.

"Yes."

I mumbled, "Congratulations."

She reached over and grabbed my arm. We stopped.

"Chris, I can't pass it up. I don't know how much longer I could keep doing what I'm doing. It's a young person's game and I'm ... well, I'm not getting younger. I'm good at catching bad guys, although it's getting more difficult and frustrating. I'm not only battling criminals, I'm fighting with the courts, attorneys, the bureaucracy, and infighting among the various outside departments, crap, even my own office." She pulled her coat tighter and leaned closer to me. All I felt was her pulling away.

"It's too good to turn down. You deserve it."

"If it was nearby, I would've accepted in a heartbeat." She sniffled.

Maybe it was the cold.

"Leaving Dad and ... you ... never mind. It was the hardest thing I've had to do."

"Hey," I said with little enthusiasm, "it's not like you're moving to France. It's just a couple hundred miles away."

She smiled, with equally little enthusiasm, and said, "A little ways up the road."

I looked at the frigid, breaking waves, and back at her. She had wiped the tears from her cheek and put her arm in mine.

"I'd love to say I'd move to Charlotte." I hesitated, then continued. "I can't, my life is here. This is what I dreamed about forever. My friends are here." I hesitated and cringed thinking about Charles being gone. "I'm sorry."

She squeezed my arm. "I love you. Like I told you before, you wouldn't be happy and that would kill everything. Besides, the company has seventeen locations, one's here in Charleston and another in Savannah. I'll be travelling with the job and some of those trips will be nearby. We'd be able to see each other. That way—"

She put her head against my shoulder and her arms around my waist. Her body shook and I thought I heard sobs through the icy wind. We stood for several minutes, neither of us wanting to move. We had seen less and less of each other the last six months and she had talked more about our age difference. I had known it was a problem from day one, and had hoped, possibly unrealistically, that it was a minor issue. If I was fifteen years younger, I would look at moving. I would look at a long life ahead of me with options. Now, I knew I won't be around for many more years and change becomes more difficult. Karen needs to move on with her life, and the new job will provide her the financial stability a single woman on a governmental salary can only dream about.

"Charlotte's not that far away," I said.

We were both mature enough to know I was lying.

She pushed away from me. "I have to go to work. Let's get back."

When she called, I had hoped to be able to share what had happened yesterday and talk through the situation and see if the detectives had more leads on who may have hired Panella. That was until I saw the look on her face as she stood in the door. Now wasn't the time to bring it up. Besides, I was freezing.

Karen kissed me on the cheek as she walked me to my door and headed to her car. The temperature in the house was forty degrees warmer than outside, but the chill from the walk and her announcement stayed with me the rest of the morning.

Chapter Thirty-Eight

Avoidance had long been one of my go-to defense mechanisms. After spending the best part of the morning thinking about how I felt about Karen leaving, the prospect of moving to Charlotte to be near her, or proposing, and her possible reactions, I had to switch gears else I'd go crazy or ram my fist through the wall. I began running through everything I knew about the threat to Barb. It didn't take long once I realized I knew almost nothing about why someone was out to get her, or who it might be. It seemed obvious that it was about her life before moving here. Her husband was involved in crimes that involved millions of dollars. Barb said she didn't know what was going on; the police believed her or she would have been indicted. Yet it seemed someone didn't buy her story and felt she was a threat.

I fixed more coffee and moved on to something that had bothered me for days. Who had broken into in my house and why? Then, while replaying the conversation with Rocky, I began to feel more confident about what I had speculated about the other day. The person who hired Panella must think I have the money he'd paid the hit man. The police hadn't found it on the body, nothing was found in his car, not much in his hotel room, and no one knew Rocky had pulled the trigger. I would have been the logical person to have killed Panella and taken the cash.

If true, the person who hired Panella would have been in the area, at least the three times my house was violated. And, according to Rocky, Panella said he had to meet at someone's house. The person who wanted Barb dead was not in Pennsylvania, but here.

My cupboard was bare so I headed to the Dog for a late lunch.

The restaurant wasn't as empty as the beach had been, but it was close. Three tables were occupied; two with regulars and the third by Jane Campbell, a lady who owned several rental properties but whom I had seldom seen in the Dog. Her arm was in a sling and her head buried in the morning's *Post and Courier*. Amber saw me and waved for me to sit wherever I wanted, so I headed to my favorite booth.

She delivered meals to a nearby table and brought me coffee. "Afternoon." She frowned. "You look like someone ran over your Corkie. You okay?"

"Rough morning."

She grinned. "Someone break in your house again?"

I smiled. "Not this time."

She took my order, brought it to the kitchen, returned to the table, and looked around the restaurant and didn't see anyone needing her attention. She slid in the booth.

"Give." she said.

Despite being friends, I was uncomfortable talking with her about my personal life. My friends didn't have that reservation and kept her updated on everything that went on with me. I'd often kidded she knew more about what was happening to me than I did. I had only been half kidding.

"Karen is taking a job in Charlotte."

"Oh."

For once, I shared something that someone hadn't already told her.

"You going with her?"

I shook my head. "No."

"Oh."

That was as close as Amber comes to speechless.

"We'll see each other from time to time. The company has an office here and she'll be back."

Amber waited for me to continue. I didn't, and she said, "They say absence makes the heart grow fonder. From what I've seen, it makes it hell on relationships. If you don't mind me saying, I don't see it working. Maybe it will at first, but not for long." She shrugged. "I'm being honest."

"I know, and don't disagree. Folly is my home and I can't see leaving."

"I don't know about the new job and why she's taking it, but I'll tell you what I do know. I'm butting in. If you want to hear it, I'll tell you."

"Amber, I've known you longer than anyone here. I always want to know what you think. I don't always agree, but ..." I smiled.

"Here it is. You're one of the most regular regulars in here. You're in a couple of times a week or more and you're my favorite by far, and that's not because you're that great a tipper. Anyway, I hear bits and pieces of your conversation with folks and I've got to tell you, you've talked less and less about Karen, and I honestly can't remember the last time she was here with you."

"Okay."

"That tells me there's drifting going on. Could be you drifting away from her or her from you; either way, something's coming on, and it hasn't been wedding bells."

I hated to admit she was right. Regardless, I didn't want to talk about it. I glanced over at Jane.

"What happened to her?"

Amber leaned closer. "She fell down the stairs of a rental she owns on West Huron." She leaned even closer and whispered. "Hear she was a tad under the weather, if you get my meaning. She missed a step. Was lucky to get off with a broken arm."

There was a reason Amber was one of the island's leading contenders for top gossip collector and distributor.

I nodded and Amber stood. "Let me grab your food."

A minute later she returned with my lunch and a question.

"Speaking of accidents, do you know if Russ Vick was in a bad one?"

"Is he in a cast?"

"No, I don't mean recent."

"Why?"

She pointed to her forehead at the hairline. "Most times I see customers when they're sitting at a table and I'm looking down at them. I've got a great view of your bald spot a lot of people can't see."

"Thanks, that's what I needed reminding of."

She smiled. "My point, Mr. Self-Conscious, is Russ has a scar right about here." She again pointed to her hairline. "Most people wouldn't see it unless they were looking."

"You think it's from a wreck?"

"Suppose so. Don't know what else it could be."

"Yoo-hoo, Amber," called Jane from across the room as she held her coffee mug in the air with her good arm.

Amber smiled at Jane, hopped up, and headed to the coffee pot. I watched her go and thought about what she had said about Russ's scar. I then remembered something that had been said when Russ, Dude, and I were in here right after I had met the T-shirt store owner. I didn't think about it at the time, but he'd said Dude wasn't anything like Barb. That wasn't profound for anyone who had met the siblings, half siblings, but unless I was mistaken, Russ had said he hadn't had a chance to meet Barb. How would he have known they were different?

Until now, I hadn't given Russ a second thought in relation to the dead man. Other than both being recent arrivals to Folly, there was no obvious connection between the two. And, Barb first met Russ the day she and I were in here, and after he left, she said she'd seen him around town. Had he hired Panella? Hadn't Barb said when her husband was caught some of the people her ex had been in cahoots with had gone missing—like cockroaches when the lights came on. Could Russ be one of them? Thinking back on when Barb had met Russ, he didn't stay long and she didn't get a good look at him. Could the scar have been from plastic surgery to alter his appearance, rather than from a wreck? The full beard could add to his disguise.

Amber had refilled Jane's mug and was occupied with a family of four who had braved the cold for a hot breakfast. Russ had also made a point of sharing he had been in Las Vegas when Panella had been murdered. In hindsight, his revelation seemed unusual to be sharing with someone he'd just met. Could he have been planting his alibi for the time Panella should have killed Barb?

Despite a new look, Russ could have figured that with both of them on the small island and having businesses within sight of each other, she would eventually recognize him as one of her ex-husband's partners in crime; one of the partners in hiding.

I left my lunch unfinished, left a substantial tip for the lady who might have given me the biggest tip, and left the restaurant to start an Internet search for Russell Vick, current resident of Folly Beach, formerly of locations unknown.

A crick in my neck was all I got after an hour searching websites and references for Russell Vick, Russ Vick, and variations of the spelling of the name. He had said he was from Delaware, so I started the search there. There was no shortage of Russell Vicks on the Internet, and many of the sights had images of the various Mr. Vicks, and even if he didn't have a beard or plastic surgery, none of them came close to looking like the T-shirt shop owner. I wasn't optimistic about the search since I figured if he went to that much trouble to change his appearance, he would have changed his name. It had been worth a try though, and besides it took my mind off Karen.

***

I had suffered another sleepless night before semi-focusing my eyes enough to brew a pot of coffee. As cold as it had been yesterday, I half expected to see a rare layer of snow outside my window. There wasn't snow, but the bleak grayness of the sky led me to believe today wasn't going to be warmer than yesterday. In the middle of the night, I had decided to call Chief LaMond and incur her ire by telling her my theory about Russ Vick. I knew she would call me every creative name someone from East Tennessee could call a jackass. In the end, she'd listen, and if a glimmer of what I said made sense, she'd investigate.

I was reaching for the phone to call the chief when it rang.

"Guess what Heather got?" Charles said.

I didn't share his enthusiasm for a daily quiz. "What?"

"No guesses today?" He sounded disappointed.

I sighed. "Okay, a pet chinchilla."

"Not a bad idea, but no. She got the prettiest little red and white gingham dress you've ever seen. Found it at Stein Mart. You wouldn't believe all the stores they have here."

I had often thought Charles would be dangerous if he had a way to get around other than by bike. Nashville's retail establishments were getting a taste of my friend.

"For her demo session?"

"She wants to look her best when she's cutting it. 'Look good, sound good,' she says."

"Has she paid for the demo?"

"Tomorrow."

"Good. I talked with Cal about it. He—"

Charles interrupted, "Do I want to hear what he said?"

Doubt it, I thought. "Let me tell you and you decide."

He didn't respond, so I told him Cal's, shall I say, less than enthusiastic, opinion of what was happening to Heather and how he felt the alleged agent was playing on her ambition and ripping her off.

Charles listened, interjected a couple of comments along the way, and when I had finished, he didn't speak for a long time, until he said, "Cal's been around the block so many times he's worn the pavement off. I trust his opinion. I sort of have a bad feeling about Starr, but you know Heather. It'd take more than a herd of buffalo to stop her once she has her mind made up."

Charles was right, yet I felt I'd be letting my friend down if I didn't share what I'd learned.

"Tell you what," Charles said. "I'll tell my honey what Cal said. I'll even, gulp, tell her I agree with him. And if she hasn't already clobbered me with her guitar, I'll try to tell her I think it's best if we *temporarily* abandoned her dream and head home, home being Folly Beach."

I smiled. "Good."

"If she tries to throw me out the window, I'm going to tell her it was all your idea."

"That's what friends are for."

"Now that you've decided what I should do, have you figured out who hired the killer man?"

"Interesting you should ask. I think so."

Charles proceeded to lambast me for not calling him in the middle of the night with my theory. I told him I would have shared it at the beginning of this conversation if he hadn't been intent on giving me a fashion update. I got down to telling him everything I'd been thinking. He asked if I had proof, the question I would have asked him when he was on one of his tangents. I said no, and he asked what I was going to do. I said I was getting ready to call Chief LaMond when he called. He said he'd step outside so he could hear the chief's scream all the way to Nashville. I said thanks.

He finished by saying, "I hope to see you soon."

I refilled my coffee and called Cindy's cell. She was in her office and said she had a meeting with the mayor in ten minutes. She added, "Of course, whatever you have to say is much more important than meeting with my boss, so take your time."

It didn't take the entire ten minutes to lay out what I suspected. I finished and she didn't yell, probably because she was in her office.

"Chris, you never cease to amaze me—not impress me, not convince me, not even make me think you're making sense." I heard her sigh. "On the other hand, it's more than the super-duper, hotshot detective Adair has come up with. I'll give him a holler and do some nosing around. And hey, when it proves to be worthless and Adair says it's the dumbest thing he's ever heard, don't worry, I'll give you credit."

Cindy had her hands full with the usual day-to-day bureaucratic and personnel issues that she had to deal with her department, and would be tied up for the next couple of hours with the mayor. Even if she got time to call Detective Adair, it wouldn't be soon, and from other things he'd said about my previous theories, he may not give credence to what she'd tell him. Barb's life was in danger, and my house was becoming a hangout for unwanted visitors, so I didn't have the luxury of waiting for something to happen. I needed to talk with Barb, so why not over a meal?

I reached for the phone, still warm from my previous two conversations, and called Barb's Books. After four rings, I had begun to wonder if she was there, but then she answered. I told her who I was and was pleased when she said she recognized my voice. I asked if she was free for supper. She hesitated, then said she needed to eat. We agreed to meet at Loggerhead's since it was across the street from her condo and close to my house. After I hung up, I wondered why I didn't go to the bookstore to talk to her. Oh well, I too had to eat.

I was standing at the steps leading to the elevated restaurant when Barb rushed across the road from her building.

"Is it always this cold in February?" she asked, as I met her in the restaurant's parking lot. "I moved here to get away from icicles hanging off my nose."

I smiled, not only because she was a pleasant sight in her black leather jacket and dark-gray wool fedora with a narrow red band around the crown, but because she'd already fallen prey to not greeting people with common courtesies.

I explained it was exceptionally cold this year and most winters she wouldn't have to worry about icicles.

"Good," She jogged up the steps.

Loggerheads, like most restaurants on the island in this weather, was nearly empty and Ed, the owner, said for us to sit anywhere. We settled in a booth along the wall and a waitress took our drink order. Barb asked for a gin and tonic with a brand of gin I'd never heard of. Neither had the waitress who said she'd see if they had it. She returned and said no and Barb ordered a Loggerhead's Draft, a step down from a gin and tonic, yet a drink the waitress was certain she could find. I stuck with the house cabernet.

Barb took off her heavy coat to reveal another bright red blouse, her trademark color, and said, "Something tells me your invitation wasn't social."

"I confess, you're right. There is something, although I could have done it on the phone."

"Hmm." She watched the waitress return with our drinks and ask if we were ready to order.

I looked at Barb and she shook her head and I told the waitress we needed a few minutes.

I sipped wine to stall and figure out how to ease into a discussion about Russ Vick.

She took a long draw on her beer and gave me a look that would have intimidated a hostile witness in court. "What is it?"

"Have you had much contact with Russ Vick?"

She tilted her head. "Russ Vick?"

"The T-shirt store guy."

"Folly Tease and SML Shirts. Just met him once, at the Dog. You were there."

"That's the only time?"

She frowned, uncomfortable with my line of questions. "Why?"

Might as well hit it head on. "I've got a theory." I held out my palm. "It might sound ridiculous, and I'll admit, it might be, but I think he hired Panella to kill you."

She took another sip and shook her head. "It doesn't make sense. I've had one, thirty-second conversation with the man. I don't know anything about him other than he caters to kids, kids of all ages, who think suggestive comments on their T-shirts are cool. What makes you think it was him?"

The waitress returned and we each ordered flounder and I began my convoluted story of why I thought Vick instigated the hit. Barb's laser focus was on me the entire time, and I suspected if she had pad and pen, she would have taken notes. I was not accustomed to getting this far into a story without interruption, and began to wonder if I was so far off track it would take a search party to bring me back.

When I finished, I expected her to laugh and tell me how stupid my theory was. Instead, she looked around at the few other tables of diners and then at me. "I'm pretty certain my ex wasn't in bed with anyone named Vick, but he could've changed his name. I'd met most of the people he either bribed or had taken money from. Business was never discussed in my presence, thank God. I don't recall anyone who looked like Vick."

"Picture him without the beard, and with more wrinkles or with his nose looking different, anything plastic surgery could change."

She didn't respond right away so I hoped she was trying to make those adjustments. She shook her head.

"What about his voice? That's harder to change than hair or facial features."

Her eyes widened. "I didn't think about it until now. I do remember thinking when I heard him in the Dog that there was something familiar about it. I didn't give it a second thought, since I could have heard it around here."

"So it's possible?"

She closed her eyes and gave a slight nod. "You're saying of all the places in the world, I decided to come to the same island where one of my ex-husband's crooked colleagues moved to hide?"

I nodded. "It's a coincidence, but I've given it some thought. It's not as big a stretch as it might seem. Most likely, your ex-husband told his buddy Russ, or whatever his real name is, about Dude and

Folly Beach. I remember the first time I talked to Dude about you, he mentioned he had visited you and Karl a couple of times and how your ex told him Folly would be a good place to escape the world. Russ also told me he hadn't owned a shop before moving here, but had worked for a large company in Delaware. I didn't ask, and he didn't offer the name of the company."

Our food arrived yet neither of us lifted a fork.

Barb looked at the plate and back at me. "And you put all this together after a conversation with Dude?"

I smiled. "I've become decent at understanding Dudespeak. I didn't think about it at the time. It wasn't until a waitress mentioned the scars at his hairline. And when Dude's employee, Rocky, mentioned the killer had told him he was meeting someone at his house, I started thinking the person who hired him may be living here."

"Whoa. Back up. What's Rocky have to do with it?"

I realized she didn't know about my close encounter with Rocky and proceeded to tell her about my pointed contacts with him and what he had said about killing Panella.

"Holy crap," she said, unlawyerly. "And I moved here to get away from drama."

I smiled. "We have our moments."

"What are we going to do about it?"

"I've shared what I told you with Chief LaMond, and she's going to talk to Detective Adair. They have the resources to follow through and will be contacting you."

"Russ could have hired someone else to kill me," she said, more to herself than to me.

That reminded me about something else. "True. Remember when you were worried about Sylvester Lopp? I was talking to Cal Ballew, a friend who owns Cal's Bar. He told me Lopp sells plastic containers and had been in the bar a few times. He'd asked Cal about you and Cal figured out Lopp had wanted to ask you out. Cal said Lopp was shy and that was why he had been in your store several times without saying anything."

Barb smiled. "Sy, that's what he likes to be called, came in yesterday afternoon. He bought three more books, stuttered a couple of times, and asked me if I was seeing anyone."

"Oh."

"Yeah." She chuckled. "I started to tell him it was none of his business, then didn't want to appear rude. I said no. He began sounding like Dude when he strung enough words together for me to figure out he was asking me to a movie. I had the feeling that if he wore a hat, he would have held it over his heart, got on his knees, before asking. He was so sweet."

"I'm glad he talked to you. Don't think you have to worry about him—being a hit man anyway."

She hesitated, twisted her napkin, and took a bite of fish. "Yeah, it's not him. Chris, I'm scared."

"I know." I put my hand on hers. She didn't pull away. "The police are good. They'll get it figured out now that they know how it could be tied to your past."

I wish I had as much confidence in the police as I told Barb. She shook her head like a dog shaking water off its back and started talking about how pleased she was with business and how much she was looking forward to the vacation season. We shared avoidance as a defense mechanism. I wondered what she had said to Sy's date request, and wondered why I had wondered.

We declined dessert and Barb said she'd had a long day and needed to get home. She halfheartedly fought for the check, but gave in and let me pay. We left the restaurant and I offered to walk her to her condo. She said it wasn't necessary, but protested less than she had about the check. Her condo was on the top floor of the four-story complex so I punched the button on the elevator. There were a handful of vehicles in the lot; a few permanent residents were the only people in the large building. As we waited for the elevator, it felt like we were in a wind tunnel as the icy ocean breeze whipped through. Barb leaned close to me until we got on the elevator and I pushed the fourth-floor button.

The elevator opened at the exterior walkway to her condo and the night went all to hell.

Chapter Thirty-Nine

Barb gave a high-pitched shriek and I took a quick step back, neither overreactions to the black, compact, Sig Sauer, semi-automatic pistol with a color-coordinated seven-inch silencer pointed at us.

"I thought you were never going to leave," said the raspy voice of Russell Vick as he nodded across the street toward Loggerhead's. "You're going to give me the death of a cold waiting out here." He smirked.

I didn't see any humor, nor did I see anyone else on the windswept walkway.

"I notice you're shivering, my dear. Shall we go in your condo?" He waved the pistol toward the door.

It took Barb three tries before her hand was steady enough to open the lock. Russ stood far enough away that I couldn't reach the gun. Still no one appeared on the walkway, and from the few cars in the lot, I doubted anyone was nearby.

Once inside, Russ ushered us down the corridor to the living area. The door closed on its own. He waved the pistol for Barb and me to stand close together and he leaned on the granite counter separating the kitchen from where we were standing.

"Mrs. Deanelli, you've caused me many sleepless nights." Russ faced Barb, yet pointed the gun at me. "I spent most everything I had getting work done on my face, growing this miserable beard, changing my name, and moving to this, as your idiotic brother Dude, says, 'Hidin' spot from *el mundo*,' to get away from your husband, and the feds." He pounded his fist on the granite counter. "Then you show up."

I didn't doubt his intentions. Barb and I would never leave here alive unless I found a way to get to the gun. To do that, I had to buy time.

I said, "So you hired someone to solve your problem, and made sure you were out of town when he was supposed to kill Barb."

Russ grinned. "Vegas is nice this time of year. Who would've thought you'd shoot the guy. Thanks a hell of a lot, Landrum?"

I caught a glimpse of Barb's head jerk toward me.

"You figured I'd shot Panella and took your money. You broke into my house to find it. Nice touch, leaving the note to throw me off from thinking you were looking for money."

He glared at me. "I'm not rich. It took all I had to remodel my body and get the stinking T-shirt shops. Panella took forty grand from me. I gave it to him the day I left for Vegas and two days before he was supposed to earn it." He waved the gun toward Barb, but I was still too far away to do anything. "I heard the cops didn't find my money on the body, in his car, or his hotel. You've got it."

Here's a way to buy more time. "Panella had no use for it."

Barb continued to stare at me.

"Where is it?" Russ asked.

"Sorry. Don't see an upside of telling you."

"Your call." He pointed the weapon at Barb.

I had to think quickly if we had chance of leaving here alive. "Shoot her and kiss your money good-bye."

"Where is it?"

"If I told you, you'd still never find it."

"Try me."

"Have you heard the stories about pirates burying treasure on Folly?"

Russ nodded.

"People have looked for it for decades. No one's found it."

"You buried my money?"

I nodded. Now what?

He looked at Barb, back at me, and pointed the gun toward the hall to the door. "Why would you bury it? That doesn't make sense."

"I didn't until you broke in the first time." I remembered the recliner was the only thing that hadn't been disturbed. "I had it with a stack of magazines under my recliner."

"Shit. You're kidding."

I grinned and hoped to keep him talking. "It was still there after the first break in, so I figured whoever broke in might try again."

"So you buried it?"

"Yep."

He glanced at the floor and gave a slight nod before returning his stare at me. "Then let's dig it up." He motioned us to the door.

Yes. A glimmer of hope. I still didn't know how I was going to get his weapon.

Barb opened the door and Russ lowered his gun hand so no one would see him holding us at gunpoint. It wasn't necessary since there was no sign of life on the outside walkway and the temperature was still dropping. I couldn't imagine anyone being nearby.

Russ stopped Barb. "Don't try anything stupid."

She turned toward the elevator with me close behind.

"No!" screamed a voice behind Russ. Then someone rammed the gunman in the back.

Russ stumbled forward. He regained his balance, twisted around and fired two shots at the person who'd shoved him. The silenced handgun still sounded as loud as a jackhammer. Russ turned back to Barb and me.

At first, I was too stunned to move, but knew this may be my only time to take the offensive. I shoved Barb in the open elevator and swung around to knock the pistol away.

Russ was quicker. I deflected the gun as he pulled the trigger. The sound was deafening and the bullet couldn't have missed my head by more than an inch. Russ, who was a couple of inches taller and outweighed me by thirty pounds, lowered his shoulder and lumbered into me. I sidestepped most of the blow. He stumbled again. I wasn't in great shape, but fortunately, I was in better shape than Russ. I knocked him sideways toward the edge of the walkway. His back hit the top of the waist-high railing. The gun flipped over the side.

Russ lunged for the weapon, missed, and glanced over the railing as the weapon bounced off the pavement. He glared at me. The distraction had given me enough time to swing at his head. He was moving toward me as my fist connected with his nose, increasing the impact of the blow. I'd never hit anyone in the face, and was jarred with the understanding why boxers wore gloves. Sharp pain radiated from my hand up my arm to my shoulder and it felt like the fillings in my teeth had been shaken loose.

Russ fared worse. He staggered sideways and smashed into the railing with all his weight. His feet left the deck. His body's momentum catapulted him halfway over the side and he teetered on the railing.

For a split second, I hoped that he would fall before I grabbed him around the waist and pulled with all my dwindling strength. My left arm felt like it was being separated from my body. And Russ was still precariously close to falling four stories to the concrete parking lot.

I screamed for Barb's help. No response. The elevator door had closed and she was probably on her way to the bottom floor. I continued to struggle to keep Russ from falling, but was growing weaker.

My shoulder was killing me. The pain was so severe that I was ready to let go when Barb peeked out the elevator door and saw what was happening. She was still on the fourth floor, and moved to the other side of Russ and put her arms around his legs dangling on our side of the railing. She pulled, slipped, and quickly regained her balance and continued to pull. Russ flailed his arms. All they came in contact with was air. I yelled for him to hold still so we could pull him to safety. He continued to thrash around. My left arm felt weaker and I was afraid we wouldn't be able to stop gravity from taking him over the edge.

I glanced at Barb. She had a death grip on his legs and a look of determination on her face. I gritted my teeth, tried to ignore the pain in my shoulder, and pulled. Russ had finally stopped trying to escape, yet it still took several seconds for us to slowly pull him back from the railing. He flopped toward me and hit the deck. I grabbed his arm and twisted it behind his back before he could push his body up. Barb rammed her right foot on his back, and I continued to twist his arm so he couldn't wiggle out of the grip.

The sirens of two of Folly Beach's patrol cars filled the air and their brakes squealed as they skidded to a stop at the entry gate to the complex.

Officer Bishop was the first cop to the fourth floor and without saying anything cuffed Russ.

With Russ in restraints, I rushed to the body of the person who had saved us. I recognized the tat-covered neck, and yelled for Bishop to get help and knelt beside Rocky. He was breathing, yet struggled for each breath. Blood was pooling under his chest.

"Hurry!" I yelled.

Rocky moved his trembling hand to my leg. I moved closer. He was trying to speak.

He blinked a couple of times. "No one going to kill Dude's sis ... couldn't leave her ..."

"You saved her."

He closed his eyes. I prayed he'd heard me.

If he had, it was the last thing he heard.

Officer Bishop, with the help of an officer I didn't recognize, had hauled Russ to his feet and to a patrol car. Chief LaMond had arrived, along with three EMTs from Folly's force. There was nothing they could do for Rocky. The chief suggested we would be more comfortable in Barb's condo, also knowing we didn't need to be outside with Rocky's body. The chief came with us, asked Barb where she kept coffee, and fixed a pot while Barb and I moved to the couch to regain our composure. Fortunately for each of us, her coffeemaker wasn't as high-tech as the one in her office. One of the paramedics gently maneuvered my arm back and forth and around and said that it was probably sprained. To me it felt like it was torn, ripped, and shredded. I struggled not to scream as he continued to manipulate my arm. He offered me a ride to the hospital. I declined, took a deep breath, and thanked him for offer. He mumbled something about me being stubborn and told me I should get ice on it as soon as possible. He said he'd get an icepack from the ambulance and left the condo.

I assured the chief and Barb that I was okay, I spent the next ten minutes telling the chief what had happened, including my lying about stealing the money.

Cindy took notes, and I said, "How'd your guys get here so fast?"

The chief looked back toward the door. "A retired principal

and his grandkids from Kentucky were eating at Loggerheads when you got there. The guy'd been standing by the window as you came up the steps and saw, and these are his words, 'a suspicious looking, slimy, young guy sneaking around outside.' Said the guy was watching you and Barb. After you ate and headed over here, the retired vacationer saw the guy hiding behind a pole, still spying on you. He figured the tattoo-covered guy was going to rob you and had the bartender call us."

I wondered how long Rocky had been looking out for Barb, how long he'd been watching to protect a near stranger because she happened to be his boss's sis. And, had given his life out of loyalty and love for Dude.

Chapter Forty

The next hour lasted an eternity. At times, Barb's condo and the open corridor outside were more crowded than the beach on the Fourth of July. Crime techs, cops, EMTs double checking to make sure I was okay, Detective Adair, and a few others I didn't know, came and went. Other times, Barb and I were alone and struggled with anything to say to each other.

Dude barged through the door. "Be okeydokey, sis?" he said, as he gasped for air.

Barb nodded and Dude wrapped his spindly arms around her waist.

"Praise be to Sun God."

Dude unwrapped himself from Barb's waist and the two of them sat on the couch.

"I'm sorry about Rocky," I said. "He saved us."

Dude looked at the ceiling. "Rockster now be celebrating with his personal deity. He be goodest, orneriest surfer me know."

I was exhausted and had to get home and Barb seemed in good, albeit strange, hands with Dude. The pain in my shoulder was beginning to ease slightly, and I said I was heading out and Barb said she'd walk me to the door. I said it was unnecessary. She insisted.

We reached the door, she hugged me, and said, "Thank you."

I didn't let her know how much the hug hurt my shoulder, and pretended it was no big deal. I said I saved damsels in distress on a regular basis.

"Right." She shook her head and smiled.

Instead of falling into bed as soon as I stepped out of the cold, I called Charles. If he had heard what had happened from anyone else, he would be the next person in line to wring my neck, and it would be worse if I waited until tomorrow to call.

Somewhere after the fifth interruption with "you're kidding," third "no way," and umpteenth "you did what?" Charles settled down and let me finish.

"See why I can't leave you even for a few days," he said.

"That mean you're coming home?"

"Sweetie and I are talking about it. I told her everything Cal had said and she didn't throw anything at me. That's a good sign. Not sure yet. Call me when you know about Rocky's funeral."

That sounded hopeful.

I thought I'd been asleep for only a few minutes when someone pounded on the door. Daylight leaking around my blinds indicated I was wrong about how long I'd been asleep.

"Yo, Chrisster," Dude said as I blinked my eyes open. "Skip along with us."

I realized the 'us' included Barb who was standing behind Dude. Both were bundled in heavy coats, hats, and smiles, and were more awake than I was.

Instead of doing what normal people would have done and asking where, what, and why, I said to give me a few minutes to get dressed.

Dude looked at my pajamas. "Be boss idea."

My arm felt better than it did last night, but still hurt. I took extra time pulling on my shirt and jacket, swallowed three ibuprofens, and told Dude to lead on.

Fifteen minutes later, Dude had ushered us to the end of the Folly Pier. It was cold, but last night's brisk wind had moved elsewhere and it didn't feel as frigid as it had been. Instead of sitting on one of the wooden benches at the end of the pier, Dude led us to the railing looking back on the Tides Hotel and Barb's condo building.

Dude said, "Me share tidbit not to be heard by copsters." He looked around like he was afraid a *copster* was hiding behind the steps leading to the second deck. No one was within three hundred yards.

"Rocky be bunkin' at *mi casa*."

"After he tied me up and said he was leaving town?"

Dude shrugged. "Be rude to do to Chrisster. Yeah, he no go bye-bye."

"You were harboring a criminal?" Barb said.

"No. Be bunkin' a bud."

"Why?" I asked, figuring an extended legal discussion between an attorney and Dude would be like talking thermodynamics with a hermit crab.

Dude looked at Barb and turned to me. "Rockster afearin' harm be visitin' fractional sis. Said not be letting that happen."

Dude bowed his head, leaned against the railing, and a tear rolled down his cheek.

"Rockster said gandering-out for sis be one good thing he ever do." He looked back at the beach. "Customers no be missin' Rockster, but should."

Barb put her arm around Dude and I inched farther away from the two so they could have their moment. So many emotions were racing through my head I nearly lost my balance. Karen was leaving. Charles may never move back. And, I was grieving over a man who had been nothing but rude to me most every time we had contact, not to mention strapping me to a chair.

Barb was saying something about Rocky's funeral and wanting to pay for it, so I stepped back to the two and asked if anything had been discussed about the funeral. Dude said Rocky didn't have any family and he was going to take care of everything and he figured it'd be in two days. Of course, he didn't use those words.

My phone interrupted Barb and Dude arguing over who would pay for the funeral. Barb seemed to think she had won and would be footing the bill, yet I knew once Dude set his mind to something, his sis—fractional or otherwise—wouldn't stand a chance.

"So when's the funeral? Heather and I don't want to miss it."

I started to remind my impatient friend that poor Rocky had only met his demise hours earlier, but instead told him what Dude had said.

"Good. Bye," he said.

"Charles," I said, hopefully in time to keep from talking to dead air.

"What? Heather's ready for breakfast."

I crossed my fingers. "Back for good?"

"Don't know," he said and hung up.

It wasn't what I wanted to hear, but it left room for hope.

Dude and I were on each side of Barb as we walked down the steps and off the pier. She put her arm around our waists, squeezed, and turned to me.

"Think we can do dinner again without almost getting killed?"

"Why not."

About The Author

Bill Noel is the award-winning author of twelve novels in the highly-popular Folly Beach Mystery Series. In addition to being a novelist, Noel is a fine arts photographer and lives in Louisville, Kentucky, with his wife, Susan, and his off-kilter imagination.

Made in the USA
Lexington, KY
05 January 2017